FLIGHT SQA016

Praise for Amanda Radley

Detour to Love

"If you're on the lookout for well-written sapphic romance with stellar characters, wonderful pairings, and outstanding plots, I wholeheartedly recommend any of Amanda's books!!"—*EloiseReads*

Flight SQA016

"I'm so glad I picked this book up because I think I've found my new favourite series!…The love brewing between these two is beautifully written and I was onboard from the beginning. I had some laugh out loud moments because this is British rom-com at its best. The secondary characters really added to the novel and the rollercoaster ride that is this book. The writing is tight and pace is perfect."—*Les Rêveur*

Lost at Sea

"A.E. Radley knows how to write great characters. And it's not just the main characters she puts so much effort into. I loved them, but I was astounded at how well drawn the minor characters were, especially Elvin and Graham. The revelations are perfectly paced in this story. We find out more about their backgrounds as they get to know each other. The reader can so easily believe everything A.E. Radley writes because she is so observant and makes the world so real in her books… The writing was beautiful—descriptive, real and very funny at times." —*Lesbian Review*

"This book was pure excitement. The character development was probably my favourite overall aspect of the book. Both Annie and Caroline need to dig deep in the feelings department because of the past and allow their feelings to show. A.E. Radley really knows how to keep her readers engaged, and she writes age-gap romance books beautifully. In fact, she probably writes some of my favourite age-gap romance tropes to date. A very intriguing book that I really enjoyed. More Captain West, please!"—*Les Rêveur*

"Absolutely amazing, easy to read, perfect romance with mystery and drama story. There were so many wonderful elements that gave twists and turns to this adventure on the sea. I absolutely loved this story and can't rave about it enough."—*LesbiReviewed*

Going Up

"I can always count on this superb author when it comes to creating unforgettable and endearing characters that I can totally relate to and fall in love with. A.E. Radley has given me beautiful descriptions of Parbrook and the quirky individuals who work at Addington's."—*Lesbian Review*

"It was an A.E. Radley story, so I naturally, I loved it! Selina is A.E. Radley's iciest Ice Queen yet! She was so cold and closed off, but as the story progresses and we get a good understanding of her, you realise that just as with any other Ice Queen—she can be thawed. I loved how they interacted, with a wit and banter that only A.E. Radley can really deliver for characters like these."—*LesbiReviewed*

"This story is a refreshing light in the lesfic world. Or should I say in the romance lesfic world? Why do you ask me? Well, while there is a lot of crushy feeling between wlw characters and all, but, honestly that's the sub-plot and I've adored that fact. *Going Up* is a lesson in life."-—*Kam's Queerfic Pantry*

"The author takes an improbable twosome and writes such a splendid romance that you actually think it is possible…this is a great romance and a lovely read."—*Best Lesfic Reviews*

Mergers and Acquisitions

"This book is fun, witty, and adorable. I had no idea which way this book was going to take me, and I loved it. Each character is interesting and loveable in their own right. You don't want to miss this one—heck, if you have read any of A.E. Radley's books you know it's quality stuff."—*Romantic Reader Blog*

"Radley writes with a deceptively simple style, meaning the narrative flows naturally and quickly, yet takes readers effortlessly over rocky terrain. The pacing is unrushed and unforced, yet always leaves readers wanting to rush ahead to see what happens next."—*Lesbian Review*

"Charming and quick witted, I think A.E. Radley is an author to watch."—*Les Rêveur*

The Startling Inaccuracy of the First Impression

"We absolutely loved the way the relationship between the two ladies developed. There is nothing hurried about the relationship that develops perfectly organically. This is a lovely, easy to read romance."—*Best Lesfic Reviews*

Huntress

"The writing style was fun and enjoyable. The story really gathered steam to the point of me shirking responsibilities to finish it. The humor in the story was very well done."—*Lesbian Review*

"A.E. Radley always writes fantastic books. *Huntress* is a little different than most of her books, but just as wonderful. The humor was fantastic, the story was absolutely adorable, and the writing was superb. This is truly one of those books where the characters really stick with you long after the book has ended. I wish I'd read it sooner. 5 Stars." —*Les Rêveur*

Bring Holly Home

"*Bring Holly Home* is a fantastic novel and probably one of my favourite books by A.E. Radley…Such a brilliant story and one I know I will read time and time again. This book has two ingredients that I love in novels, Ice Queens melting and age-gap romance. It's definitely a slow burn but one I'd gladly enjoy rereading again."—*Les Rêveur*

Keep Holly Close

"It was great to go back into the world of the Remember Me series. The first book in the series, *Bring Holly Home*, is one of my favourite A.E. Radley books. I love Holly and Victoria; they tick all the boxes for me when it comes to my favourite tropes. Plus, Victoria's kids are adorable, especially little Alexia. She melts my heart."—*Les Rêveur*

"So much drama…loved it!!! I already loved Holly and Victoria from the first book in the series, *Bring Holly Home*, so it was brilliant to be back with them. Victoria hasn't changed and I adore her as much as before. She was utterly brilliant at every moment of this follow-up story and she even managed to surprise me from time to time. The Remember Me series is so beautiful and one of my all time favourites. 5 of 5 stars."—*LesbiReviewed*

Climbing the Ladder

"What a great introduction to what will undoubtedly be another fantastic series from A.E. Radley. After I finished it I just kept thinking that this book is amazing and it's just the start...enough said!"—*Les Rêveur*

"Radley has a talent for giving us memorable characters to love, women you wish you knew, and locations you wish you could experience firsthand."—*Late Night Lesbian Reads*

Second Chances

"This is an absolute delight to read. Likeable characters, well-written, easy flow and sweet romance. Definitely recommended."—*Best Lesfic Reviews*

"I always know when I get a new A.E. Radley book I'm in for a treat. They make me feel so good after reading them that most of the time I'm just plain sad that they have finished...The chemistry between Alice and Hannah is lovely and sweet...All in all, *Second Chances* has landed on my favourites shelf. Honestly, this book is worth every second of your time. 5 Stars."—*Les Rêveur*

The Road Ahead

"I really enjoyed this age-gap, opposites attract road trip romance. This is a romance where the characters actually acknowledge their differences and joy of joy, listen to each other. I love it when a book makes me feel all the feels and root for both women to find their HEA. Hilarious one minute, heart-tugging the next. A pleasure to read." —*Late Night Lesbian Reads*

Fitting In

"Writing convincing love stories with non-typical characters is tricky. Radley more than measures up to the challenge with this truly heart-warming romance."—*Best Lesfic Reviews*

By the Author

Romances

Mergers & Acquisitions

Climbing the Ladder

A Swedish Christmas Fairy Tale

Second Chances

Going Up

Lost at Sea

The Startling Inaccuracy of the First Impression

Fitting In

Detour to Love

Under Her Influence

Flight SQA016

The Remember Me Series

Bring Holly Home

Keep Holly Close

The Around the World Series

The Road Ahead

The Big Uneasy

Mystery Novels

Huntress

Death Before Dessert

Visit us at www.boldstrokesbooks.com

FLIGHT SQA016

by

Amanda Radley

2021

FLIGHT SQA016

ISBN 13: 978-1-63679-045-9

This Trade Paperback Original Is Published By
Bold Strokes Books, Inc.
P.O. Box 249
Valley Falls, NY 12185

First BSB Edition: July 2021

CREDITS
Editor: Ruth Sternglantz
Production Design: Stacia Seaman
Cover Design by Tammy Seidick

Acknowledgments

This rerelease of my first ever published novel is special to me in so many ways. It's been a surprising and wonderful journey, and I'd like to thank everyone who read *Flight SQA016* the first time around. Your support enabled me to embark on a fulfilling career which I never thought would be possible.

For the readers.

CHAPTER ONE

If First Officer Tom Kent piloted a Boeing 747 with the same laid-back attitude with which he drove his red Chevrolet Camaro, he'd have been fired from Crown Airlines immediately.

He weaved in and out of traffic with one hand lightly resting on the wheel while the other busily gesticulated to his tense passenger. "But, Em, you're used to those itty-bitty planes. This," he said and smiled, "this beautiful piece of engineering is a Boeing 747-400, four Rolls-Royce engines, the best in the business."

Emily White stared straight ahead out of the windscreen, her gaze fixed on the blurred line of cars they were overtaking. If she was going to die, she wanted to know which make and model took her from this world.

"And what are the odds that we'd occasionally fly the same schedule?" Tom asked as he happily smacked his hand down on the wheel. "It works out perfectly—I can drive you to and from work on those days. I have to admit this journey was starting to get a bit boring, but now I have someone to talk to."

He turned to Emily and offered a big, friendly smile, which she quickly returned, so he could refocus his attention back to driving like a bat out of hell. He slammed his foot on the brake then weaved around another car that had joined the freeway.

"You okay?" Tom asked with a frown. "You've not said a word since we left home."

"Yeah," Emily quickly answered. "Yeah—sorry, Tom, I'm just a bit out of it. Nervous, I guess."

"You'll be great," Tom enthused. "You completed all your training, and you're good to go."

Emily laughed at his childish enthusiasm for everything. "It's my first time serving first-class passengers, real ones! Not just people from the training course putting on a posh accent."

"You'll be fine," Tom said. "How bad can it be?"

"Three weeks of intensive training before you're even allowed on a real flight says they think it can be pretty bad," Emily said with a chuckle. "This is nothing like I'm used to. In my old job you didn't have different classes. You just sat them down, checked their seat belts, did the safety demo, and tried to sell them as much overpriced merchandise and gifts as possible before we landed. This is proper service—they pay a lot for these seats, and they expect the earth."

"And you'll be great." Tom reached into the centre console and picked out a sweet from an open bag and threw it into his mouth. "You've had the training, you passed the course. And think of the money." He rubbed his thumb and finger together.

"That's the only reason I'm doing this." Emily sighed. "The schedule stinks, and I'll hardly see Henry, but the money makes it worthwhile."

Tom nodded half-heartedly. "I still think that two transatlantics a week are going to be too much for you, Em. You'll burn out," he said seriously.

Emily shrugged. "It's the only way I get to spend time with Henry. What's the point in having time off if I'm in the wrong country? And the more I work, the quicker I can pay you and Lucy back."

"You don't need to pay us anything. We love having you and Henry stay with us." Tom's reply sounded genuine.

Emily smiled and reached over to gently squeeze his shoulder. "You're both so kind, but you know me—I have to pay my own way. I've got to pay you guys rent, not to mention pay Lucy for all her babysitting services. Especially now! She's going to see Henry more than I am. He's only five. He's going to think she's his mother."

They both shared a laugh, and Emily stole a sweet before returning her hands to her lap and nervously rubbing them together.

"Lucy loves Henry. She loves watching him while you're away. You don't owe us anything—you focus on paying off your debts first."

"Okay, I'm getting depressed," Emily told him with a sigh. "Tell me more about this fancy plane of yours. Any advice?"

"Well, we seat three hundred and sixty-seven passengers in total," Tom began as if reading from a well-rehearsed presentation. "Two hundred and seventy-one in standard, seventy-two in premium, and twenty-four in first class. There are ten cabin crew on board, and your senior cabin crew manager is Iris Winter. Have you heard of her?"

"Nope." Emily shook her head.

"She's a bitch," Tom said simply. "Don't mess with her, do what she tells you, and you'll be fine. If you don't agree with something, ignore it—it's not worth it. I've heard stories of her busting first-class cabin crew back down to economy for talking back to her, and that would be a hell of a pay cut for you."

"What?" Emily said. "Surely she can't do that?"

"Her husband is head of cabin operations in New York. She does what she likes, and he lets her." Tom shook his head. "Needless to say, she rules with an iron fist because she can. So keep out of her way."

"Gotcha." Emily nodded.

"First-class has four cabin crew. Two attend to the upper deck first-class area, while the other two look after first class at the front of the plane, the nose," Tom explained. "If you can get the nose, do. There are fourteen seats on the upper deck but only ten in the nose. It's quieter and more of the frequent flyers take the nose because it's nearer the door for disembarking."

Emily nodded. "Okay, try to get the nose, got it."

Tom looked at his watch. "Wheels up at seven this evening, so we've got three hours until then. You'll have an hour in the debriefing room and then an hour on board until passengers start to arrive."

"When do we land at Heathrow again?" Emily asked.

"Seven thirty in the morning. This will be a busy flight because it's Sunday evening. Anyone who does a week's work in London wants to get there for early Monday morning, so this is the flight."

"One hell of a commute." She laughed.

"Not if you're in first class."

Emily groaned. "True. Oh, I hope they all just want to go to sleep."

"They will," Tom said. "They lose a few hours going to London. We take off at seven in the evening and land at seven in the morning, but it's only a seven hour flight, so between take-off and landing they only have five hours to sleep, max."

They arrived at JFK airport, and Tom pulled into the Crown Airlines parking lot and his assigned space. Emily fussed with her deep purple skirt to ensure it was as pristine as when she removed it from the dry-cleaning bag that morning.

"You look great," Tom reassured.

"Great isn't good enough," Emily told him. "I need to look impeccable all the time." She smoothed her white shirt down and got a compact mirror out of her bag to examine her hair and make-up. "It's okay for you guys," Emily continued as she fussed with a few strands of long blond hair that had fallen out of the intricate updo she had chosen that morning. "White shirt, tie, black suit. Done."

"Don't forget the hat." He placed his first officer's cap on his head and slung his uniform jacket over his shoulder.

Emily opened her carry-on luggage and removed her matching purple jacket. She replaced her flat shoes with the impressive high heels she was supposed to wear when not serving. She fiddled with the high collar of her jacket and then picked up her name badge from her bag, affixed it to her lapel, and looked at Tom for approval.

He smiled at her and nodded. "Perfect, you look one hundred percent Crown first class."

"Good." Emily zipped her bag up. "Let's hope I still look like this after a nine-hour night shift."

Tom lifted out her carry-on luggage and gestured towards the Crown Airlines staff entrance. They walked across the car park and into the building.

CHAPTER TWO

Emily walked confidently along the carpeted corridor, dragging her work-issued wheeled luggage behind her. She looked out for the cabin crew debriefing room for Flight SQA016 to London Heathrow. Animated chatter drifted from a nearby meeting room. Emily poked her head around the door and asked, "Flight sixteen to Heathrow?"

"Yes, and you must be Emily White," a friendly Australian girl replied.

"That's me." Emily held out her hand.

"Jessica, Jessica Martin." She shook Emily's hand. "I work first class, so hopefully we'll be paired up. I used to work with Michael, who you replaced."

"What happened to Michael?" Emily asked.

"Promotion, he got a cushy desk job over in Training." Jessica sighed. "What we all want when we're sick of waking up and not knowing what day it is or what country we're in."

"Well, that should be a little easier for me now." Emily smiled as Jessica led her to a small table with assorted refreshments. "It'll either be London or New York. If I'm in a hotel, then it's London."

Jessica laughed. "After a nine hour shift, you'll still get confused, trust me. Have you done transatlantic before?"

"No," Emily admitted quietly. "Never even been out of this country. With my last job, I was on short haul all over the place, really fast paced. Will be nice to not have to deal with turnarounds."

Jessica filled up a small coffee cup and nodded. "Yep, when we're done with that plane, we're outta there. No going straight back for us."

"So are you on the upper deck?" Emily asked casually as she took the cup Jessica offered her.

"No, I'm in the nose, fewer passengers." Jessica winked. "I just hope Iris keeps it like that."

"The cabin manager?"

"Yup, she's a bitch," Jessica said softly.

"Yeah, I'd heard."

The chattering in the room suddenly stopped, and the staff fell silent as a short, well-groomed woman with light brown hair entered the room and looked around at the group.

"Good afternoon, crew," she said as she parked up her luggage. "Two hours until take-off, so let's get this debriefing under way."

Emily was quickly introduced to the team by Iris, who gave her the quickest of polite smiles. A wave of relief washed over Emily when it was announced that she would be paired up with Jessica, and they would be taking responsibility for the forward first-class compartment, the coveted nose.

The briefing lasted exactly forty-five minutes. Emily wasn't at all surprised that the agenda was adhered to with military precision.

After the meeting, the cabin crew scrambled to get their bags and to get to the gate to begin boarding preparations, but Emily found her exit from the room cut off by Iris.

"Miss White, I'm glad to have you with us," Iris said in a frosty tone.

"Thank you, Mrs. Winter," Emily said, keeping her professional face firmly in place. "I'm eager to get started and be an asset to the team."

That seemed to please Iris, and she gave a stiff smile. "Good. Welcome to the team. Stick close to Miss Martin—she knows first class very well and will be able to show you all the intricacies of working on board a real flight, things that they probably don't teach you in training."

"Absolutely." Emily nodded, deciding that the less she said, the better.

Iris stepped to one side, and Emily quickly exited the meeting room. She was relieved to see Jessica waiting for her down the corridor, for although she had worked in JFK before, she had never even set foot in the long-haul sections of the airport and was unsure where to go.

"Hey, thanks for waiting."

"Been sufficiently welcomed to the team?" Jessica asked with a knowing grin.

"Yeah," Emily said. "I feel all warm and cosy now."

Jessica laughed. "If you're lucky that will be the last time you talk to her one-on-one, aside from when you call her on board to say we're ready for take-off or landing."

"Fingers crossed." Emily smiled as they walked through a set of security doors.

❖

A few passengers had gathered at the boarding gate and looked up with interest as the cabin crew glided past.

Emily glanced out of the windows along the air bridge and admired the sheer size of the 747. She stepped onto the aircraft; some of her colleagues turned right to head towards the economy section, while she followed Jessica to the left, up towards the front end. They passed through the premium section before dropping their bags off in the first-class crew galley.

"Have you seen the new first-class cabins?" Jessica asked, removing her dress jacket and hanging it neatly in the galley closet. "They have only been in service a couple of months."

"No, the training course had the old stock," Emily replied as she hung her jacket next to Jessica's.

"Ta-da!" Jessica threw back the curtain that separated first class from the galley.

Emily stepped through and looked around with an impressed nod. She walked further into the cabin. There were ten luxurious seats, five on either side of the aircraft, the aisle narrowing towards the front but still wide enough to give each passenger privacy. There was a faint glow of purple in the dimmed ceiling lights. Even in the low light Emily could see that everything about the cabin was magnificent, and she understood why people would choose to fly in such luxurious surroundings.

Jessica explained the layout. "So, the seat rows are six through ten. On the left we have seat A and on the right we have seat K—that's just so we're in sync with the seating in economy."

Emily nodded and looked up at the row numbers to familiarise herself with them.

Jessica approached seat 8A and began a quick demonstration. "As you can see, each chair has a high-backed, curved wall behind it, which gives the passengers more privacy, and there is a large storage bin below the window. All seats fully convert into flat beds." She sat down and pointed at the screen embedded in the shiny wall in front of her. "Each also has a private touch-screen television, which is dead simple to use, and the ground crew check it as part of their maintenance routine, so we don't need to worry." To the right of the screen sat a permanently fixed stool with a half-height back on it. "These are for people travelling together who want to work during the flight or dine together." Jessica pressed a button on the wall next to the television, and a panel popped out. She lifted out a table and folded it out to full size. "These new tables can accommodate two full dinner services."

She folded the table away and stood, then indicated a panel of buttons to the side of the seat and identical buttons at eye level on the curved wall. "You can use either of these panels to make the bed," she explained, pushing a button that caused the base of the chair to slide forward while the back reclined automatically. "When the chair is a bed, the stool becomes the end of the bed."

Emily nodded as she took it all in. "And we make the beds for all the passengers, right? We don't want them to do it themselves even if they want to."

"Right, health and safety," Jessica agreed. "Most will say they want to go to bed and will go to use one of the three washrooms over by the galley. When they go, you need to lower the chairs, get the padded bed sheets, the pillow, and the quilt from the galley, and make the bed up. We stagger the meals slightly to make sure that everyone doesn't want to get ready for bed at the same time. As with all service, we move from the back to the front of the cabin."

"Okay." Emily pointed to a device embedded in the armrest. "Is that the inflight phone?"

Jessica looked to the inner armrest. "Yep, well, it's everything. It's a phone for voice and text services. You can also watch TV, play games, or use it to call other passengers if you know their seat number."

Emily blew out a breath. "Wow, do they use all that?"

"Nah." Jessica laughed as the chair stopped moving once in its fully reclined position. "It's just a gadget to sell seats."

Emily looked at the control panel. "This makes it go back into a seat, right?"

"Yep. In the morning we slowly turn up the cabin lighting, and they wake up and go to the washrooms. Once someone leaves, you strip the bed and press that button, so when they get back it will be a chair again. It's much easier than making the bed."

Emily pressed the button and watched as the chair started to move again. "Cool," she said, "seems easy enough."

Jessica smiled and started to walk towards the galley, and Emily followed her. "So," she said, "this is a scheduled weekend flight, which means we have a few regulars on this trip. Some of our passengers live in New York and work in London, so they have a weekly commute. These frequent flyers are the most important to us. They pay around twelve thousand dollars a flight, twice a week for most of the year. That's more than a million dollars a year each, and if they're not one hundred percent satisfied, they won't hesitate to complain, and then the airline is in trouble. Simple as."

"Well, that's done nothing to help my nerves." Emily giggled nervously.

Jessica removed a cabin trolley from the galley and guided it into the cabin. "There's nothing to worry about. You've done the training, and you'll have me by your side. We're going to smash this." Jessica smiled and Emily felt immediately better to have an ally.

Jessica set up the first seat. "So, bottle of water, overnight bag with all they'll need, pillow, and a selection of today's newspapers."

"Got it." Emily nodded and started to repeat the process on the next seat.

"The frequent flyers we have with us today are, first, 9K, Liam Jones," Jessica said as she angled her head towards the seat and grimaced. "He's nice enough, he's in the music business, and as long as you keep the alcohol flowing, he is fine. Bit of a groper, though."

"Nice." Emily grimaced.

"Yeah, but in 9A we have Dr. Charles Harvey, and he is lovely." Jessica smiled as she set up the seat. "He's a surgeon and travels back and forth to a training college in London. Let me tell you, if the whole plane was filled with Charles Harveys, everything would be great."

"Cool." Emily smiled. "It will be nice to see a friendly face."

"He doesn't fly every week, but he'll be with us today," Jessica said. "Lastly, we have 10A, Olivia Lewis. I don't know exactly what she does—she's a businesswoman of some sort. Doesn't talk much, commutes regularly. She has this seat because it's nearest to the exit door. Every Sunday she's on flight sixteen to London and then returns on Friday's flight nineteen. Same thing every week."

"Oh, that's my return. I'll see her twice a week." Emily looked around the cabin to make sure that all the seats had been set up correctly.

Jessica frowned. "You're in London for a week before your turnaround?"

"No." Emily gave a soft laugh. "I have kind of a gruelling schedule. I'm over to London today, and then after the required twenty-four hour break, I'm back to New York on the Tuesday morning flight."

"Whoa." Jessica blinked. "And then back out and back home again within a week?"

"Yeah," Emily admitted. "The Tuesday morning London flight gets me in to New York for early Tuesday afternoon, which means I can spend Tuesday evening and all of Wednesday with my five-year-old kid, Henry. Then I'm back to London on Wednesday night, arriving Thursday morning, and then back to New York on flight nineteen on Friday."

Jessica nodded in understanding. "And then you get Friday afternoon, all day Saturday, and Sunday morning with Henry. You're not kidding about that being a gruelling schedule."

Emily pushed the trolley back to the galley. "Yeah, I know. I need the money to clear some debts. I figure I can do this for six months, and then I'll have some breathing space. I've worked it out, and it's just within company policy."

"What about childcare?" Jessica asked before blushing. "I'm sorry, that's none of my business. You've only just met me, and here I am, asking personal stuff."

"No, it's fine." Emily smiled. "My best friend, Lucy, runs a childcare service from home, and she takes Henry. We live with her and her husband, Tom, at the moment, so I'm really lucky there."

"Tom and Lucy? You mean First Officer Kent and his wife?"

Emily flushed. "Yeah, that's the one. They're both good friends."

"They're lovely people," Jessica said. "But keep that a secret. You don't want Iris finding out, or she might say something."

"Yeah, I figured she wouldn't like cabin crew fraternising with the cockpit." Emily winked and Jessica laughed.

Jessica helped Emily secure the trolley and started to show her the rest of the galley. "And just remember, if the passengers are using the toilets on either side of the galley and they are queuing in the corridor, then they can probably overhear what we're saying."

"Gotcha. Be professional at all times."

"Exactly. Now, they'll be boarding soon, and they start with first class, so we better get some champagne flutes set up."

CHAPTER THREE

Iris Winter had just completed an unscheduled inspection of the first-class compartment and, aside from needlessly moving a few items a few centimetres, declared it suitable. Jessica assured Emily that *suitable* was the best they were going to do and told her to get ready to greet the passengers who would be boarding within the next five minutes.

In the small washroom beside the galley, Emily checked her hair and make-up meticulously, knowing that even a hair out of place or a stray smudge of mascara could make a difference. When she was satisfied, she removed her dress jacket from the hook and put it on, ensuring the white collar of her blouse and the collar of her purple jacket balanced, as per regulations.

With a deep breath she pulled on a pair of white gloves and went to wait in the cabin while Jessica stood in the corridor to greet the passengers—by name, if she knew them.

Before long Emily heard Jessica greet Dr. Harvey and welcome him on board. As she told him that Emily would assist him with his carry-on luggage, Emily waited for him to appear. She couldn't help but smile. He was dressed in khaki trousers, a woollen shirt and tie, and a tweed jacket. His messy red hair spoke of a man who didn't fuss about his appearance.

"Hello, Emily," he said warmly as he held out his hand to her. "Charles Harvey."

Emily shook his hand, surprised but delighted that her first ever first-class passenger was so friendly. "Dr. Harvey, it's a pleasure to meet you," Emily said.

"Oh, please, call me Charles," he said as he handed her his overcoat.

Emily gave a gentle laugh. "I think my boss would prefer it if I call you Dr. Harvey."

He nodded in reluctant agreement. "Very well, shall I put my bag in the closet?"

"Oh, no." Emily smiled. "I can do that."

"It is rather heavy," he apologised.

"Not a problem," Emily said politely and took the bag. "Can I get you a drink? Champagne?"

"Oh, just orange juice for me," he said and took his seat.

Emily placed his coat and bag in the closet before serving him a pre-poured glass of orange juice. The next two passengers to enter the cabin were a married couple on holiday. They were seated up front in 6A and 7A. Emily checked their boarding passes to ascertain their names without the need to ask.

"Here you are, Mr. and Mrs. Archer. Can I get you both some champagne?"

They seemed bewildered by the whole experience, and Emily got the impression that she wouldn't be the only person enjoying their first trip in first class that evening. They eagerly accepted the champagne and asked Emily to explain the various buttons on their seats.

While Emily showed the Archers how everything worked, Jessica greeted three incredibly tall and thin women who just had to be fashion models going by their dress and poise. They were shown to seats 6K, 7K, and 8K and all given champagne.

Next a dark-haired, unshaven, leather-clad man approached the cabin. He was talking animatedly on his phone and looked Emily up and down lewdly as he waved his boarding pass in her face.

"Mr. Jones." Emily knew who he was before she'd even read the pass and followed him into the cabin.

"Champagne, please, love." He checked out the models and fell into his seat with his leg hooked over the arm.

"I'll get that for him," Jessica offered. "Can you seat the next passengers?"

Emily greeted the next two passengers. She glanced around the cabin. Only one seat was still empty, 10A, but no sooner had she noticed than another passenger arrived. This had to be Olivia Lewis.

She was a little under average height but made up for the fact with expensive-looking high-heeled shoes. Her slightly olive skin tone and beautiful dark hair made it difficult for Emily to place her ethnicity, but Miss Lewis was easily more attractive than the models seated a few rows in front of her. She wore a navy business skirt suit and quickly took her seat after handing her overcoat and one of her small luggage bags to Jessica, who had arrived to greet her.

Jessica looked at Emily in a silent indication to join her in the galley, and both of them exited the cabin. While she hung up Miss Lewis's overcoat, Jessica explained, "Miss Lewis won't want a drink—she prefers to stick to water. She's happy with the bottled water provided, but she'll need a glass. And you need to get her a fresh bottle if she finishes the first one, and obviously take the empty away with you."

"Okay." Emily pulled out a tray, got a glass tumbler out, and held it up to the light to check it was spotlessly clean.

"For service tonight I want you to take row A, and I'll take K. If you need anything, I'll be right next to you," Jessica said with a smile as she picked up a couple of glasses of champagne and took them into the cabin. Emily followed and walked over to 10A.

"Good evening, Miss Lewis, here is a glass for your water."

Miss Lewis had settled into her seat and was reading one of the provided newspapers. A pair of black-rimmed spectacles perched on the end of her nose. She looked up at the interruption.

"Thank you"—she looked at Emily's name badge—"Miss White."

"Emily." Emily supplied her first name with a polite smile as Olivia placed her glass on the drinks table built in to the armrest.

It quickly became clear that Olivia wasn't about to say anything else, so Emily went to check that Dr. Harvey and the rest of her allocated passengers were comfortable and had everything they needed.

When she was happy that her five wealthy passengers were satisfied, she walked back to the galley, removed her white gloves, and swapped her high heels for her flats for service. She quickly entered the washroom and checked to see if she was still looking up to first-class standards before returning to the galley.

"It's all going well so far." Jessica kicked off her own heels and put on her flats before removing her jacket.

"Yeah," Emily agreed. "But we've not even taken off yet."

The internal crew telephone bleeped once and lit up. Jessica answered the call, and Emily assumed it was Iris asking for an update. Jessica reported that her section had boarded and were seated, and a few seconds later she hung up the phone.

"Okay, first and premium are all in. So it's just economy now, but they're usually pretty quick, so we need to do another sweep of the cabin, check everyone is okay, and then the safety video will be played."

Emily returned to the front of the cabin and attended to Mr. and Mrs. Archer, politely conversing with them about their trip to London, which turned out to be a wedding anniversary trip. After a brief conversation with the Archers, she approached Dr. Harvey.

"Can I get you anything, Dr. Harvey?"

"No, thank you," he replied. "Is this your first flight with us?"

"Yes," Emily admitted. "I transferred to Crown three weeks ago."

"I'm sure you'll enjoy it," he told her enthusiastically. "I've been flying with Crown for fifteen years, and I've always had the very best time."

"We aim to please." Emily smiled at him as she moved on to her final passenger. "Can I get you anything, Miss Lewis?"

Olivia looked up from her newspaper and regarded Emily for a moment before shaking her head. "No, thank you, Miss White."

Emily smiled politely and returned to the galley.

"Everything okay?" Jessica was putting things away in preparation for take-off.

"Yep, they're all fine."

"Great. Once economy is seated, we prepare the cabin for take-off while the safety vid is on, and then we tell Iris we're good to go and take our seats." Jessica picked up a stack of menu cards and flicked through them while Emily checked that the correct trolleys had been delivered by the ground services team and signed for them. She then checked and signed the passenger manifest.

"I'll go take this to Iris."

Emily walked through the premium cabin towards the main galley where Iris was located. "All trolleys have been checked, and our passenger manifest is correct," she said. Iris checked every item meticulously before finally signing and handing the paperwork back.

Tom Kent's voice came over the intercom system, introducing

himself and welcoming everyone on board, and Emily smothered a smile at his professional tone.

Sean, the steward working in economy, appeared and told Iris, "Everyone's seated, and Captain Locke said we are clear for push back."

"Roll the safety video," Iris told him. Emily quickly excused herself and made her way back to her own cabin as all the televisions in the premium cabin sprang to life.

She entered the first-class cabin and checked seat belts were fastened and the aisles were clear. She could hear Jessica having a discussion with Mr. Jones to encourage him to end his phone call.

Once she was satisfied the cabin was secure, Emily took her seat by the emergency exit, which was located between the last seat in row A and the first-class washrooms, where three folding jump seats were available for crew members. A few moments later Jessica took the seat next to her. She picked up the telephone tucked in the wall next to her and pressed the button to indicate that their cabin was secure and that they were both seated and ready. Emily looked out of the porthole window and watched as the airport slowly rolled past them.

As a scheduled flight leaving on time, Flight SQA016 had priority access to the runway, and before long the four giant engines were sending the aircraft up into the air. Ten minutes into the ascent, a single light indicated to the cabin crew that they could leave their seats and begin their duties. Emily and Jessica quickly entered the galley and began opening trolleys for the dinner service.

"Okay," Jessica said as she turned the ovens on. "We work from back to front. First we hand out menus. There are two choices of starters and three choices of mains. Take Miss Lewis's order straight away—she likes to be served quickly, so she can get to sleep. Everyone else you can give a few more minutes. Take their full order including wine or any other drinks, and then we'll get everything cooking, again working back to front."

A few minutes later, the sound of the seat belt warning light being turned off was accompanied by the sound of approximately one hundred and fifty seat belts being simultaneously removed. Moments later, Iris Winter's voice filled the cabin as she welcomed everyone on board and reminded them, pointlessly, that although the seat belt sign had been switched off, it was recommended to keep the belt securely fastened when not moving around the cabin.

Jessica and Emily entered the cabin and began handing out menus.

"Can I take your order now, Miss Lewis? Or would you like a few more minutes?" Emily asked politely.

"Salad starter, I'll have the chicken for main, no dessert, please," Olivia said as she handed the menu back.

"Any wine with your meal?"

"No." Olivia shook her head. "I'll have some more water, though, still water."

"I'll get on that immediately." Emily pushed the button to release the table and unfolded it before heading into the galley where she gathered the cutlery, tablecloth, and condiments and put a chicken meal in the oven to heat through.

Jessica appeared and said to Emily, "Don't bend over when you serve near Jones. He's wasted already, and he'll probably try to grab you."

"Ugh, thanks for the warning."

In the cabin, she approached Miss Lewis's table and prepared it to the exacting standards she had practiced over and over during training. Miss Lewis ignored her, content to flip through the in-flight magazine silently.

Emily returned to the galley and picked up another bottle of water and a clean glass. "Miss Lewis doesn't talk much, does she?"

Jessica shook her head. "Nope, at first I used to think she was a bit of a snob, but now I think she's just quiet."

Emily placed a salad, bottle of water, and glass on a tray and exited the galley to serve the starter. "Here you are, Miss Lewis."

Olivia wordlessly unwrapped her metal cutlery from her thick linen napkin while Emily stepped forward to speak with Dr. Harvey.

"Can I take your order, Dr. Harvey?"

"One of everything." Dr. Harvey laughed in a way that indicated that wasn't the first time he had told the joke.

Emily quickly took all of the orders up the row, and on her return cleared away Olivia's starter dish and cutlery. In the galley, she removed the main course for Olivia from the oven and turned to Jessica. "So she'll want this now?"

"Yes." Jessica nodded. "She doesn't want a break between courses."

Emily quickly plated the meal, went back into the cabin, placed the dish on Olivia's table, and put some fresh cutlery beside it. "Can I get you anything else, Miss Lewis?"

Olivia looked happy at the speed of delivery and shook her head. "No, that's wonderful, thank you, Miss White."

Emily quickly poured wine for her row and began serving the starters when she noticed that Olivia had finished her main meal.

"All finished?" she asked and, at Olivia's nod, removed the plate. "Would you like me to clear everything away?"

"Yes, I'm going to prepare for bed," Olivia said as she picked her wash bag from out of the storage bin by the window.

"I'll have your bed ready for when you get back," Emily said with a smile. She cleared all the items from the table, folded it back into the wall, and clicked it into place.

In the galley, Emily quickly deposited the dishes and used linens into the appropriate trolley, opened a storage locker, and removed a stack of bedding. The sound of the washroom door closing indicated that Olivia had left her seat, and Emily rushed into action to close the window blind and make the bed.

When she had finished, she stepped back to review her work. Jessica passed by and nodded. "Looking good, Em."

Emily continued serving the remaining meals. At one point she looked up to see Olivia exiting the washroom. She wore pyjamas and the airline-provided slippers, and her face was scrubbed clean of make-up. She got into bed, switched off the dim night light, and then donned a face mask and earplugs.

Back in the galley Emily said, "So, Miss Lewis takes her sleep seriously, eh?"

Jessica laughed. "Yep, and nothing wakes her. I don't know how long she's done this journey, but she's just out like a light, so don't worry about tiptoeing past her."

Over the next hour, Emily and Jessica finished the dinner service and slowly set up all the beds, except for Liam Jones's because he had passed out in his seat. They both tried to wake him, but he was out for the count, which Jessica said wasn't unusual. They placed a blanket over him and left him alone. Once everyone was tucked up in bed,

Jessica turned the cabin lights to the dimmest setting and drew the curtains as she entered the galley.

"So, what do you think?" Jessica asked Emily with a smile.

"Yeah," Emily nodded. "Hard work!"

"Yep, but as long as you have a good partner, then it's all fine. You did really well tonight—you should be proud."

"I don't know about that," Emily said shyly. "It was okay. I need to speed up a bit."

"That comes with time," Jessica said. "Now, let's get the galley cleared, and then we can prep for breakfast, which we'll serve in"—she looked at her watch—"three hours."

CHAPTER FOUR

By the time breakfast service had begun, Iris had called to advise Emily and Jessica that the captain was benefitting from a strong tailwind, which meant they were landing twenty minutes earlier than expected. That meant that breakfast needed to be served, eaten, cleared, and everything stowed for landing within the next forty-five minutes, or there would be a delay. They quickly served breakfast, consisting of a hot meal for those who wanted it and cereals for those who didn't, as well as tea and coffee.

As Emily poured Miss Lewis her second cup of tea, she noticed her checking her watch for the second time. "We're running a little early due to a strong tailwind, around twenty minutes early."

"Oh, I see," Miss Lewis replied. "I had wondered."

Emily smiled and removed the breakfast plate from the table.

"I'm very conscious about time," Miss Lewis confessed, almost awkwardly.

"So am I, especially in this job," Emily replied with a smile.

Knowing that Olivia Lewis chose to sit in 10A to get a quick getaway, Emily prepared her items first, and as soon as the aircraft stopped in the arrival gate and the seat belt light was switched off, she was beside Olivia with her belongings.

"Oh, thank you," Olivia said in pleasant surprise as Emily helped her into her overcoat, knowing that the London morning chill would require it.

Jessica and Emily provided everyone with their belongings and stood by the exit to say farewell. As soon as their passengers deplaned they returned to their cabin to check for any left belongings.

"Dr. Harvey's left you a tip and a note," Jessica said as she handed Emily a fifty-dollar bill and a folded piece of paper.

"Oh my God," Emily said with surprise. "That's so nice." The note was a rambling thank-you, stating he hoped to see her again soon. "So I can keep this, or do I have to report it to…?"

"No." Jessica shook her head. "First-class passengers often tip. It's an unspoken rule that we just don't tell anyone."

Emily nodded and read the note again.

"Looks like Miss Lewis likes you too," Jessica said, pointing at seat 10A. Emily picked up an origami swan made from a folded bill.

"Wow, that's amazing." Emily held the delicate paper in the palm of her hand and looked at it in awe.

"Better pocket it before Iris comes up here. She's funny about tips—she thinks they should be given back to the passengers."

"Isn't that rude?"

"I think so," Jessica agreed. "And I'm not about to chase down a passenger and tell them to keep their money!"

After a quick inspection of the cabin, they disembarked the aircraft, and following a swift meeting in the Crown offices, they were dismissed for the day. Jessica hugged Emily and said she couldn't wait to see her again next Sunday. Emily waved her off before catching a shuttle bus to the hotel she was booked into.

Emily stared up at the ceiling from her hotel bed and smiled. It was going to be damned hard work, but she knew it was worth it. She reached into her pocket and took out the fifty dollars and the note from Dr. Harvey and read it again with a smile, hoping that she would see the kind man again.

From her other pocket, she took out the origami swan. It seemed almost a shame to unfold it, but she knew she had to as she couldn't let money go to waste, no matter how beautifully it was presented.

Emily slowly unwrapped the swan, careful not to rip it, and looked at the bill in shock. It was a one-hundred-dollar bill. She carefully flattened it out and stared at it for a moment in surprise as she wondered what on earth she'd done to deserve one hundred and fifty dollars' worth of tips.

Summoning some energy, she got changed into jeans and a sweater and bagged up her work uniform. She quickly went down to reception to drop it off, double-checking that they would have it back to her by that evening. She returned to her room exhausted and peeled off her jeans and sweater to crawl into bed. The last thing she did was set her phone alarm to wake her at one in the afternoon, so she could call Henry and tell him about her adventures.

It barely seemed like ten minutes had passed before her alarm was bleeping. Emily had to double-check her phone with the clock in the room to assure herself that she had slept for over three hours. Exhaustion soon gave way to excitement as she connected her phone to the hotel's Wi-Fi service and opened a free call application and called Lucy.

She wiped at the sleep in her eyes and smothered a yawn as she held the phone to her ear and waited for an answer.

"Mommy!"

Emily smiled as she realised that the second Lucy's phone had rung, Henry had grabbed it.

"Hey, Henry!"

"Mommy!" he shouted again, his excitement clear in his voice.

"Yep." Emily giggled. "How are you doing?"

"Mommy, are you in London now?" Henry asked, ignoring her question.

"Yes, I'm in London now."

"Wow," Henry whispered in awe, his grasp of time and distance still not quite developed.

"And it's the afternoon here," Emily told him, keen to help him understand the intricacies of travelling through time zones.

"It's the morning here," Henry told her.

"I know—you just had breakfast, right?" Emily smiled, her heart clenching as she wanted nothing more than to reach through the phone and hold him tight.

"Yep, pancakes," Henry announced with pride before his tone became serious. "When will you be home?"

"Tomorrow afternoon," Emily told him, feeling like it was an eternity away.

"Okay," Henry said casually. "Lucy wants to talk to you now. I love you, Mommy."

"I love you too, Henry," Emily said before she heard the shuffling of the phone being handed over.

"Hi." Lucy's voice replaced the shuffling. "How's London?"

"I have no idea. I'm exhausted," Emily admitted. "Is everything okay there?"

"Yes, everything's fine," Lucy replied, and Emily could almost hear the rolling of Lucy's eyes at this frequently asked question. "We played games, had dinner, and then Henry had a bath and went to bed. He woke up half an hour ago. He has barely had time to miss you."

"I suppose you're right," Emily said sadly. "It's so weird being so far away from him."

"I know, but I promise you I'm taking good care of him, and I don't let him out of my sight."

"I don't know what I'd do without you," Emily admitted, trying to fend off the tears that had formed in her eyes.

"You'll never have to find out," Lucy told her seriously. "Now, tell me all about the people in first class. What are they like?"

Emily sighed deeply and expelled a small laugh, and they began talking about the adventures of Emily's first service in the first-class cabin.

CHAPTER FIVE

Emily had never thought that time could pass so quickly. It was Friday morning, and she was in the Crown Airlines staffroom at London Heathrow, clutching a cup of coffee and holding back a yawn. She'd completed two more transatlantic flights since her first one, six days ago.

Her daytime flight back to New York on Tuesday had been eventful, in that it had been delayed for two hours once the passengers had boarded, and she and her crewmate, Ashley, had their work cut out for them dealing with the frustrated first-class passengers. The day flight had been hard work, and the constant stream of meals, drinks, and conversations with the passengers had her longing for the night flights.

On Wednesday evening, she returned to London on a night flight with Anna, another stewardess, who had given her lots of helpful advice on how to cope with jet lag and disturbed sleep schedules. Not that the information helped much with a schedule as packed as Emily's. She took another sip of coffee as she tried to wake herself up for her return trip to New York, set to depart at nine o'clock that morning.

"You must be Emily White."

Emily looked up to see a tall, long-limbed brunette in a Crown Airlines uniform approach with a friendly grin.

"Yes, that's me." Emily stood up and smiled.

"I'm Kerry." She held out her hand. "Jessica told me all about you. I'm your partner in crime for this flight."

Emily shook Kerry's hand. "Oh, great to meet you."

"Likewise," Kerry said and they both sat down. "Jessica told me about your schedule, so I didn't know if I'd find you upright or not."

Emily laughed. "Well, it's been an experience, that's for sure."

"I'll bet." Kerry nodded to the stern looking woman who had just entered the staffroom. "Have you met Iris Winter yet?"

"Yes, she was on my Sunday flight out here." Emily smiled at Iris but wasn't surprised when the woman ignored her and joined a group of other cabin managers.

"Ugh." Kerry shook her head. "You have to put up with her twice a week?"

"Yep." Emily nodded. "She's left me alone so far, though."

"Good," Kerry said. "You really don't want to cross her."

"So I hear."

Silence fell over the room as Iris began her briefing session.

The low rumbling sounds of air turbulence began again, and Kerry let out a sigh as she grabbed hold of the workbench in the galley to steady herself.

"I hope this stops before we serve the hot meals," Emily commented, catching an empty plastic bottle that had started to roll towards the edge of the workbench.

"That's the fifth time the captain has put the seat belt sign on," Kerry said as she picked up the intercom and requested that the first-class passengers take their seats.

Emily secured the trolleys and checked that there was nothing that could move during turbulence before heading out into the cabin to check that all the passengers had their seat belts on. Quickly passing through the cabin, she noticed that Olivia Lewis's seat was empty and looked towards the occupied washroom before returning to the galley.

"Miss Lewis is in the washroom, and everyone else is sitting down," Emily said, bracing herself against the wall as the aircraft lurched.

"Iris has just called and asked me to help out in economy." Kerry rolled her eyes and grabbed a handful of sick bags as she exited the galley.

"Miss White?"

Emily turned and gasped. Olivia stood in the washroom doorway, a small trickle of blood running down the side of her face. Emily grabbed the first aid kit and stumbled into the washroom as another jolt of turbulence hit the aircraft.

Emily manoeuvred Miss Lewis so she was sitting down on the toilet seat in the cramped washroom. Blood smeared the shelf over the sink. It was clear to Emily what had happened.

"Are you okay?" Emily asked as she leaned in to examine the cut.

Olivia immediately stiffened. "I think so."

"It doesn't look too bad. I'll need to clean it, though." Emily placed the first aid kit on the sink and unzipped it. "My hands are clean but just to follow procedure…" Emily explained as she took out a pair of latex gloves and snapped them on.

She held Olivia's face carefully in both hands and tilted her head up so she could see the cut clearly. Their eyes met briefly, and Emily gave her a reassuring smile.

"I'm so stupid," Olivia mumbled as she studied the wound.

"Not at all, the turbulence is quite severe," Emily soothed. "Do you feel dizzy or light-headed?"

"No." Olivia shook her head and then winced at the movement.

Emily opened a cleansing wipe and started to carefully clean around the wound. "Any blurred vision?"

"No."

"Nausea?"

"No."

"Headache?"

"No more than usual." Olivia let out a sigh. "Sorry to take you away from your duties."

"You are my duty." She paused as Olivia's eyes flicked up to meet hers with confusion. "I mean, the well-being of all passengers is my duty."

The aircraft lurched again, causing her to fall closer to Olivia before she braced herself against the wall.

"Sorry," Emily mumbled softly.

Olivia sat still with her head angled upward as Emily pressed a piece of gauze to the wound to stem the bleeding, before placing a small sticking plaster over the cut. This close, Emily noted the nervous swallowing and the heightened colour in Olivia's cheeks as she gently cleaned the blood.

"There, good as new." She pulled off the latex gloves and threw them in the bin. "Are you sure you're okay? It looks like you're starting to bruise."

"Much better, thank you for your assistance, Miss White."

"Please, call me Emily."

"Very well, E-Emily." Olivia smiled gratefully.

❖

"I drewed the plane you work in." Henry held up a piece of paper for Emily to look at.

"You drew the plane," Emily gently corrected. She took the paper and looked at the multiple scrawls. "Very good, Henry, should we put this in your book?"

He scampered towards his bedroom to pick out his scrapbook. In the half an hour Emily had been home, Henry had told her about every single thing that had happened while she had been away.

"He's okay, you know." Lucy placed a tray of hot drinks on the coffee table and sat beside Emily.

"I know, it's me who's not okay," she said with a sigh. "I knew it would be hard to be away from him, but I miss him so much already. The distance makes it worse."

Henry dashed back into the living room with his arms full of paper, pens, and his scrapbook and sat on the floor in front of the television.

"Just keep reminding yourself that it's not forever. You just need to get a little money together, and then you can pull back on the hours," Lucy said softly so Henry wouldn't hear. "And then you can start living life again, maybe start seeing people."

Emily let out a sigh. "I don't have the time or the energy for dating."

"Are you sure?" Lucy picked up a mug of coffee and curled up on the sofa. "I think you could do with the break. You know we're happy to watch Henry whenever you need."

"I feel like I hardly see him as it is," Emily pointed out. "I want more time with him, not less. I wouldn't feel right going out when I could be spending time with him."

Tom entered the living room and ruffled Henry's hair. He picked up his coffee. "Did you tell Lucy about the tips?" he asked and flopped heavily into an armchair.

"Yes, she did," Lucy said. "So much extra money coming in is great."

"Yeah, I just feel like I'm not actually earning it," Emily said.

"They must think you deserve it," Lucy commented.

Henry got up from in front of the television and started to walk backwards to his mother, eyes still stuck on the screen. As he bumped into Emily's legs she laughed lightly and took the scrapbook out of his hand.

"Do you want some help with the glue, Henry?"

Henry nodded, still staring at a documentary about wild giraffes in Africa.

"Haven't we seen this?" Emily indicated the program on the screen.

"Oh yes." Lucy laughed. "We're up to about three times a day now."

Emily smiled at Henry and gently pulled him up into her lap, so she could hold him close while he was distracted by the television.

"You should spend some of those tips and go to the place that starts with the last letter of the alphabet," Tom said cryptically, not wanting to get Henry too excited about an expensive visit to a zoo that might not be happening anytime soon.

"Absolutely." Emily smiled as she hugged Henry again. "Just a couple more payments and I should have some breathing room, and then we can have a treat."

Chapter Six

Olivia stared at the abstract painting and slowly raised an eyebrow. She had no idea what the artist was trying to convey.

"Miss Lewis, how lovely to see you again." The gallery owner approached her and looked at the painting along with her. "It's wonderful, isn't it? Such depth of character, it really speaks to the soul, don't you think?"

"Yes, absolutely," Olivia lied. "How much?"

"Four thousand," he replied.

"Add it to my account, and send it to my office."

"Of course, Miss Lewis." The smarmy man removed the painting from the wall and gently carried it away.

Olivia picked up her mobile phone, which had started to vibrate in her bag, and answered the call. "One moment, Nicole," she said before calling out a farewell to the gallery owner and leaving the building. Once she was out on the busy New York street, she spoke into the phone again. "I just bought another painting."

Nicole laughed down the phone. "I thought you were done with buying art for the office."

"So did I," Olivia admitted. "I went for a walk and ended up here. I'm sure the people in the office will enjoy another piece of art to look at."

"What is it called?"

"*Untitled.*"

"Oh, deep," Nicole drawled. "I suppose that means the artist had no idea what it was supposed to be either."

"Apparently it has depth of character and speaks to the soul."

"Did it?"

"Maybe. Not for me, but then maybe my soul is hard of hearing," Olivia deadpanned.

"Don't be hard on yourself," Nicole ordered gently. "You know, just because you don't see what other people see, or pretend to see, in those paintings doesn't make you wrong."

Olivia hummed dismissively, and Nicole changed subject. "How was your flight home?"

"Awful, the turbulence gods were against us, and somehow I managed to cut my forehead on a shelf in the washroom."

"Are you okay?" Nicole asked with concern.

"Yes, my embarrassment was greater than my pain. I intended to ask a member of the cabin crew for a sticking plaster, but she went a step further and cleaned the cut and bandaged me up."

"Like a kindly grandmother figure or more a sexy nurse?" Nicole asked mischievously.

Olivia smiled and shook her head. "The second one."

"Oh, get a name? Number?"

"Name, but I knew that already. Not that it matters—I might be seeing Kay tonight."

Nicole groaned. "Kay? She's crazy. Why are you still seeing her, Liv?"

"Lack of alternatives?" Olivia offered.

"Neither of you has feelings for the other."

"Maybe. But it's better than being alone all the time."

"Your call, but a woman like you can do better. Maybe the sexy nurse dash cabin crew could be that person?"

Olivia laughed softly. "Ever the romantic, Nic."

"I know, I know," Nicole replied. "Now, tell me more about her…"

Emily looked around the upper level of the busy terminal to see how she could entertain herself for the next half an hour. Something that wouldn't cost any money and would hopefully keep her awake. She walked past a number of coffee shops and eateries, knowing that any more caffeine and she'd be able to fly home to New York without an aircraft. She saw the large duty-free shop and decided to go in and have a look at the luxury products on sale. Even though she had no chance of ever affording them, she could still look.

She started with perfumes and quickly moved on to make-up before examining the handbags and purses with interest, shooing away several salespeople who were hoping to make a sale out of her. A beautiful silk scarf caught her eye, and she lifted the garment and held it up to her chest while looking at herself in the mirror.

"It suits you, Miss White."

Emily spun around to see Olivia Lewis looking at her with a wry smile. "Oh, Miss Lewis, hello." Emily stumbled over her words as she quickly put the scarf back, embarrassed that she had been caught daydreaming by the wealthy woman.

"Please, call me Olivia."

Emily nodded and looked at the cut on Olivia's forehead. "That seems to be healing nicely."

"Yes, thanks to prompt medical attention."

Emily smiled nervously. She hadn't expected to bump into Olivia and especially not when she was window shopping for items she had no hope of ever affording. Her conversational skills abandoned her and an awkward silence filled the air between them. Emily opened her mouth to speak, when she heard her cell phone ringing from inside her purse. Only one person would be calling her at this time. She checked the name on the screen and knew it was important.

"I'm sorry, I need to take this," Emily said to Olivia as she answered the call. "Lucy?"

The background music and the sound of shoppers drowned out Lucy's voice, and with a sense of panic Emily mouthed another apology to Olivia and rushed out of the shop to a quiet seating area. She leaned against a large window. "Okay, I can hear you now, what's happened?"

❖

From a distance, Olivia watched Emily stifle a cry of anguish. Tears began to roll down her face. Concern flooded Olivia, and she anxiously moved forward, then stopped. What could she say or do?

Again, she gathered her courage to approach Emily to try to offer some help. But what? What was happening? While she struggled with her indecision, Dr. Harvey appeared at Emily's side. Olivia hid behind a pillar and watched.

Dr. Harvey sat Emily down and talked to her. He was nodding his head in understanding as Emily explained her problem, all the while gesturing with her phone. Olivia watched the scene unfold while out of sight. Who was Lucy? A pang of jealousy hit her as soon as she heard the name. Emily was still crying, and Dr. Harvey handed her a handkerchief and patted her shoulder softly.

Olivia let out a sigh when she saw the kind gesture. She wished that she had reacted quicker so that she knew what was happening and could be the one providing comfort. Though she knew in her heart that she would probably not have reacted that way. She didn't have the natural skills that Harvey had. Emily had been so kind to her when she had hurt her head, and now, when it was her turn to provide help, she had once again failed miserably. With a rueful shake of her head, she turned and walked away.

Emily rushed into the preflight debriefing with seconds to spare. When the meeting was finished she said to Kerry, "I have to talk to Iris quickly. I'll meet you on board."

"No problem, I'll start prep work, and I'll see you soon."

Ten minutes later Emily was speedily walking through the terminal and towards the gate. As she approached the departure desk, she saw Dr. Harvey reading a book and Olivia Lewis nearby on her phone.

Emily smiled brightly at the doctor and paused to speak to him quietly. "She's going to ask, but she doesn't think it will be a problem. I have to get on board now, so I'll talk to you soon, okay?"

Dr. Harvey smiled warmly and nodded at her. Emily looked at Olivia and gave her a polite smile, not wishing to interrupt her telephone call. However, Olivia looked away as soon as eye contact was made. Distracted, Emily turned for the air bridge and rushed towards the aircraft.

"I am so sorry about that," Emily said to Kerry as she wrestled her carry-on luggage into the crew closet.

"No problem, is everything okay?" Kerry asked as she lined up champagne flutes on the workspace.

"Yeah, well, no, but...kinda," Emily admitted before taking a deep breath. "Iris has asked that I don't talk about it until she's made a few phone calls. I'm sorry, Kerry."

Kerry smiled genuinely. "No problem, as long as you're okay. If you need anything, then let me know."

Emily smiled in return. "Thanks, Kerry, I really appreciate that."

She entered the first-class cabin and began setting up the seats, noting that the passenger manifest showed that the cabin would only be half full, which would give her and Kerry some breathing space.

All too quickly the call for boarding came, and they welcomed their passengers on board and served drinks.

When Olivia entered the cabin, she was immediately greeted by Kerry and handed her coat and bag over, while subtly looking at Emily for any clues as to what had happened earlier in the terminal.

She had spent the time waiting by coming up with theories as to who Lucy was and why Dr. Harvey had been so helpful. She considered that maybe Emily was unwell and that was why she seemed to welcome the doctor's assistance.

"Can I get you anything, Miss Lewis, other than a glass for your water?" Kerry asked.

Olivia silently shook her head, awkwardly avoiding eye contact in the hope that Kerry would leave her to her analysis of Emily. She watched as both women headed towards the privacy of the galley. Taking her seat, she started to unpack her belongings while considering how to find out more information.

Emily quickly worked her way through the inventory paperwork, anxious to go and speak to Iris. As soon as she was finished, she held up the papers and said to Kerry, "I'll just take these to Iris, back in a minute."

She walked through the premium cabin and into the main galley and waited for Iris to finish berating a nervous looking stewardess who Emily hadn't seen before. When the young girl scurried away, Iris turned around and noticed Emily.

"Ah, thank you." She took the paperwork from Emily and looked around to check they were alone.

"I have spoken to the airline and they have agreed." Iris signed the paperwork and then jotted a telephone number on the piece of paper she returned to Emily.

"Call that number when you are home, and ask to speak with Margaret. She will be able to sort out the details for you," Iris said with a stiff smile.

"Thank you so much, I can't tell you what this means to me—"

"Yes, well, repay me by doing your job to the best of your ability today. I'm still not one hundred percent convinced that your hectic schedule is advisable. I don't want standards to drop. I'm keeping an eye on you, Miss White."

"I understand," Emily replied. "I won't let you down."

Iris looked her up and down one last time before nodding. "Very well."

Emily decided that it was a good time to leave and headed back to the first-class cabin, noting the safety demonstration video starting on her way through the premium cabin. Entering first class, she did her standard safety check for seat belts and window blinds, and that floor areas were clear. Olivia Lewis was the only person who didn't look her way as she passed, choosing to stare defiantly at her newspaper instead.

Kerry appeared from the galley, where she had been preparing for departure.

"Everything's secure," she told Emily.

"And the cabin is ready," Emily replied professionally.

The two women took their jump seats behind 10A, and Kerry lifted the intercom and pressed the button to advise Iris they were ready for take-off in their cabin.

The sound of the engines roaring to life drowned out anything else they wanted to say, so Emily just looked out of the porthole in the emergency exit and watched as London Heathrow raced past the window.

The call from Lucy had shaken her, but the job was too important, and she couldn't let anything prevent her from delivering the very best service. Iris Winter would be on her, and if she lost her job, then things would be even worse. She kept reminding herself that she just had to get through one more flight, eight more hours, and she'd be home.

❖

When Emily began the food service, Olivia seized her opportunity.

"I do hope everything is all right?" she asked as she slowly perused the menu that she already knew by heart.

"I'm sorry about rushing off like that," Emily replied as she waited patiently for Olivia's order.

Olivia took a deep breath and finally released the statement she had been preparing in her mind. "If there is anything I can do..."

"No, thank you, Miss Lewis. Have you decided what to have for lunch, or do you need a few more minutes?"

Olivia inwardly winced at the polite yet direct dismissal and quickly gave her lunch order and handed the menu back.

For the rest of the lunch service, Olivia stewed over the conundrum that was Emily White. For some reason she was unable to get the incident at the airport out of her mind. Neither did she know why Emily was so upset nor who the mysterious Lucy was. So many unanswered questions were eating at her. Over lunch she considered her other options. But each time Emily approached, she lost her nerve and remained silent.

Once the lunch service was over, Olivia sat staring out of the window, silently berating herself for not being able to start a simple conversation or offer some comfort to someone who had clearly been distressed. She decided another attempt was in order and grabbed the empty water bottle from her armrest and approached the galley. She could hear Emily and Kerry talking privately, and she froze in front of the curtain, not wanting to interrupt their conversation.

"That cheesecake looks amazing," Emily said.

Kerry laughed. "You can have it if you like. It will just get thrown out anyway. The amount of food the airline wastes is criminal."

"Split it with me?" Emily asked.

"Okay, but just the tiniest bit, I'm watching my weight," Kerry replied.

"Watching your weight?" Emily repeated in horror. "You're almost see-through!"

"Aw, you're sweet. My boyfriend says I've been getting a bit of a belly lately."

"Dump him," Emily said plainly. Olivia smiled at the statement, which she fully agreed with.

Kerry laughed, clearly also amused by Emily's forthright attitude. "What about you? Any boyfriend?"

"No, I broke up with my girlfriend six months ago and no one since. Life's been…hectic since then."

Olivia frowned and shifted nervously. She hated eavesdropping on the conversation but also relished the information she was picking up. Clearly Lucy wasn't a love interest if Emily hadn't dated for six months.

"Oh, sorry, girlfriend," Kerry corrected. "Although, I'm not surprised with your work schedule."

"Oh, this is a new thing. To be honest, and I don't like saying this out loud, I'm in debt up to my eyeballs. I need the money so I've gotta work, work, work."

"I hear ya," Kerry said.

The curtain swished open, and Kerry stared at Olivia in shock. "Oh! Miss Lewis," Kerry exclaimed in surprise.

Olivia held the empty water bottle that she had been worrying in her hands. Kerry grabbed the bottle before Olivia had a chance to speak. "I'll bring you another water immediately, Miss Lewis."

Olivia awkwardly nodded her gratitude. "Thank you," she said as she quickly retreated back to her seat.

Kerry closed the curtain, and Emily put her head in her hands and whispered, "Shit, she heard everything, didn't she?"

"Yep." Kerry laughed. "Oh well, nothing you can do about it now. What's her opinion matter anyway?" Kerry leaned closely into Emily as she whispered, "She's weird."

Emily pondered the comment for a moment. While she didn't wish to use that terminology, she could tell that Olivia Lewis was somehow different.

"Yes," Emily whispered back. "Do you know what her story is?"

Kerry shrugged and placed a fresh bottle of water on the tray she was carrying. "Beats me," she said and left the galley.

❖

Thankfully the rest of the flight sped by, and before long Emily and Kerry were completing the final safety check of the cabin prior to landing. Emily watched New York slowly appear from her jump seat and listened to Kerry tell her stories about her boyfriend, grateful for the distraction.

Eventually they touched down, and Iris's voice sounded through the intercom as she gave her standard speech about welcoming passengers to JFK. When the aircraft came to a stop and the seat belt sign was switched off, Emily and Kerry quickly provided everyone with their jackets and luggage and wished them a safe onward trip.

As soon as the passengers disembarked, they checked their cabin. Emily found another thank-you card and fifty-dollar bill from Dr. Harvey.

Kerry seemed occupied with something one of her passengers had left for her, and Emily noticed that Olivia Lewis has left her something too. Emily picked up the flat hundred-dollar bill with a business card fastened to it by a paper clip.

It was Olivia's business card—she was CEO of a financial services firm. She turned the card over and her heart sank. On the back of the card was a large advertisement for a freephone number for a debt helpline. Emily stared at it for a moment and felt her heart thundering in her chest. Olivia had been listening in on the conversation, she'd heard everything, and this was her response.

"Ouch," Kerry said as she looked over Emily's shoulder. "That's cold."

"I know, right?" Emily spun around. "I'm not overreacting, am I? This is really rude, right?"

"That she eavesdropped on our conversation and heard you were in debt and then left you a debt advice-line card? For her own business. Yeah, it's really rude."

Emily felt her rage building as she screwed up the card and shoved it into her jacket pocket.

CHAPTER SEVEN

Olivia Lewis stepped aboard Flight SQA016 bound for London Heathrow. She walked through the premium cabin towards Jessica, who was waiting to greet her by the curtained entrance to the first-class cabin.

"Good evening, Miss Lewis," Jessica said. "Can I take your luggage?"

"Thank you." Olivia nodded and handed one of her bags and her overcoat to the stewardess before taking her seat. A moment later, an empty glass was placed on the drinks tray on her armrest as it was every Sunday evening.

A quick look around the cabin and Olivia could see that none of her regular fellow travellers were on board, and the cabin was, in fact, half empty, not at all surprising considering it was a short working week in Britain due to the public holiday on Monday.

She picked up a newspaper from her armrest and glanced at the front page with disinterest while she waited for Emily White to make an appearance. She hadn't called. Olivia didn't know why, and she certainly wasn't about to ask, but she still wanted to see her to try to piece together some information that might help her to ascertain what she had done wrong. This time.

Olivia hadn't spent much time seeking out an exact diagnosis regarding the difficulties she had communicating with people. Her mother had called her odd, her sister said socially awkward, and her friend Nicole had thrown around words like Asperger's. To Olivia's way of thinking, putting a name to the reason why she always said and did the wrong thing in social situations wasn't going to help her in any way.

With a frown she turned her head to see if she could figure out why there was a sudden commotion behind her in the crew galley and what the hushed whispers were about. Both Emily and Jessica were absent from the cabin, and Olivia strained around, to see what was happening, but to no avail. As the conversation quietened, she turned to look out of the window and watch the seemingly endless stream of passengers boarding the aircraft via the air bridge.

The telltale sound of high heels alerted her to the presence of a member of the cabin crew leaving the galley and walking into the cabin. Olivia looked up.

"Good evening, Miss Lewis, I hope the girls are treating you well?" Iris Winter asked as she stood by Olivia's seat and smiled.

"Yes, yes, they are," Olivia replied with a frown as she wondered why the cabin manager was making a rare appearance.

"Good, good," Iris said with a wide smile. She glanced expectantly at the galley.

Olivia turned to see what Iris was looking at and blinked in surprise as a young boy emerged, holding Emily White's hand. Olivia tried not to stare but found it difficult. The boy was helped up into the large leather seat by Emily, who was quietly speaking to him as she fixed the seat belt around his small hips.

"I hope you have an enjoyable flight with us, Henry," Iris said with a smile and a prim nod before she left the cabin again.

Olivia tried to stop staring. Luckily, Emily was giving the boy her full attention and didn't notice her gawping.

Jessica stepped into the cabin and bent down beside Henry with a grin.

"Wow, Henry, the big seats! How exciting. Wasn't it nice of Mrs. Winter to let you sit up here instead?"

Henry nodded and smiled at Jessica as he looked around the cubicle with fascination. He was around five years old with a mess of dark brown hair, and he wore blue jeans and a light blue T-shirt with a cartoonish giraffe printed on it.

Olivia snapped her attention back to the newspaper in her hands as she realised that this was most certainly not like every Sunday. This was rapidly becoming a very different Sunday.

Olivia cast a glance sideways and saw Jessica stand up and start to check on the passengers in the cabin while Emily tightened Henry's seat belt and ruffled his hair before heading into the galley.

The safety video began to play, and Henry explored all the options on the screen of his armrest handset with interest, and Olivia did her best to look at him without making it too obvious what she was doing. When she heard footsteps, she turned back to her newspaper and peeked over the top of it while Jessica did a final check of the cabin, the window blinds, and the seat belts, and ensured that all the overhead lockers were firmly closed.

Jessica closed the locker above Olivia, and the plane began to move away from the terminal building. Henry looked up in surprise at the movement. Jessica walked over to him and smiled calmly. "Don't worry, Henry, we won't take off for a while yet, and when we do, your mommy will come and sit with you."

Olivia frowned as she intensely studied the same article in her newspaper that she had supposedly been reading for ten minutes but had yet to take in a word of. She wondered who the boy's mother was and why a young child was flying in first class. Her question was answered a few moments later when Emily returned to the cabin and strapped herself in the seat opposite Henry.

The distance between the main seat and the temporary seat was enough that Emily could only reach Henry's feet that pointed straight out, as he was far too short for the chair. She held on to an ankle and soothingly rubbed it as she gently spoke to the boy. Olivia couldn't catch what was being said but could see the boy was looking at his mother and smiling.

The journey to the runway took ten minutes, and then the sound of the large engines roaring to life echoed loudly throughout the plane. Henry's eyes flew wide open as he stared at his mother with panic. Emily smiled at him and seemed to offer comforting words and encouraged him to look out of the window to his right, as the aircraft picked up speed and the outside scenery began to whizz past the window.

Slowly, the aircraft started to climb, and Oliva watched as Henry held his breath and pushed himself back into the comfort of the chair. He stared at his mother for reassurance, which she gave by way of a smile and a gentle squeeze of the ankle that she continued to hold. Throughout the five-minute ascent, Henry seemed to calm down and occasionally peeked out of the window with interest at the clouds and the cityscape that became visible to him when the aircraft banked heavily to the right.

An electronic sound in the distance had Emily looking up and removing her belt. She leaned forward to Henry and gave him a kiss on the forehead and handed him the telephone device from the seat armrest again, so he could access the television screen and presumably the accompanying games. Emily said a few more quiet words to him before leaving the cabin for the galley.

Another five minutes went by, and Olivia decided that she couldn't possibly stare at the boy throughout the entire flight, and her newspaper was providing her with little in the way of distraction. With a sigh, she folded the newspaper and put it in a netted compartment by the window, then closed her eyes and leaned back in her chair. Her mind raced with questions about the boy and his presence on the aircraft. She started to feel uncomfortable, like she was being watched, and she slowly opened her eyes and turned to see the boy staring right at her. He was smiling.

Olivia looked away, out of the window, but could still feel his gaze upon her. She slowly turned back and swallowed hard as he smiled a big, toothy grin at her and offered a small wave.

CHAPTER EIGHT

Olivia looked out of the window and wondered what to do. She could barely speak to adults, never mind small children. She glanced up, and the boy was still smiling at her. Olivia offered a tight, nervous smile back. Henry held up his hand and waved again at her. She anxiously returned the small wave.

"Here's your menu for this evening—oh, I'm so sorry, Miss Lewis," Emily said as she looked from Olivia to Henry in their mid-wave. "Henry! Sweetheart, I told you that you have to be good if you're going to sit up here. You can't disturb Miss Lewis."

Henry blushed and looked down at his feet, and Olivia felt she had to step in. "It's quite all right, Miss White. I know how flying alone can be."

Emily was about say something when Henry spoke up. "I don't like flying, Mommy. It's noisy and scary."

While Olivia wasn't good at reading people, she could see the panic forming in Emily's eyes. Her son was frightened, and she very clearly had a job to do and no free time to comfort him.

"He can sit with me," Olivia offered and indicated the temporary chair in her own cubicle. "That's if you think that it might h-help?" For the life of her, Olivia couldn't understand why she made such an offer. She knew nothing about children, and the whole idea terrified her, but somewhere in the back of her mind the idea had taken shape and her mouth had blurted it out.

"I can't ask you to do that," Emily whispered, but her face looked like she was seriously considering it. She looked from a lip-quivering Henry and back to Olivia.

"You're not asking, I'm offering," Olivia explained with a confused frown. "He can sit here."

"Are you certain?"

Olivia nodded. The truth was that she wasn't certain at all. Emily walked over to Henry's seat and whispered something in his ear. Initially his face lit up in a smile, but very soon he was nodding his understanding seriously. When Emily seemed assured he had understood her, she unlocked his seat belt and helped him down from the large leather chair. She continued to hold his hand as he stumbled across the aisle, not certain about the shaky movement of the aircraft. Emily put him in the temporary seat in front of Olivia, which fit him perfectly, and quickly bent down and fastened the seat belt.

"Henry, you must keep this seat belt on, okay? If you want to go back to your seat, you need to let me or Jessica know—don't go yourself," Emily told him as she tightened the belt.

"Okay, Mommy." Henry looked at her with a frown. "Where's Tiny?"

Emily looked up to the vacated seat. "Over there. I'll go and get him." The boy looked over at Olivia with another big grin, causing her to swallow in fear. Emily returned with a tatty stuffed giraffe and handed it to Henry.

"Okay, Henry, this is Miss Lewis, and she's very kindly agreed to let you sit here, but you have to be really good and not bother her because she's very busy, okay?" Emily said seriously and Henry nodded.

"Okay, Mommy."

Emily picked up the stack of menus and handed one to Olivia. "Thank you so much. I think he'll be happier just being near someone. But if you want some privacy, then press the call button, and I'll put him back in his own seat."

Olivia nodded as she took the menu but stared at Henry like she wasn't sure what to do with him now he was there. Emily continued to walk up the rows handing out menus and talking to passengers.

"This is Tiny," Henry said as he thrust the giraffe forward for her to see.

"That's a silly name," Olivia frowned. "Giraffes are big. Why is he called Tiny?"

Henry frowned as he looked at the giraffe and then shrugged. "Giraffes only sleep for two minutes at a time."

"Really?" She raised an eyebrow. "They have perfected the art of the power nap, then."

"What *should* I call him?" he asked, confusing Olivia by his sudden return to the previous topic.

"Big?" Olivia suggested but shook her head when she realised it was ridiculous. "Or Stretch?"

"In the movie the giraffe is called Melman," he added helpfully.

"Why?" she asked with a frown. "How about Spotty?"

Having tended to the other passengers, Emily approached them again. "What can I get for you this evening, Miss Lewis?"

Olivia looked at the menu in her hand and realised she hadn't even checked it and quickly scanned the familiar options.

"What's for my dinner, Mommy?" he asked.

"I brought you some pasta." Emily softly brushed her hand through his hair. "How are you feeling?"

"I'm okay." Henry shrugged and Olivia attempted to pretend she'd missed the exchange but now wondered if the boy was ill and, more importantly, if it was catching.

"I'll have the salad to start and then the salmon, no dessert," Olivia told Emily as she handed her the menu.

"No dessert?" he whispered in horror. "Were you naughty?"

"Henry," Emily hissed. Olivia looked at him before plucking the menu back out of Emily's hand and studying it again. "Very well, the chocolate fondant," she said smartly before handing it back to a surprised Emily.

"You don't have to…" Emily started but paused at the meaningful look from Olivia. "Be good," she whispered to him one last time before returning to the galley.

"Why are you eating salad?" he asked with a tilt of his head, "It's just leaves."

"Giraffes eat leaves." Olivia grinned.

"But you're not a giraffe." Henry shook his head.

"Why are you eating pasta?" she asked, not knowing what else to ask the boy.

"Because it's yummy." Henry grinned and fidgeted in his chair before squeezing Tiny tightly to his chest. "I like Tiny being called Tiny. Me, Tiny, and Mommy are going to London."

"Yes." Olivia nodded. "We're all going to London." She indicated the plane with her finger.

"Why are you going to London?"

"I work in London."

"Why do you work in London? Do you live in London? Why were you in New York? Was it a vacation?" Henry asked in quick succession.

"Er, no, I live in New York, but I work in London," Olivia replied.

"What?" Henry exclaimed. "That's really, really far. Mommy says it's so far the clocks are different!"

"That's true," Olivia conceded. "It is a long way."

"You should get a new job in New York. Then you could stay in New York, and we can be friends."

Olivia opened her mouth to reply but had no response to that and was relieved when Emily returned and began to unfold the table. "Henry, you should probably go back to your seat now."

"But I want to talk to Miss Lewis." Henry pouted at his mother as she laid a linen cloth on the table.

"He can stay," Olivia said. "He isn't doing any harm."

"He's a messy eater," Emily warned, smiling towards her son.

"I can be good," Henry replied in his best big-boy voice.

"It really is no trouble," Olivia added. "He is telling me all about giraffes."

Emily laid the cutlery down on the table and smiled at the admission. "Oh, I see. Well, that may be a very long conversation, I'm afraid. They are Henry's absolutely favourite animal in the world."

"Ever." Henry nodded with enthusiasm towards Olivia.

"Ever," Emily agreed. She stood up straight and looked at Olivia. "If you're okay to sit with him a while longer, then I can serve you together."

"Sounds wonderful." Olivia nodded, and Emily ruffled Henry's hair as she made her way further into the cabin to set up other passengers' tables for dinner.

"Olivia," Olivia said softly.

"What?" Henry asked.

"My name, it's Olivia. You don't have to call me Miss Lewis, and you don't say *what* when you don't hear someone, you say *pardon*."

"Pardon," Henry said with a nod as his young brain accepted the information.

"Very good," Olivia said proudly.

"What do you do in London?" Henry asked as he brought Tiny up and placed him on the corner of the dining table. Olivia looked at the boy for a moment as her brain struggled to think of an appropriate way to describe the complicated world of taxation, investments, offshore accounts, and personal finances.

"I help people look after their money," Olivia decided upon finally.

"Like my piggy bank?" Henry asked.

Olivia paused. "Yes, kind of."

Henry crinkled his nose. "Seems like a funny kind of job."

"Yes, it is," Olivia agreed.

"I'm having an operation," Henry told her as he picked up a spoon from the table and pretended to feed Tiny. "So is Tiny."

Olivia hesitated. "Oh? What operations are you both having?"

"My heart needs to be looked at by special doctors," Henry said with a disinterested shrug.

"I see." Olivia's eyes flicked from the boy to his mother in the distance. "And Tiny?"

"He gets neck aches," Henry said.

"Of course he does." Olivia nodded her understanding and regarded Henry with concern. Now that she knew the boy had a serious condition, she wondered even more if she was the right person to be watching over him, but he seemed well enough. Henry continued to feed Tiny imaginary food with the spoon, and she regarded him with a tilt of the head. "What are you feeding him?"

"Soup."

"Do giraffes eat soup?"

"Tiny does," he pointed out as if it was obvious. Olivia noticed that Emily looked at them as she walked past and back into the galley, trying to determine if everything was still all right between the odd couple.

"Is that because his neck aches?" Olivia asked.

He looked at her in awe, as if the thought had never crossed his mind. Then he nodded approval.

Emily returned with a salad for Olivia and placed it in front of her and held another dish in her hand. "Are you sure you're okay to sit with him while he eats?"

Olivia nodded with little understanding as to why she was agreeing to dine with a child, but somehow she knew she wanted to spend more time with the boy. Emily placed a bowl of heated pasta shapes in front of Henry and handed him a child's fork. "Please don't give any to Tiny today."

"Tiny's had soup," he told her as he plunged his fork into the bowl. Emily paused for a moment and looked at him, clearly still worried about leaving him there.

Olivia unwrapped her knife and fork from a linen napkin and looked at Emily. "To soothe his neck ache."

Emily smiled brightly. "I see," she said before retreating back to the galley. Olivia felt herself blush and looked down at her plate with an intense feeling of pride at making Emily smile.

"Does your mom make you eat salad?" Henry asked.

"No, my mother is dead."

"Oh. My daddy is dead."

"Oh." Olivia looked at the boy, moving around pasta shapes with his fork. "I'm sorry to hear that. My father is also dead."

"I don't remember my daddy. Mommy says I was an egg when he died," Henry said with a shrug. Olivia didn't know what to do with that information and began eating. Henry held up a pasta shape on the end of his fork for Olivia to see. "A giraffe!"

Olivia nodded. "Yes, it is."

"You eat it," Henry insisted as he held the fork aloft for her.

"I can't eat your dinner—that's for you to eat," Olivia told him.

"One giraffe," Henry pleaded. Olivia regarded him for a minute before spearing a thin slice of cucumber on her own fork. "I will eat one giraffe if you eat one slice of cucumber."

Henry regarded her for a moment, his five-year-old brain ticking over whether the payoff would be worth it. His mind made up, he used his hand to pick the slice of cucumber from the end of her fork and held it in between his finger and thumb suspiciously. Taking his cue, Olivia picked the giraffe pasta shape off Henry's fork and held it.

"You first," she told him.

Henry took a nibble of the cucumber and carefully chewed it as

Olivia put the pasta in her mouth. Henry looked at the cucumber with surprise and put the rest of the slice in his mouth and happily ate it.

"When I was a little girl, cucumber sandwiches were my favourite," Olivia told Henry as she continued to pick at her salad. "Would you like to try some lettuce?" Henry crinkled his nose and shook his head, clearly having gone as far as he wanted on his culinary exploration for the day.

"Would you like some more cucumber?" Olivia asked and handed him a piece at the very moment Emily returned from the galley. She saw the interaction and paused in shock as she watched her son eating a slice of cucumber. Then she smiled and shook her head before walking on.

"Have you been to London before?" Olivia asked Henry, making conversation with him as if he was an adult.

"No, I've never even left New York before." Henry smiled. "Now we're going to London because I went to the hospital on Friday."

"Oh, dear." Olivia frowned. "I am sorry to hear that. Are you feeling better now?"

Henry shrugged. "It still hurts, but it always hurts. But Mommy says that Dr. Harvey's friends will fix it, and Dr. Harvey says that I'm special, and because my heart is sick his friends will be able to teach lots more of Dr. Harvey's friends how to fix hearts like mine and make people all over the world feel better again."

Olivia smiled at his understanding of what she presumed was a teaching hospital. "Well, that really is something to be proud of."

"Tiny is scared, but I'm not," Henry said as he continued to push his pasta around his bowl.

"That's only natural. If I was Tiny, I'd probably be frightened too. But with a best friend like you, I'm sure he will be fine. As long as you eat your dinner, so you're able to be big and strong for him."

Henry's gaze angled up towards Olivia, and he gave her a look that said he knew what she was doing, but he reluctantly ate some more pasta regardless.

Emily arrived at the table and smiled at Olivia. "Can I take your plate for you?"

"Thank you." Olivia nodded.

"And would you like your main course now?" Emily asked,

though they both knew it was only a formality as Olivia always wanted her main course immediately after her starter.

"Yes, that would be lovely."

Emily picked up the plate and cutlery and returned to the galley.

"So, are you married?" Henry asked Olivia. "Do you have kids?"

"No and no," Olivia answered.

"Oh." Henry frowned. "You'll be a great mom one day."

Olivia smiled at Henry's simplistic outlook on the world. "Thank you, Henry."

"Are you lonely?" Henry asked suddenly, and Olivia looked at him in surprise.

"Why do you ask that?" Olivia asked, avoiding the question.

"You said your mommy and daddy are dead, and you're not married, and you don't have any kids, and you travel a lot." Henry shrugged and picked up a piece of pasta shaped like an elephant and put it in his mouth.

Emily returned and placed a plate of salmon, new potatoes, and green beans with hollandaise sauce in front of Olivia. Henry peered at it with part suspicion and part disgust.

Emily noticed Henry's reaction. "Eat your own, and don't worry about other people's dinner."

He nodded and continued moving his dinner around his bowl.

Emily looked at Olivia. "Can I get you anything else?"

"No, thank you," Olivia said and unwrapped her fresh cutlery.

Emily quickly returned to the galley, and Henry looked up at Olivia's plate. "What is that?"

"Salmon," Olivia explained. "Would you like some?" Henry shook his head quickly and looked back at his bowl. "Do you intend to separate all the animals into piles and then eat them or just separate them into piles?" Olivia realised what Henry was doing. He scowled slightly and started to eat the animals from the lion pile.

"Salmon is fish," Henry told her with a serious expression.

"Yes, it is."

"What is pasta?" Henry asked as he looked at a lion-shaped piece on the end of his fork.

"A mixture of flour and water," Olivia answered as she methodically cut her potatoes to release the hot steam.

"Sounds horrible," Henry said with a wrinkled nose as he looked at the pasta piece.

"Does it really matter what it is as long as you like the taste of it?" Olivia questioned.

"How do planes fly?" Henry asked suddenly, as his attention was captured by the window to Olivia's left.

"A balance of thrust, lift, weight, and drag," Olivia replied. Henry looked at her and blinked. "The plane has really, really big engines," Olivia said, trying again.

"Cool." Henry smiled. She nodded in satisfaction that he had accepted her answer and returned to her meal.

"What's a chocolate fon ant?"

"Fondant," Olivia corrected lightly. "It's a chocolate cake that melts in the middle."

"Wow." Henry's eyes lit up.

"Indeed, however I'll most likely be too full to eat all of it, so I had intended to share it with you, but only if you'd finished your pasta." Olivia had barely finished the sentence before Henry started shovelling pasta into his mouth and happily finished up his meal.

"Are we in space?" Henry asked her as she lowered her cutlery to her empty plate.

"No."

"Are we near space?"

"It depends on how you think about it," Olivia said. "If you consider how far above the ground we are, then we are relatively close to space. We're closer to space than we are to the ground."

"If we stood on the roof of the plane and stretched up really high, would we be able to touch space?"

"No." Olivia shook her head. "You'd blow off of the plane. And freeze to death on your way back down to earth."

Emily had clearly been listening in on some of the conversation and quickly approached their dining table. "All finished?"

"Yes, it was delicious," Olivia confessed.

Emily looked at Henry's empty bowl. "Wow, Henry, you finished your dinner too?"

"Yep." Henry smiled with pride.

"Miss White, if it's okay with you, I'd like two spoons for dessert," Olivia said.

Emily looked at her blankly for a second before realising what she meant. "Oh, you don't have to do that, Miss Lewis."

"I'd like to, if I may, Miss White." Olivia knew better than to randomly feed someone else's child—except for the cucumber, but that was mainly water anyway.

"Her name is Emily," Henry provided helpfully, and Olivia found herself smiling at the awkward social situation they all found themselves in, which wasn't nearly as uncomfortable as it usually was for her.

"That's very kind of you, Miss Lewis," Emily replied with a smile. "Just don't let him eat it all because he will, given half a chance."

Olivia smiled, and Emily returned to the galley.

"Why does Mommy call you Miss Lewis but I call you Olivia?" Henry asked with a frown.

"Um, well…" Olivia tried to think of a way to explain it. "Well, it's because she's at work."

"So if we went to the park, you can call her Emily?" Henry clarified just as Emily returned with spoons and napkins. His mother had clearly heard Henry's comment and started to blush.

"I'm sorry if he is being a chatterbox," she said.

"Not at all," Olivia replied as Emily placed the cutlery on the table. "He's quite the gentleman."

"Yes, he is," Emily admitted with pride. "I'll just go get your dessert."

As Emily left Henry picked up Tiny and brought the stuffed giraffe to his ear.

"Tiny says he wants to go to the park with you and Mommy."

"Oh, really?" Olivia grinned. "What about you?"

"What do you mean?" Henry frowned.

"Well, if it's Tiny who wants to go with us, what will you do while we are all at the park?" Olivia questioned lightly.

"Oh." Henry suddenly realised his mistake and quickly gave a shrug. "I'll have to come too."

Olivia laughed. "Well, I think you and Tiny need to concentrate on getting better first."

Emily returned and placed the dessert in the middle of the table and looked sternly at Henry. "It will be hot in the middle, so be careful."

Once Emily had left, Henry dropped Tiny to the floor and edged forward in his seat so he could be nearer the delicious looking dessert. He looked up at Olivia with excited eyes.

"Let's cut it in half," Olivia said as she lifted her heavy silver spoon and delicately cut the sponge in two and watched as the steaming hot chocolate sauce in the middle oozed over the plate.

"Wow," Henry whispered with low reverence. Olivia thanked whoever had invented chocolate fondants. Not only did the dessert make him smile, but it also had the bonus of keeping the boy quiet for a while. A few minutes later they were finished, and Olivia leaned forward and wiped chocolate from Henry's face with her napkin.

"If you could be any animal, what would you be?" Henry asked seriously.

"Um, I don't know," she said honestly.

"You must know," he told her as if the topic came up every day.

"Well, I don't know, a cat?" Olivia tried.

"A cat? That's so boring." Henry rolled his eyes. "Lucy wants to be a sparrow. That's boring too."

"Who is Lucy?" Olivia asked. She genuinely wanted to know more about this woman.

"Me and Mom live with her," Henry said. Olivia's chest began to hurt. "And her husband, Tom."

"Oh, I see," Olivia said and smiled, her mood turning and the pain going as easily as it had arrived. "Are they family?"

"No, I don't think so," Henry said with a shake of the head. "But they are like family."

"What animal does Tom want to be?" Olivia asked, mainly for inspiration.

"A hawk," Henry said. "He likes flying."

"Ah." Olivia nodded her understanding.

"Are you really sure you want to be a cat?" Henry asked, clearly hoping that Olivia would choose something better on a second attempt.

"I'll tell you what," Olivia said seriously. "I'll give it some thought, and I'll get back to you. Is that okay?"

Henry smiled widely.

"Okay, little man," Emily said as she approached and started to clear the plates. "You need to go to bed."

"But I'm talking to Olivia about what animal she wants to be," Henry grumbled.

"Well, you'll have to finish that discussion later, because Miss Lewis needs to go to bed, and she can't do that if you're talking about giraffes."

"I'd be a giraffe," he told Olivia.

"I probably would have guessed," Olivia admitted.

"Do you tell Olivia when to go to bed too, Mommy?" he asked as Emily removed everything from the table and onto a tray she was holding.

"Yes," Emily said seriously. "I set bedtimes for everyone on board."

"Wow," Henry whispered, clearly impressed with his mother's wide-ranging powers. Emily placed the tray to one side and folded the table back into place.

"I'm going to put these things in the galley. Say goodnight and thank you to Miss Lewis. I'll be back in a moment."

Henry made a sad face as Emily left.

"I'm sorry, Olivia," he said sincerely. "I know it's early for bedtime, but Mommy is very strict."

Olivia bit her lip to smother her laugh. "It's probably for the best. Thank you for your company over dinner, Henry."

Emily returned with some bedding and started to convert Henry's chair into a bed.

"Tiny says he likes you," Henry said as he picked the giraffe up.

"Well, I very much like Tiny, and you," Olivia admitted.

"Will you be here when I wake up?" he asked as he looked over to where his mother was making up a bed and knew that it wouldn't be long before he was also relegated to sleep.

"I certainly will." Olivia smiled. "Maybe we can have breakfast together."

Henry smiled happily. "I'd like that."

"Okay, Henry, time to get ready for bed," Emily announced as she approached with a tiny Iron Man rucksack that apparently contained his travel necessities. She bent down and unfastened his seat belt and held his hand as he stood up.

"Night night, Olivia," he said as his mother led him away. Emily looked over and mouthed her own thank you, and Olivia watched as they disappeared towards the washrooms.

CHAPTER NINE

Everyone's asleep," Emily commented to Jessica as she entered the first-class galley.

"Great. Henry okay?"

Emily nodded as she began to put the dirty crockery and cutlery into a shelved trolley. "Yes, he woke up once, but he seems to have drifted off again now."

"He's adorable." Jessica grinned while she filled in some paperwork. "Such a great kid."

"Thanks," Emily said with pride. "I'm very lucky with him."

"And he's taken to Miss Lewis," Jessica pointed out with a grin.

"Yeah." Emily sighed. "Henry is such a chatterbox. I dread to think what he has said to her."

"Well, whenever I passed them, all I heard was stuff about giraffes," Jessica said. "Miss Lewis seemed to really get on with him."

"Henry doesn't usually take to other people like that, but for some reason he connected with her right away. I just can't figure out if she was being nice or if she really didn't mind him sitting with her. You know how kids can be, making demands, and some people don't want to say no."

"She seemed happy enough," Jessica said with a smile. "And you said she had him eating cucumber, so she's clearly a good influence on him."

Emily laughed. "I thought I was going to pass out from shock. Henry doesn't eat anything green, ever. He asked if he can have cucumber sandwiches when he gets home."

"Aw, he is so sweet. It's good that he had some distraction. He must be frightened about the operation."

Emily shook her head. "No, he's fine, but Tiny on the other hand is very scared."

"Ah." Jessica nodded knowingly. "Poor Tiny."

"Exactly," Emily replied. "I wish he'd talk to me, but more and more everything goes through Tiny."

"At least he has Tiny, or you'd not hear anything," Jessica said.

Iris Winter entered the galley. "Are all the passengers settled?"

"Yes, they're all asleep," Emily replied.

"And how is young Henry?" Iris asked.

"He's sleeping at the moment. Thank you so much for allowing him to move up here, so I can keep an eye on him," Emily said.

"It made sense as there were spaces in your cabin. I had a call from the marketing department. It seems they wish to interview you about Henry for the internal staff magazine. Just a small piece about the airline agreeing to fly him to London for his operation."

"Okay, that sounds fair."

"They would also like a photograph of Henry, for the article," Iris continued.

"Okay." Emily thought for a moment. "I have a few nice ones at home that I can send to them."

"I rather think they wanted one that was more up-to-date," Iris commented. "Maybe even one of him after his operation. One that speaks to the readers a little more."

"You mean one in the hospital?" Emily asked, quickly catching on to the unspoken meaning.

"Why, yes, that's a very good idea," Iris said as if the thought had never crossed her mind. "And, of course, another one on his flight home. Maybe with a couple of key members of the crew, the captain, myself, et cetera."

Emily quickly plastered a false smile on her face. "Yes, of course."

"Wonderful, I'll call and tell them once we get to London," Iris said. "I assume you'll be taking the shift down here for the next few hours?"

"Yes, I want to be near to Henry," Emily confirmed.

"Good, I'll leave you and Sean down here, so ensure you keep an eye on the call buttons in the premium and economy cabins as well,"

Iris said and then turned to Jessica. "And I shall expect to see you in the crew quarters shortly." Iris left and drew the curtain behind her. Jessica peeked through the curtain to assure herself that the woman had gone and couldn't hear before turning around and looking at Emily open-mouthed.

"Did you know they wanted to use Henry for publicity before they offered free travel?" Jessica asked, already knowing the answer.

"No," Emily said bitterly. "They didn't mention a thing."

"Sounds like they want to make it into a real sob story as well, a photo of him in his hospital bed and everything." Jessica shook her head. "This is Iris's doing."

"How so?" Emily frowned.

"Oh, it's common knowledge that she's been after the marketing manager's job for a while now," Jessica explained. "She probably orchestrated the whole thing."

Emily sighed. "Well, I don't have a choice. There's no way I could afford to get Henry to and from London on my own. I have so many loans that there's not a bank in America that would go near me, and all my credit cards are maxed out with medical bills. I need them, and Crown knows it. I'm just going to have to suck it up. I never thought I'd get the money for Henry to have the operation he needs, but with Dr. Harvey's help…Well, I couldn't turn it down."

Jessica walked over and put her arm around Emily's shoulders. "The important thing is that Henry is going to have the operation he's been needing, and you don't have to pay for it. Then he'll be better, and you'll do a few months more of your schedule, and you'll get rid of those debts."

Emily smiled and shook her head. "Oh, this schedule won't get rid of those debts. It will mean I can get back within my credit limits. I'm over on everything and can barely make the minimum payments. I've worked out if I keep this schedule for eight months, then I'll be in a situation where I'm back within the maximum limits, rather than over."

"Wow, you're in real deep then?" Jessica questioned softly.

"Yeah." Emily sniffed and took a deep breath. "When it's your kid, you'll do anything, you know?"

"Absolutely." Jessica nodded. "I'm not a mother, so I can't imagine what you've gone through, but I know I'd do exactly the same."

Emily took another deep breath to get herself together again, and Jessica stepped away and finished up what she was doing.

"I better get going before she comes back," Jessica muttered.

"Okay, I'll see you in a few hours," Emily said.

❖

Olivia jolted awake to find Henry staring at her. For a moment she wondered why she could see him through her sleep mask but then realised that his hand was on her face where he had pushed the mask up. That was what had woken her. "Henry?"

He was kneeling on her bed in his long-sleeved giraffe pyjamas. "We're gonna crash," he told Olivia solemnly. "And I can't find Mommy."

Olivia sat up on her elbows and realised that the aircraft was flying through some turbulence, the engines rumbling slightly. Glancing to the panel above her, she noticed the seat belt sign was on display. "We're not going to crash, I promise."

The aircraft shook violently, and Henry fell forward onto Olivia's stomach before sitting himself back up on his knees again. He looked at her with something near to panic. Olivia pushed her pillow back against the wall behind her, sat up, and patted for Henry to sit beside her, thankful for his small form in the cramped space. He didn't need telling twice and quickly crawled up the bed and sat beside her, folding his legs under the quilt without invitation.

"I'm scared," he told Olivia. As her brain scrambled for something comforting to say, she noticed a rectangular lump under his T-shirt, about the size of a USB stick, located over his heart. She stared at it for a moment while she tried to figure out what it was, and Henry followed her gaze and pulled up his T-shirt to show her his chest.

"It's so Dr. Fisher knows when I'm sick," Henry said as he put his hand to the protruding lump with its angry scar and accompanying yellow bruising.

"I see," Olivia said and took the T-shirt from his hands and gently pulled it back down again.

The aircraft lurched, and Henry gripped Olivia around her middle, resting his head against her silk pyjamas. She put an arm around him and looked about her in a panic. She decided that distraction was probably the best plan of action, so she turned on the reading light, pulled out a newspaper, and flipped it open. The pages immediately caught Henry's attention.

"What's that word?" He pointed at a headline.

"Auschwitz," Olivia said quietly.

"That's a funny word," Henry said.

"Yes, it's a name of a place," Olivia said and quickly moved on. "Oh, look, China is planning to invest thirty billion dollars to create an economic corridor with Pakistan." Olivia mentally kicked herself for thinking he would understand any of the words in that headline, but she kept turning pages.

"The White House!" Henry pointed at a picture.

"Yes." Olivia breathed a sigh of relief. "And who lives there?"

"The president," Henry said quietly as he looked at the picture with interest.

"Very good, and what is the president's name?"

"Nibbles!" Henry declared happily.

Olivia frowned. "No, not Nibbles."

"I need to go wee-wee." Henry kicked back the quilt and started to crawl down the length of the bed before turning and looking at Olivia. "Come on."

"Me?" Olivia panicked.

"I can't go alone," Henry told her insistently.

Olivia pushed down the quilt and followed the small boy to the end of the bed. Once she stood up, he held out his hand for her and dragged her towards the washrooms. As she passed the galley, Olivia quickly looked in to see if Emily was there, but it was empty. She sighed. She had no idea if what she was doing was appropriate, as she was technically a stranger to Henry.

The small boy pushed the door open with his free hand and continued to hold Olivia's hand as he pulled his pyjama trousers down and edged himself up to sit on the toilet. Olivia remained in the corridor. She averted her eyes and kept her arm outstretched into the washroom where Henry still held her with a tight grip.

The curtain separating the first-class washrooms from the premium cabin moved, and Olivia felt cold dread wash over her as

Emily appeared before her with a frown of confusion. Emily angled her head into the washroom and saw her son.

"He won't let go of my hand," Olivia whispered, hoping that Emily would understand how she came to find her son and a stranger in such an odd situation.

Emily's face fell. "I'm so sorry. Did he wake you?"

"He was frightened because of the turbulence."

"I couldn't find you, Mommy," Henry called from the washroom.

"I'm sorry, Henry. I had to look after a little girl who had been sick," Emily explained as she squeezed into the small washroom.

Olivia stared fixatedly away from the scene and listened to the sound of Henry's clothes being readjusted and the flushing toilet.

"Henry, you have to let go of Miss Lewis's hand now," Emily told him.

"We read a newspaper in her bed," Henry told his mother, and Olivia felt her breathing constrict.

"Well, that was very nice of Miss Lewis," Emily said lightly. "But you shouldn't be disturbing people when they're asleep."

Olivia felt Henry's hand loosen, and she managed to step away.

"But I couldn't find you and I was scared," he whined.

"It was no trouble," Olivia said.

"You've done so much already," Emily said. "I'm mortified that he woke you."

"He really is a lovely boy," Olivia said and made tentative eye contact with Emily.

"Me and Olivia are friends," Henry told his mother as he washed his hands. Olivia didn't know what to say to that so stood silently by as Emily dried Henry's hands with a paper towel.

"Right, Henry, I'm taking you back to bed, and then I need to talk to Miss Lewis, okay?" Emily said and looked up at Olivia. "I'll be, like, twenty seconds…"

Olivia nodded and stood frozen in the corridor thinking that Emily was about to berate her over some kind of impropriety.

True to her word, twenty seconds later Emily reappeared and gestured for Olivia to step into the galley for a little more privacy. Olivia folded her arms defensively over her chest, feeling quite out of place standing there in her pyjamas.

"I am so sorry," Emily began, and Olivia looked at her in surprise, having expected to be reprimanded.

"What are you sorry for?" Olivia frowned.

"That my son has just woken you, crawled into bed with you, and forced you to take him to the toilet," Emily explained as if Olivia hadn't been there for any of it.

"It's quite all right, Miss White," Olivia replied. She couldn't understand why Emily was apologising.

"I should have been here," Emily said.

"You had to work," Olivia said. "As I said before, he is a lovely boy. I don't mind."

Emily looked at Olivia and smiled. "Thank you, I really do appreciate that."

"Miss White," Olivia said and fidgeted nervously, "I didn't hear from you, after Friday, and I...well..."

"Oh yes, the business card," Emily said and folded her own arms. "Look, thank you for trying to help, but it really isn't...I mean, I have it under control."

Olivia frowned. "I'm sorry, I don't understand."

"The debt advice, I don't need it," Emily clarified. "I'm not some dumb blonde. I can manage my own finances."

"Oh." Olivia felt perplexed and looked down at her shoes. She could sense Emily's eyes upon her as she struggled to catch up with the conversation and could feel an embarrassed blush creeping onto her cheeks. With abrupt clarity, the pieces clicked into place and she lifted her gaze to meet Emily's. "I gave you my business card."

"Yes."

"No, I mean, I gave you my *business* card."

Emily looked lost, so Olivia tried again. "I mean, I gave you my card in the hope you would call *me*. Not for financial advice."

"Oh!" Emily said with realisation. "You wanted me to *call you*-call you?"

"Why are you saying it twice?"

"You wanted me to call you, so we could talk, socially?"

"Yes." Olivia smiled, relieved at finally being understood. "I wanted to ask you out. For dinner. Or drinks. Or both."

"You attached a hundred-dollar bill to it," Emily pointed out.

"That was a tip." Olivia's frown returned. "Like I did before. I always leave a tip. Was that wrong?" she asked at Emily's prolonged silence.

"You don't think it's unusual to ask someone out on a date and pay them money at the same time?"

"Oh." Realisation dawned. "Oh!" Olivia's hand flew to her mouth as she realised her mistake. "I don't think of you like that, like...like a..."

"Like a hooker?"

Olivia felt horrified. "I'm so sorry, I didn't think."

"It's okay, I'm teasing. I mostly thought that you were offering debt advice."

"Which would also have been considered rude?" Olivia enquired nervously.

"Well, some people might think it rude if it was unsolicited and based upon a conversation you were not supposed to have heard," Emily pointed out.

"I apologise for my miscalculation. I'm prone to it."

Emily offered a comforting smile. "No need to apologise."

Olivia regarded Emily silently for a few seconds. "So?"

"So?" Emily asked, not understanding the question.

"I left you my number," Olivia prompted.

"Oh," Emily said, on realising Olivia was asking her out. "Oh, I..."

Olivia gave a tight smile at Emily's discomfort. "I understand. I'm sorry for bothering you," she said and began to turn away.

"No, wait." Emily stepped forward. Olivia paused. "I'm in a difficult place at the moment. Henry is very sick."

"So I understand," Olivia admitted.

"He is my priority, and I don't have time for anyone else in my life. This isn't some brush-off. I just have a lot going on at the moment," Emily explained with a sad smile. "If the situation was different, then my answer would be different."

Olivia strained to smile brightly but couldn't quite make it reach her eyes. "Thank you, you don't have to say that. I understand your situation. Of course, Henry is going to be your priority. I'm sorry for the confusion with the business card. I really didn't mean any offence."

Emily nodded. "Thank you for explaining."

"I'm going to go back to sleep." Olivia indicated towards her seat with her finger.

"Can I get you anything?" Emily asked.

"No, thank you, Miss White," Olivia replied and left the galley.

CHAPTER TEN

E mily was pacing the galley when Jessica returned.
        "Jess! Thank goodness."

Jessica frowned. "What's wrong? Is Henry okay?"

"Yes, he's fine." Emily reassured her then whispered, "Miss Lewis asked me out."

"Ooh." Jessica laughed.

"No, no, not *ooh*." Emily shook her head. "Absolutely no *ooh*."

"You don't want any *ooh*?" Jessica questioned.

Emily took a deep breath and leaned on the workspace. "She explained about the business card."

"Okay. So what's the scoop?"

"It was all a misunderstanding. She was leaving me her number... to *call* her."

"Like I suggested," Jessica pointed out.

"Yes," Emily hissed. "And you were right."

"So, what happened?" She looked at her watch. "I am so glad I came down here early. I love a bit of juicy gossip."

"This has to stay between us, Jess," Emily implored as she checked the curtain to make sure no one was eavesdropping. "If Iris finds out, I'm dead. I'm sure she has a rule about dating passengers. Especially those worth a million dollars."

"Of course," Jessica replied seriously. "I'd never tell anyone anything you tell me, I promise."

Emily stood opposite her and leaned on the wall. "There was a little girl being sick, and Sean called me to go and help—that man is useless."

Jessica nodded her agreement. "Yes? And? Come on, get to the juicy bit."

"While I was there, Henry woke up. He was scared because of the turbulence, but I wasn't here…" Emily drifted off and raised her eyebrows at Jessica.

"Oh my God, he didn't." Jessica covered her smile with her hand.

"Yep, he woke her up. Even climbed into bed with her." Emily shook her head, mortified. "Apparently she read to him from a newspaper."

Jessica tried to stifle her giggle but failed.

"Oh, wait, it gets better. He made her take him to the bathroom."

Jessica stared at her with wide eyes. "No way."

"Yep," Emily replied. "I came through that curtain and she's standing in the corridor, he's on the toilet holding her hand, and she's looking away to give him some privacy."

"That's adorable," Jessica said with a smile.

"I could have died." Emily shook her head. "So I put Henry back to bed and asked her to stay here, you know, so I could apologise to her."

Jessica nodded with excitement. "Yes, and…?"

"So, I'm apologising, and she's telling me what a lovely boy he is, and then she brings up the business card, and I say thanks but I've got it covered. So she's looking all confused, and then she explains, in her own way, that she wanted me to call her socially. And I say that it's weird that she put a hundred-dollar bill on the business card, and then she seemed to get why I was confused and she apologised for her…What did she call it?" Emily pondered for a moment. "Oh yes, a miscalculation. She apologised for her miscalculation and said she was prone to it," Emily continued. "And it was weird because I kinda understood her a bit better then, you know? She seems a little…stilted, like she's a bit socially awkward or something. So I tell her it's all fine, and she asks me out."

Jessica quietly clapped her hands together. "And? Then what?"

"Well, I said I can't," Emily admitted. "I don't have time to date, not while all this is going on with Henry."

"Oh." Jessica pouted. "But she's so nice—she's great with Henry, clearly."

"But what does she really know about me?" Emily questioned. "I bring her food and bottles of water, I make her bed and retrieve her luggage. We have nothing in common."

"How do you know that until you've been out with her?" Jessica asked. "Two people can come from different walks of life and still be perfect for one another."

Emily paused for a moment before shaking her head. "I have to think of Henry first. I don't have time for anyone else. My schedule is packed, and I have to take time out while Henry has his operation and recovers. Then it's the schedule from hell again. And she's a passenger. It could get awkward, you know?"

"Well, I think you're right that Iris wouldn't like it," Jessica agreed. "Look, you know what's best, and if you're not ready to see someone, then that's that. It's just a shame. She's always seemed so nice."

"Yeah, I think she is," Emily said and let out a wry chuckle. "But maybe hard work."

"The awkward thing?" Jessica smiled.

"Yeah, Henry asked me what an economic corridor is." Emily rolled her eyes "And then he said something about fish sticks, or ass witches, he wasn't sure."

"But then she is getting him to eat cucumber."

"True." Emily nodded.

Jessica smiled. "Can I ask you something?"

Emily narrowed her eyes. "Sure, what?"

"Do you think she's hot?" Jessica let out a quiet giggle.

Emily felt herself blush as she whispered, "Jess…"

"No, go on," Jessica pushed. "Do you?"

"Of course, anyone can see she's hot," Emily admitted.

Jessica grinned and turned around to press some buttons on the control panel that regulated the first-class cabin lighting to begin the slow lights-up procedure.

"What's that grin for?" Emily laughed.

"You know," Jessica said quietly.

"It's just bad timing." Emily shook her head. "I have too much on my plate right now."

Jessica took her hand and gave it a comforting squeeze and smiled at her. "Things will work out—they usually do."

"Thanks Jess, it's good to be able to talk to someone. Someone who's not five. Speaking of which, I better wake him up."

"Okay, I'll get the menus ready," Jessica said.

"Done it," Emily called over her shoulder.

"Oh, great, the ovens." Jessica looked up and noticed they were already on.

"I've been freaking out for about an hour and a half. I've done everything." Emily laughed and left the galley.

Entering the cabin, Emily could see the lighting was still on its dimmest setting. She went over to Henry's seat to find an empty bed. She quickly looked over at Olivia's bed and saw Henry sitting on the edge of it, playing with Tiny while the woman slept.

"Henry," Emily hissed. He looked up and smiled. "Henry, what did I tell you?" Emily whispered as she tentatively approached the bed.

"To not wake Olivia," Henry repeated seriously and then turned to point at the sleeping woman. "I didn't wake her, Mommy. She's still asleep, see?"

Emily could feel her heart beating out of her chest as she tiptoed closer and picked him up and carried him back to his own bed. "I meant don't go over there and bother her at all, Henry. Miss Lewis is very important and needs her sleep."

"She's a piggy bank," Henry told her as Emily balanced him on her hip.

She crouched down to pick up the overnight bag which held his toiletries and clothes, as Henry continued, "And I told her she needs to get another job, so we can all be friends in New York."

Emily pressed a kiss to his hair. "You'll be the death of me, Henry White."

"Why can I call her Olivia but you have to call her Miss Lewis?" Henry asked as Emily carried him into the washroom to get him ready, passing a sniggering Jessica on her way.

❖

Olivia woke up as the cabin lights started to come up and people started to move around the cabin. She sat up and pulled off the sleep mask and looked across the cabin to where Henry was in his chair with headphones on, watching the television screen in front of him. With sleepy disorientation, she began to remember the night before— the dinner she shared with the boy and then the middle of the night discussion with Emily. Sighing, she reached for her wash bag and clothes and smiled at Henry as she headed towards the washroom to get ready.

Another ten minutes passed before Olivia emerged in a charcoal grey pantsuit with her hair and make-up prepared for the start of her workday. She returned to her seat, which had been stripped of its bed linen and returned to its upright position, sat down, and began to sort her belongings for disembarking the aircraft.

"Good morning, Miss Lewis." Emily's voice announced her arrival. Olivia sat up and smiled as Emily handed her a breakfast menu. She noticed Henry was looking at her expectantly.

"Miss White," Olivia began, "will Henry be joining me for breakfast? I believe he wanted to."

Emily looked at Henry, who still had his headphones on and was unable to hear what was being said but was still managing to smile pleadingly at his mother.

"You really don't have to do that," Emily said with a soft smile.

"I'd like to," Olivia admitted. "And I did promise." Emily hesitated, so she added, "I have no ulterior motive if that's what you're wondering."

"What? I mean no, I didn't think that even for a moment."

"But you're hesitating," Olivia said with a frown.

"Are you sure you don't mind him sitting with you? I know he can be a handful and, truthfully, he can sit on his own."

"Mommy," Henry took his headphones off, "can I have breakfast with Olivia?"

"I'd enjoy the company," Olivia addressed Emily.

"I'll hand out the rest of these, and then I'll get you set up."

Once the menus were handed out, Emily whispered a few words to Henry. He nodded seriously before she released his seat belt and held his hand as he walked over to Olivia's chair.

"Don't forget Tiny," Henry reminded his mother as she sat him down and put his seat belt on him.

"Yes, master," Emily joked.

"A horse," Olivia said to Henry.

"What?" Henry asked and then corrected himself. "I mean, pardon?"

Olivia smiled her appreciation at his correction. "If I could be any animal, I'd be a horse," she clarified as Emily returned with Tiny.

"I like horses," Henry said thoughtfully, much happier with Olivia's revised decision.

"So do I." Olivia smiled, happy to have something in common with the boy.

"I'd be an elephant," Emily chipped in with a smile.

Olivia and Henry considered this as Emily unfolded the dining table between them.

"Mommy, you can't be an elephant."

"Why not?"

"Yes, how can you be completely happy with me being a horse but your mother can't be an elephant?" Olivia placed a napkin on her lap.

"She's too little."

"Well, that is true." Olivia regarded Emily's slim frame out of the corner of her eye.

"Maybe I'll eat more pancakes."

Henry let out a small sigh. "I think you're being silly, Mommy." He turned his attention back onto Olivia. "You have a scar on your cheek." He pointed out the faint mark on Olivia's left cheekbone.

"Henry!" Emily reprimanded him and began to blush. "I'm sorry," she said to Olivia.

"Why are you sorry?" Olivia questioned. "I do have a scar."

"But he shouldn't bring it up. You might be uncomfortable with it."

"Oh. Well, I'm not." Olivia shrugged.

"How did you get it?" Henry pressed. Emily rolled her eyes and headed towards the galley, obviously at a loss with the rules of the relationship her son and Olivia had formed between themselves.

"I fell off of my bike when I was a child," Olivia told him.

"Did it hurt?" Henry asked as he looked at the scar.

Olivia frowned as she considered it. She hadn't thought about the incident for many years, and no one had ever asked her that question before.

"I believe it did," she finally agreed. "But I forgot about it quickly."

"I'll have a scar," Henry told Olivia distractedly as he played with Tiny. "But Tiny says it won't hurt. What do you think?"

Olivia wanted to kick herself for her lack of forethought regarding Henry's questioning. Her mind raced to find the correct thing to say, but she had no idea how to deal with this kind of conversation, and she began to look helplessly around the cabin for Emily.

"Well…" She strained around and saw Emily and the relief was tangible.

Emily quickly approached the table. "Everything okay here?"

Henry was preoccupied with Tiny, and Emily looked at Olivia with a questioning glance. Olivia hesitated for a moment. "Henry was just saying that he will have a scar after his operation," she said.

"Olivia said her scar hurt." Henry looked up at Emily accusingly, and Olivia shifted nervously in her seat.

"But her scar was caused by an accident, right?" Emily confirmed with Olivia who nodded quickly. "Your scar is going to be made when you're sleeping and by people who are very clever."

"Okay." Henry considered the point and then nodded and shrugged, indicating that his interest in the conversation was waning.

"I'm sorry." Olivia looked up at Emily apologetically. "I didn't—"

"Oh, it's fine." Emily smiled sincerely. "Now, what about breakfast?"

"Toast!" Henry looked up at his mother with a smile.

"Toast, what?" Emily looked back at him with a grin.

"Toast, please." He tried again.

"I'll have the croissants and jam," Olivia replied. "And coffee."

"Can I have coffee?" Henry asked with a cheeky smile.

"No, you can have hot chocolate." Emily ruffled his hair as she returned to the galley.

"When we get to London, will you come with Mommy and me?" Henry asked.

"Oh, I can't, Henry," Olivia said sadly. "I have to go to work. I have meetings."

Henry nodded his understanding and stared at the table. Olivia could sense the young boy had a lot of things on his mind and clearly was thinking about his upcoming operation. Over the course of breakfast, Olivia tried to make conversation, but he steadfastly answered with one-word answers or a nod or shake of his head. She kept encouraging him to eat and even shared some of her jam with him to make the toast a little more appealing, but Henry's mood for the day seemed to be set.

When breakfast was over, Olivia said goodbye to Henry as Emily moved him back to his own seat. Once he was settled, Emily returned to clear the breakfast things away.

"I'm sorry," Olivia said. "I don't think I was much help."

Emily looked over at Henry, who was drawing something on a piece of paper.

"He's often a little shy in the morning. And he is nervous, so I don't think anything would help much today. But I know he appreciated your company, so thank you."

"I wish I could do more, but I'm not good with children."

"You're great with him—he adores you."

Olivia looked surprised and looked to Henry, who was fiercely concentrating on his colouring project. "I…" She drifted off, unsure of what to say.

"Thank you again, for everything," Emily told her sincerely. "You've made a really stressful journey easier for him. And for me."

Olivia smiled as Emily returned to the galley to prepare for landing. Not long after, both Jessica and Emily were checking window blinds and seat belts. Emily took the temporary seat in front of her son and watched him as he leaned on the solid armrest and continued to colour. Absorbed in his colouring, Henry was unaware how close they were to landing and would have missed the experience if not for Emily shaking his foot to get his attention. Surprise filled his face as the aircraft came down, and the gentle impact shocked him, but after a reassuring smile from his mother he smiled back at her and looked out of the window.

Once the aircraft was docked at the gate, Emily and Jessica set about gathering the passengers' belongings, and as Olivia stood up, she saw Henry beckoning her over. He was still strapped into his own seat.

He held out a piece of paper and she took it with a smile. "Is this for me?"

Henry nodded. "It's you, me, Mommy, Tiny, and all his giraffe friends in the park."

Olivia tilted her head but couldn't really make out any of the figures that Henry was claiming he'd drawn. "Thank you, Henry, it's lovely," she said. Henry smiled up at her with pride.

Emily approached with her bag and coat.

Olivia was uncertain what to say. After a few moments, she said somewhat formally, "Goodbye, Henry, I hope to see you again someday."

Emily nodded her gratitude and handed over her bag and coat.

"Have a safe onward journey, Miss Lewis," Emily said politely.

Olivia nodded and took one final look at Henry before leaving the cabin, wondering if she'd ever see the boy again.

CHAPTER ELEVEN

The next Friday, Olivia sat at the departure gate scrolling through email messages on her smartphone, but her mind was elsewhere. She had spent most of the week looking forward to the flight home, not because she wanted to go home and not because she enjoyed the flight. She was looking forward to seeing Emily White again, and finding out about Henry's operation, or maybe even seeing him again. All week she had been kicking herself that she had not asked Emily if there was anything she could do for them while they were in London. She didn't even know which hospital Henry was in.

She was unsure where to start that kind of conversation and reminded herself that she was practically a stranger in Henry's life. Sure, he had connected with her on the flight, but he had been frightened and lonely, and she figured that it probably meant little.

The announcement came for first-class passengers to begin boarding. She took a deep breath as she entered the aircraft and nodded politely at the cabin crew by the entrance. In the cabin, she saw a flash of blond hair but quickly realised it wasn't Emily. The stewardesses on this flight were Ashley and another blond girl she didn't recognise. With disappointment as she realised she couldn't see either Emily or Henry anywhere, she moved to her usual chair.

It wasn't until much later on in the flight that it occurred to Olivia that Emily would probably have changed her schedule to accommodate Henry. With frustration, she realised she didn't know if the pair had already returned to New York or if they had remained in London. A thought she had been attempting to keep silent traitorously surfaced, and she wondered if Henry had even survived the operation. This depressed her further as uncertainty tore at her.

She considered the appropriateness of asking the crew for information on Emily and Henry. But she was unsure of the social protocol for such things and wondered if they would be willing to divulge the information if they even had it.

Deeming the risk in asking was too great, and her mind now too confused to focus on work, she picked up the airline-issued headphones and plugged them in to the armrest.

She pressed the touchscreen television in front of her and quickly scrolled through the enormous number of movies on offer, none of them catching her interest.

She sighed deeply and scrolled through the television offerings, stopping when she came to a documentary about giraffes. With a sad smile, she selected the show, took a sip from her water glass, and settled down to find out more about Henry's favourite animals.

❖

Olivia appreciated and required order in her life. So the fact that her entire weekend schedule had been completely wrecked by her incessant worrying about Henry was not a welcome change. She had tried to call Nicole but belatedly remembered that her friend was on a weekend break, leaving her to fret alone.

No amount of distraction seemed to be able to take her mind off the questions her brain continued to present regarding the whereabouts and well-being of young Henry White.

Two days later and Olivia anxiously waited to board Flight SQA016 to London Heathrow. She gripped her smartphone firmly in her lap as she looked around the terminal for Emily but didn't see her. Over the last few days, she had made the decision that she would ask Jessica, a member of the cabin crew she felt she knew well enough to speak openly to, if she knew anything.

Olivia also hoped that Dr. Harvey would be on board. Although she by no means knew the man well, she had made small talk with him a few times in the many years they had flown together.

She looked longingly at the coffee shop where she usually sat and ate an afternoon snack following her priority check-in. Instead, she now sat in the front row of the departure gate waiting for the arrival of anyone she knew who might have some information. After an uncomfortable hour of waiting, the gate staff finally arrived and, thirty minutes later, the cabin crew. She looked for Emily but couldn't see her in the crowd. She did see Jessica Martin talking to Iris Winter. Olivia continued thinking about how she would phrase her question to Jessica once they boarded.

Boarding was finally announced, and Olivia felt emotionally drained by all her worry. Worry that she didn't really understand. She barely knew Henry or his mother, but in a short amount of time she had become very attached to them both. Olivia's life was restrained and orderly, and the change to her personal schedule caused by Emily's absence unsettled her. Coupled with the fact that she had no idea what had happened to the little boy, and her anxiety levels were peaking to unacceptable levels.

Upon boarding the aircraft, Olivia quickly made her way to first class and was surprised to find Iris Winter and one of the male cabin crew from the premium cabin greeting her.

"Where is Miss Martin?" Olivia asked Iris with a frown.

"Miss Martin is working upstairs on this flight," Iris answered with a polite smile. "We have a full house upstairs today and only half capacity here, so that means that Sean will be looking after this cabin."

The change was one that Olivia hadn't planned for, and she glanced at the nervous looking man for a few moments before taking her seat. Realising that her opportunity to question Jessica about Emily was gone, she clenched her fist in frustration and angrily berated herself for her cowardice in not questioning Iris when she had the chance.

"What has that salad done to you?"

Olivia looked up with a frown. "I'm sorry?"

"That salad." Her friend pointed to the plate in front of Olivia. "You've been stabbing at it for the last fifteen minutes."

She looked down at her meal and laid her fork down. "I'm sorry, Nicole, I'm a little distracted."

"I know." Nicole picked up her wine glass and took a sip. "You were distracted all last week, and this week is shaping up to be the same. So something is obviously bothering you."

"I'm sorry," Olivia repeated as she picked up her tumbler of water and sipped the lukewarm liquid, the ice long since melted.

"Don't be sorry. Just stop telling me that everything is fine and tell me what's up."

Olivia regarded Nicole thoughtfully. She had been deliberately avoiding telling her about her latest social faux pas, hoping that the feelings of inadequacy would pass as soon as she saw Emily again. But Emily's prolonged absence meant that she continued to feel distracted and out of sorts.

While Nicole was her best friend and her go-to person for advice, it often took Olivia a little time to open up. It seemed that the greater her distress, the more susceptible she became to Nicole's investigative behaviour. It was always easier to talk about the little things.

She looked around the busy restaurant which was located off Southampton Row and directly opposite Olivia's London office. They'd lunched there most Tuesdays and Thursdays for as long as either of them could remember.

"It's silly," Olivia said quietly.

"I don't think it is," Nicole replied. "You don't often get distracted, so something must be upsetting you."

Olivia placed her linen napkin on her plate to indicate that she was finished and debated whether or not to say anything further.

"I..." Olivia paused as she contemplated her words. "I met someone. She works for the airline."

"Oh yes?" Nicole smiled at the news.

"Yes, I told you about her, the attendant who helped clean my wound."

"Oh, right, of course, the sexy nurse."

"I left her my business card," Olivia explained, ignoring Nicole's comment. She paused as a waiter came and removed their plates.

At Olivia's continued silence, Nicole prompted, "Did she call?"

"No," Olivia shook her head. "And on the following Sunday, there was a boy in first class, about five years old. It turned out he was her son."

Nicole frowned. "You're losing me, darling. There was a five-year-old boy in a first-class seat?"

"Yes." Olivia nodded to assure her that this wasn't just another misunderstanding as it so often was. "His name was Henry, and we had dinner together."

Nicole stared at her incredulously. "You had dinner with a five-year-old boy in a three-thousand-pound first-class seat?"

"Yes." Olivia sighed and closed her eyes for a moment while she arranged her thoughts. Nicole waited patiently, well-versed in an average Olivia Lewis conversation.

"He was frightened, you see. He'd never flown before. I didn't know why he was on board, but I later found out that he was coming to London for an operation. It seems he has a problem with his heart," Olivia explained.

"Oh, how awful." Nicole frowned. "So, you had dinner with the boy?"

"Yes, and the mother, her name is Emily, well…" Olivia let out a long breath as she attempted to replay the events in a format that would make sense to a stranger. "He—Henry—woke up in the night. He wanted me to take him to the washroom since he couldn't find his mother."

Nicole tried to hide a smirk behind her hand. "Okay."

"Emily came along and took Henry to bed, and then we spoke in private. She hadn't realised I had left her the business card because I wanted her to call me," Olivia explained.

"Why else would you have left it?" Nicole asked, searching out the missing piece of the puzzle.

"On the Friday flight, I overheard her speaking with her colleague and found out she had an ex-girlfriend and was in debt."

"Right," Nicole said, but she was clearly still clueless.

"So when I left my business card attached to a tip and with the debt advice line on the back, she thought I was offering financial advice," Olivia explained.

"You didn't leave a note?" Nicole asked. "Wait a minute, you left your phone number for someone to call you…attached to some money?"

Olivia nodded. "Yes. But it's okay now. I realise that was wrong."

Nicole smiled. "Okay, so she thought you were offering financial advice?"

"Yes, so I clarified the matter, but she said she isn't in a position to date anyone at the moment because her son is ill, and she needs to focus her attention on him," Olivia explained. "Which I understand, of course. But I've not seen her since then and I...I don't know what happened to Henry. I don't know if he had his operation, if he survived, if he is still in London, if he is in New York. I can't find Emily, and I don't know who to ask. It's disturbing my sleep. The not knowing."

"I see." Nicole nodded her understanding. "You want to know if Henry is okay—that's perfectly natural."

"But I'm aware that Emily doesn't want to see me socially, and essentially I'm a stranger to them," Olivia pointed out.

"Did you argue?" Nicole asked.

"Not to my knowledge," Olivia answered thoughtfully.

"Did she look angry?"

"No, she smiled. She thanked me a lot for watching Henry," Olivia said after consideration.

"Okay," Nicole said. "So Henry is five years old, give or take. Do you know his surname?"

"I believe it's the same as his mother, White," Olivia answered with confusion. "Why?"

"And he was having a heart operation in London?" Nicole continued.

"Yes." Olivia nodded.

"Okay, I have a friend who works at the National Health Service. I'll see if I can find anything out for you. However, it wouldn't be entirely legal."

Olivia considered it for a moment, uncertain of what to do.

"Of course they wouldn't give any sensitive information, only confirmation of where he is, if indeed they know that much."

Olivia slowly nodded. "Yes, please see what you can find." Olivia was suddenly nervous. "But what would I say?"

"Hello, Henry, I hope you're feeling better?" Nicole chuckled. "But let's not get ahead of ourselves—we need to find them first. Leave it with me."

"Thank you, Nicole." Olivia smiled genuinely for the first time in a while.

"Well, it's not like you to leave your number with someone. This Emily White must really be something." Nicole grinned.

Olivia nodded slowly. "Yes, there is something about her that I find endearing. But the timing isn't right."

"Well, one step at a time, eh?" Nicole said and took another sip of wine.

CHAPTER TWELVE

Simon Fletcher, Olivia's PA, was signing for a parcel at the main reception desk as Olivia stepped into the building.

"Nicole is in your office—she said it was important," he told her.

Olivia nodded and quickly walked down the long corridor. Every step of the minute-long walk she panicked about what Nicole was there for and what she had found out.

Nicole was standing by the window looking down on a bustling Southampton Row below.

"Nicole?" Olivia asked, her voice slightly shaky.

Nicole turned around and smiled widely. "Come here," she said.

Olivia put her coat and bag on a chair and joined her.

Nicole pointed out of the window. "What do you see?"

"London."

"More specifically, what is that building there?" Nicole indicated a building not far away. Olivia smiled. She knew it well. The construction of the new wing had been something she had taken a personal interest in, convincing a large investment bank to donate an enormous sum of money for the state-of-the-art facility.

"Level six," Nicole said. "Bear Ward."

"Unbelievable," Olivia whispered as she looked at the building she had watched take shape from her office over the past five years.

"I know. Who would have thought he'd end up at Great Ormond Street Hospital for Children? A five-minute walk from your office. Sounds like fate to me."

"How is he?"

"I don't know his condition," Nicole admitted. "They wouldn't give me any information over the phone. I also don't know when he might be released, so if I were you, I'd clear your diary and get over there quickly."

Olivia balked at the idea. "But I have meetings." She looked at her watch in mild panic. "And I have work to do and…and calls to make."

Nicole smiled. "Yes, and a ton of other excuses too. But if you don't go and see him now, you won't know. And trust me, not knowing is worse."

A quiet knock on the door frame caused them both to turn towards Simon. "Will you be wanting coffee?" he asked.

Nicole picked up her coat. "Not for me, thank you, Simon. I'm just leaving." She collected her bag and turned back to Olivia. "Call me later, and let me know what happens."

Olivia watched her leave then turned to the hospital, staring at it for a few moments.

"Olivia," Simon asked quietly, "did you want any coffee?"

"No," Olivia whispered. An idea forming in her mind. "No, but I need you to clear my diary for the rest of the day." She stepped towards her desk and paused. "What do you buy a child who has had an operation?" she abruptly asked.

Her PA stepped into the office. "How old is the child? Boy or girl?" He adjusted his thick-framed glasses and looked thoughtful.

"Five, and a boy," Olivia replied.

While Simon was only in his mid-twenties, he was sensible and intelligent and always seemed to be a couple of steps ahead of Olivia's rambling thought process, so she felt safe asking him such a strange question.

"Sweets? Toys? What does he like?" Simon asked with a smile.

"Giraffes. He loves giraffes."

"Giraffes?" He picked Olivia's coat up from where she had dropped it and hung it up in the closet. "Well, presumably he has a toy giraffe already."

"Yes, his favourite toy is a giraffe called Tiny," Olivia agreed.

"Cute."

"It's silly." Olivia sniffed.

"It's ironic," Simon corrected as he leaned on the back of a chair facing her desk. "Well, there's no point in getting him a toy giraffe—nothing will replace Tiny. How about one of those helium balloons? The ones with little weighted feet?"

"Why would he want that?" Olivia frowned.

"It would be shaped like a giraffe," Simon clarified.

"Oh!" Olivia caught on. "Yes, I think he would like that."

"But helium balloons fade, so you might want to get him something more permanent," Simon suggested as he got his smartphone out of his back pocket and started to type.

Olivia sat at her desk and moved the mouse to wake her computer up and opened her emails.

"Okay, here we go," Simon said as he read off his screen. "Giraffe-themed gifts seem to be big business. Books, mugs, water globes, cushions, balloons, rucksacks, key rings, slippers, stickers, money boxes, bookmarks—"

"Money box." Olivia's head snapped up. "A giraffe money box. I couldn't think of a way to explain my work to him, so I said I looked after other people's money, and he said I was like a piggy bank."

"Okay." Simon smiled. "A giraffe money box, anything else?"

"The balloon with the feet." Olivia looked thoughtfully at Simon. "And something else. The giraffe rucksack."

"Sure, money box, rucksack, and balloon." Simon nodded. "Do you want a giraffe get-well-soon card?"

"Do I?" Olivia asked him curiously.

Simon shrugged. "It's traditional, I guess."

"Then one of those too," Olivia said. "How long will it take you to get these things?"

"When do you need them for?" Simon regarded her with a knowing look.

"As soon as possible. Money is no object. I need these things today. This morning, in fact...Oh, and wrap them in giraffe paper."

Simon smothered a smile. "Giraffe paper, no problem," he said and made to leave the office.

"Oh, and don't forget to clear my schedule for the rest of the day," Olivia repeated as he got to the door.

"Of course," he called back and left.

"Oh, and Simon?" Olivia looked up.

He poked his head back through the door and looked at her expectantly.

"Could I have that coffee?" Olivia asked him with a cheeky smile.

Simon laughed. "Sure, coffee, cancel day, giraffes, back in a flash!"

He returned quickly with coffee, and a few minutes later Olivia saw cancellation notices being sent out regarding her afternoon meetings. She turned around in her chair and looked at the London skyline, her eyes drifting towards the famous Great Ormond Street Hospital as she remembered the years of fundraising efforts and the many meetings she had attended. When she had first begun working in the London office in Bloomsbury, she was quickly informed of the importance of the historic London hospital and the special place the charitable trust held in Britons' hearts.

The hospital was founded on Valentine's Day in 1852 and was the first hospital providing services specifically for children in the whole of England. Through the patronage of Queen Victoria and Charles Dickens it quickly boomed from a ten-bed hospital to one of the world's leading children's facilities. Such was the public love for the hospital that playwright JM Barrie donated the copyright to Peter Pan to the trustees of the hospital on the provision that the amount of money generated was never disclosed. Olivia's father had begun working with the hospital when Olivia was a child, and since then the family business worked closely with the board of trustees. It held a special place in her heart.

Now it seemed to come full circle, and after so many years of looking after the hospital's best interests, it seemed to Olivia that the historic institution was looking after something for her. Knowing that Henry and Emily were so close, she began to experience the familiar nerves again as she wondered if she was doing the right thing, specifically wondering if she would be a welcome visitor. Admittedly, she hardly knew them and had used her contacts to track them down in a manner which Olivia wasn't one hundred percent sure was civil, never mind legal.

Lost in her work, it was an hour later when Simon walked into her office with his arms full. He placed everything on a chair and then, one by one, handed the items to her.

"One giraffe rucksack," he said. She took the item and looked at it with a smile.

"One giraffe money box, rubber so it won't break." He took the rucksack back and handed her the bank, which she looked over with a nod.

"I made an executive decision," he told her with a grin and held up an item of clothing. "Giraffe hoodie!"

Olivia chuckled at Simon's enthusiasm as he showed off the dark blue garment with a large giraffe print emblazoned on the front before holding up the hood to show two giraffe horns and ears.

"I know," Simon said. "It's adorable, but don't get excited because it doesn't come in adult sizes."

He handed her the hoodie and she examined it with a smile. "It looks perfect."

"Great." Simon held up two sets of wrapping paper. "Which do you prefer?"

Olivia looked at the choices and pointed to one. Simon nodded and then picked up two get-well-soon cards. "Giraffe with a bandage on his leg or giraffe with a scarf?"

"Scarf," Olivia said after a moment of deliberation.

"Great, the balloon is on the way. I'll get these wrapped up while you sign this." He handed her the greeting card.

"What should I write?" Olivia looked at Simon with a frown.

"What's his name?"

"Henry White."

"How about, Henry, get well soon. Love, Olivia," Simon suggested.

"That's all?"

"You could add that you hope he enjoys the gifts."

Olivia nodded. "Very well."

Simon smiled. "Everything will be ready for you in about fifteen minutes."

"Good, make sure you bring a jacket—it's a little chilly today," Olivia told him as he got to the door.

He paused and turned around to regard Olivia with a confused expression. "I'm coming with you?"

"Yes," Olivia replied as if it were obvious.

"Okay." Simon shrugged and left the room again.

Olivia sighed. She knew it was a cop-out, but she needed someone to accompany her. For her, it was a strange situation that she was heading into. Simon was chatty and friendly and could charm the birds out of the trees. Olivia knew that having him there would help any potential awkwardness that might arise. As well as helping her to identify any awkwardness that had already arisen, as she was often unaware.

Thirty minutes later, they had walked the short distance to Great Ormond Street Hospital and were on their way to the Bear Ward for children with cardiac conditions.

Olivia held a large, brightly coloured paper gift bag with giraffes on it, which Simon had provided to carry the wrapped gifts in. Simon walked beside her with a giraffe-shaped helium balloon with weighted feet that made it seem as if the balloon was walking. Olivia had steadfastly refused to walk through the streets of Bloomsbury with the balloon, but Simon happily stepped out with it, making conversation with people as he went.

Approaching the reception desk on Bear Ward, Olivia slowed slightly as her nervousness started to amplify.

Simon leaned on the desk and smiled at the nurse. "Good afternoon." The nurse smiled at him and looked at the giraffe balloon.

"We're here to see Henry White," he said while Olivia looked around the brightly coloured hospital ward with interest. It wasn't like any ward she had seen before with its murals, and mood lights in the ceiling, and she found herself comforted that Henry was being treated in such a friendly place.

"Henry and his mother are in room seven," the nurse said and stood up to give directions.

Olivia tuned out the rest of the conversation and kept her head down as she walked behind Simon in the indicated direction. Suddenly she found herself nearly walking into him as he stopped and turned to face her.

"Do you want me to come in with you?" Simon asked her casually as he indicated a large cartoon bear painted on the wall next to him with an equally large number seven. Olivia nodded. He turned around and gently knocked on the open door to room seven and walked in with a friendly smile.

Olivia fell into step behind him and saw Emily in a chair beside Henry's bed. The boy was asleep, his body connected to various monitors and machines by wires and tubes. Henry was pale and looked so tiny in the large bed, and Olivia felt her breath constrict. She quickly looked at Emily, who rose from her seat. She looked surprised and confused to see Olivia there, but not unhappy.

"Miss Lewis?"

"Hello, Miss White," Olivia said. "I—I was worried about Henry's condition and didn't know how to contact you to ask."

"I'm Simon." He stepped forward and held out his hand. "I work with Olivia."

"Emily." She shook his hand, still looking at Olivia in surprise. "How did you find us?"

"A friend." Olivia was vague. "I'm sorry if we're intruding."

"No, it's good to see a friendly face."

"The website tells me that this is giraffe balloon zero-zero-one-four," Simon said as he gestured to the balloon. "But I'm sure your son will come up with a much better name."

The joke cleared the air, and Emily let out a small chuckle as she looked at the balloon and said, "Thank you so much, he'll love it."

Olivia frowned as she looked at the motionless boy.

"The first operation didn't go too well, so they had to keep him in and operate again," Emily explained softly. "He's recovering nicely now, though."

"May I ask what was wrong?" Simon asked as he parked the balloon by the wall.

"He has an underdeveloped heart," Emily replied. "He needed surgery to fix three of his heart valves."

Simon nodded his understanding. "And the valves have now been repaired?"

"Yes, when he had his first operation, they realised it was worse than they thought, but now he's all patched up." Emily smiled at Olivia directly. "Thank you for coming."

Olivia took a step towards Emily and held out the bag. "Some gifts, for when he wakes up."

Emily smiled brightly as she took the bag. "Thank you, you really didn't have to."

"I better head back to the office to do that thing, unless you need me for anything else," Simon said.

She opened and closed her mouth, realising she had no logical reason to ask him to stay. Seeing the twinkle in his eye, she simply said, "I will see you tomorrow."

Simon grinned and turned to Emily. "Lovely meeting you, Emily." He waved his goodbyes.

Olivia watched the traitor leave and then turned to look at Emily nervously. "I…" She pointed at the bag that Emily held. "Giraffes."

"Yes," Emily said with a wide smile. "He'll be ecstatic. He's not had any visitors since he's been here. We don't know anyone in London."

"Well, you do now." Olivia nodded and looked at Henry again, disconcerted by the boy's pale complexion.

"Would you like to sit down? It's nice to see a friendly face," Emily said as she took her own seat again.

"I imagine it has been very difficult," Olivia admitted as she perched on the edge of a visitor's chair. "Where are you staying?"

"Here," Emily said and pointed to a sofa on the other side of the room. "It's a sofa bed and there's a bathroom." She pointed to a door.

"You've stayed here the whole time?" Olivia questioned. "For a week and a half?"

"Yes." Emily nodded. "Where else would I go?"

"You must be exhausted," Olivia commented. She couldn't imagine watching over a sick loved one for that long and never leaving their hospital room.

"Well," Emily said with a shrug, "you do what you have to do." Emily looked at Henry and gently took his hand. Olivia noted how pale she was. She had to be almost sick with worry. Freed from the brutal airline conformity of make-up and hair, Emily looked younger and maybe even vulnerable.

"Are you eating properly?"

Emily smiled. "Is that a nice way of saying I look like hell?"

Olivia hesitated because frankly that was exactly what she was saying. "You have to keep your strength up." She settled on what she hoped was a diplomatic answer.

"Why did you come here?"

"Should I leave?" Olivia asked, already preparing herself to go.

"No, I'm just curious. You're a passenger, and I'm cabin crew. We hardly know each other, and yet you're buying my son gifts and visiting his bedside."

"I've been told that my behaviour is not always predictable," Olivia said seriously.

Emily laughed lightly. "Yes, I can somehow believe that."

Olivia sighed as she tried to collect her thoughts. "You weren't working on my usual flights, and I was worried about Henry's condition, and I wanted to see for myself how he was."

"I see," Emily said. "Well, he's still recovering from the second operation, but hopefully he will be more like himself tomorrow."

"And you?" Olivia asked gently.

"I'll be fine." Emily gave a tight smile, and even Olivia knew it was faked.

"Is there anything I can do?" Olivia asked.

Emily gestured at the balloon and the bag of gifts. "You've already done so much."

They sat in silence for a few minutes. Nervously wondering what to say next, Olivia reached into her handbag and pulled out a business card and handed it to Emily. "I had them reprinted—no debt helpline."

Emily held the card and looked at Olivia curiously.

"My office is literally a five-minute walk away, and I stay at the Hilton, which is even closer," Olivia told Emily nervously, refusing to make eye contact. "I know you hardly know me, but you said that you don't know anyone at all in London. Now you do. So if you need anything at all, please do call me, even if it's something minor."

Emily looked down at the business card thoughtfully for a moment, and Olivia took it as her cue to leave. She stood up and looked at Henry one last time before heading towards the door.

"Coffee?"

Surprised, Olivia turned around and looked at her.

"If you have time, maybe we could have coffee? Maybe tomorrow? You could come and see Henry open his presents," Emily suggested.

Olivia smiled and her heart lightened at the prospect. "I'd like that very much."

"Lunchtime? Around one?" Emily asked.

Schedules and meetings were again thrown out of the window as Olivia nodded her agreement. "Tomorrow at one," she replied with a smile.

Chapter Thirteen

Emily paced around the fountain in the small garden located outside the hospital, with her phone pressed to her ear. "I can't accept that." She sighed.

"Look, Em," Tom's friendly voice spoke softly back, "once Henry is released by the hospital, he isn't going to be well enough to fly for at least another week. You need to stay somewhere with him, and we both know that London isn't cheap."

"I can't take more of your money. You've done so much already," Emily told him as she sat on a bench and leaned forward, her head on her free hand.

"This isn't about you or me or money," Tom told her seriously. "This is about Henry. He needs to be near his doctors for check-ups, and even with the grant from the hospital, you're still looking at over twelve hundred dollars for a week in a hotel. Then you need to add food expenses to that, and I know you don't have any money coming in at the moment since you've extended your vacation leave."

"I've been looking around, and I've found another option," Emily explained. "There are hostels around, well, not right here but in London. Henry and I can stay in a hostel for about four hundred for the week. I can just about do that."

"A hostel? What kind of hostel?" Tom's voice started to build in concern.

"It's not a dive, Tom—it's fine," Emily said as she shot to her feet and began pacing again.

"Hostel?" Lucy's voice could be heard in the background and then she obviously gained control of the phone. "Emily, you can't go to a hostel."

"Lucy, I don't have much choice. It's been a godsend that I can stay with Henry in the hospital—otherwise I'd be in a cardboard box or a shelter by now. I can't keep borrowing money. I know you guys are struggling too. I can just about afford the hostel with what you've already loaned me," Emily explained. "I've seen pictures of it online. They have lots of different rooms, and the ladies' dorms are only twelve beds to a room."

"Twelve beds?" Lucy sounded panicked. "Emily, you can't do that. Who knows what kind of people will be there, and Henry will be recovering from an operation."

"Give me some credit. I have checked it out." Emily sighed. "It's safe and it's clean."

Lucy took a deep breath and sighed. "I'm sorry, Emily. I know you're trying to do what's best, but we just feel so useless stuck all the way over here."

Emily looked up at the grey London sky and realised belatedly that she should have taken a coat with her, as the wind started to pick up and she was only wearing jeans and a thin grey sweater.

"I know, it's okay," Emily said gently. "Just another week or two and Henry will be safe to fly, and then things will get back to normal." She looked at her watch. "Look, I have to go. Thank you again for the transfer. I really don't know what I'd do without you two."

"We love you both," Lucy said. "Call us again when you can."

"I will. Love to you and Tom," Emily said. She disconnected the call and sighed. She looked around the small park which was surrounded by tall London buildings, a preserved oasis in the middle of the city. It was then she saw a familiar face sitting on a park bench with a takeaway coffee in one hand and eating a chocolate bar with the other. "Simon?" Emily questioned as she approached him.

Simon looked up at Emily and smiled happily. "Emily, hello again."

"You really do work locally, huh?" Emily smiled.

"Yep." Simon pointed down at the park gates. "Through the gates, onto that road, and on the main street. I come here to get out of the office sometimes. Do you want to join me?"

Emily sat on the wooden bench beside him and stared ahead at the central fountain while Simon took another bite of chocolate. She usually wouldn't just start up a conversation with a practical stranger, but Simon was endearing and seemed harmless. And having been stuck in the hospital for so long, she was desperate for a conversation with another adult.

"How's Henry?" Simon asked in between chews.

"Awake and doing better," Emily replied. "I just came outside to make a call while he's watching TV."

"From your accent, I assume you're not from around here."

"New York."

"Oh, so is that where you know Olivia?"

"Kinda. She didn't tell you?" Emily asked, using the opportunity to quiz the man about his boss and her somewhat unusual behaviour.

Simon shook his head and smiled wryly. "Olivia's not great at explaining things."

"Yeah." Emily nodded. "I'm kinda getting that about her. I work for Crown Airlines as cabin crew. I served Olivia a couple of times. I hardly know her. I was so surprised to see her turn up yesterday."

Simon took a sip of his coffee and nodded.

"You don't seem surprised," Emily commented. "Does she do this a lot?"

Simon shook his head. "No, never, she's not got a thing for cabin crew if that's what you're wondering." He chuckled.

"How about kids she doesn't know?" Emily asked.

Simon regarded her seriously. "I've worked for Olivia for four years, and I promise you that there is nothing you need to worry about. I know that's coming from a stranger, but she just…expresses herself a little differently than other people. She doesn't know all the social rules, so sometimes she comes across a little odd, but she is a genuinely nice person."

Emily looked at him for a moment before nodding. "I just don't know what to make of her," she admitted. "She seems nice, but then she does strange things like turn up at children's hospitals unannounced."

Simon chuckled. "I didn't know your connection to her, or I would have advised her to call first or something."

"So, what do you do?" Emily asked.

"I'm her PA."

"And does that often involve delivering giraffe balloons to hospitals?"

Simon laughed. "Well, I have to admit that being Olivia's assistant doesn't always stick to the job description. But I put my hand on my heart and say that yesterday was the very first time I took a giraffe helium balloon to a hospital. And, in fact, the first time Olivia's been in a working hospital for many years. She hates them."

"Well, no one likes them," Emily pointed out.

"True," Simon said. "But she has an irrational fear of them."

"Oh." Emily frowned and pondered the statement for a moment. "But she agreed to meet me again today at one o'clock to watch Henry open his presents."

Simon nodded in sudden understanding. "Oh, that's why she cleared her diary for the afternoon."

"She was busy?" Emily said. "She cancelled things for us? To go to a hospital that she's scared of."

Simon laughed lightly at Emily's confusion. "Yep. Look, Emily, the best way to deal with Olivia is to take logic and just chuck it out of the window. She doesn't do things the same way that the majority of people do. She sees the world a little differently, she says things and does things that may seem weird, but it's just the way she interprets things. As I said, she is a genuinely nice person, just not good in social situations. But give her a chance, and she'll be a great friend." Simon checked his watch. "And with your boy being in the hospital and you being stuck so far away from home, it looks like you could do with a friend."

Emily shrugged. "I'm just not that good at trusting people, especially not when Henry's involved. The gifts are lovely, and it's only right that Henry knows who they're from and Olivia gets to hear a thank you from him directly. But after that I'm planning to tell her to not come back. I just don't think it's appropriate."

Simon took a sip of his drink before replying. "May I ask why?"

"I don't know her," Emily explained.

"You don't know me, but here we are sharing a park bench and a personal discussion. Who knows, we may go on to become best friends. You have to start somewhere." Simon grinned.

Emily rolled her eyes but smiled at the charismatic man. "Okay, I see that, and I agree with you, but I can't put my job at risk. I need my job, and Olivia is worth a million dollars a year to the airline."

"When I first started working for Olivia, I'd been with her for only a day when she had a meeting way out in the countryside. She took the train to the nearest station and then a taxi to the client's farmhouse. I forgot to book the taxi coming back. She walked two miles in the rain and wind, down small muddy trails, *in heels*. There was no signal on her mobile, so she couldn't call a taxi for herself. She missed her train, and there's only one train an hour out there, so she sat on the platform as there was no waiting room, soaked-through from torrential rain, for over an hour waiting," Simon explained.

Emily was horrified. "Well, you're still working for her, so I assume she didn't fire you."

"Once she got a signal while on the train, she called me, and she asked me to push back her four o'clock meeting because she would have to go to the hotel and get changed." Simon chuckled at the memory. "It wasn't until the next day that I heard her telling her friend Nicole what had happened. I was mortified. I thought she was probably planning to fire me, and I decided to go in and take it like a man. So once her friend left, I walked in and told her I was sorry I forgot to book the second taxi and that she'd had a horrible afternoon and missed her train. You know what she said?"

Emily shook her head.

"She said, and I quote, *If I had walked faster, maybe I would have made the train.*" Simon shook his head. "Blaming me never even occurred to her. Over time, I realised she doesn't have a malicious bone in her body—it's like that thought process is missing from her. Some might say she's naive, but I think the world would be a better place if there were more Olivia Lewises around."

Emily smiled. "Is she paying you to say all this?"

"Yeah." Simon nodded. "Is it working? She said I could totally borrow her yacht if you fall for all this."

Emily sighed. "I just have a lot going on in my life, you know?"

Simon nodded his understanding. "Sure, but give her a chance as a friend. Maybe you'll find some common ground. I don't think I've ever met anyone who couldn't do with another friend."

Emily smiled. "Okay, you're right. I'll keep an open mind when she comes by for coffee this afternoon."

"Speaking of which, how do you take your coffee?" Simon asked.

Emily looked at him with confusion.

"If you're meeting for coffee, she'll want to take coffee with her as a gesture, which she'll ask me to get, and if I know how you take your coffee, then that will totally give me bonus points." Simon grinned. "Need to keep the boss lady sweet."

Emily laughed. "A latte will be fine."

Simon stood up. "I better get back."

Emily stood too. "Me too, thank you, Simon. Really, it's nice to talk to someone who isn't a doctor or a nurse."

Simon tossed his chocolate wrapper and empty cup in the bin beside the bench. He reached into his back pocket and pulled out his wallet.

"Here," he said and handed her a business card. "Whatever you decide with Olivia, here's my number. I literally work over there, and I live not too far away, so if you want to chat or meet up."

Emily took the business card with a grin. "Does everyone at"—she looked at the card—"Applewood Financial hand out their business cards to people they've just met?"

"Yeah, it's company policy," Simon said with a cheeky smile. "But mainly if they look like they could use a friend."

"Thank you, Simon."

"Catch you later, hopefully." Simon put his wallet back into his pocket and headed for the gates.

CHAPTER FOURTEEN

Emily had decided not to tell Henry about the potential visit from Olivia in case she didn't show. She'd also hidden the giraffe presents in the en-suite bathroom just in case she did.

"Try to eat a little more," Emily said gently. She pulled the trolley closer to where Henry sat up in bed.

"I'm not hungry, Mommy," he whined.

The nurses on Bear Ward had instantly fallen in love with Henry, and they all fawned over him. He usually lapped up the attention, but his strength was low following the second operation, and the medical staff, as well as Emily, were struggling to keep his spirits up.

Emily looked at the uneaten apple slices, a cheese sandwich with one tiny bite taken from it, and the untouched chocolate chip muffin. "Maybe drink a little more milk?"

Henry shook his head and looked away sullenly. Emily sat on the edge of the bed, mindful of the leads that were connected to the monitor embedded in the wall behind her. "Henry, I know you don't feel well, but you will feel better if you eat something."

"I don't want this, Mommy," he said. He put his hand on the trolley and carefully pushed it away.

"Am I interrupting?"

Emily looked up to see Olivia standing in the doorway with a nervous look on her face and a tray of takeaway drinks in her hand.

"Olivia," Henry cried out happily, and Emily blinked in surprise at the sudden enthusiasm on her son's face. "You're here!"

Olivia blushed at the attention and hesitantly stepped into the room. "Yes, I wanted to see you," she explained as she placed the drinks down on a table by the door.

Emily stood up. "Thank you for coming," she said with relief that Henry's melancholy seemed to be disappearing rapidly.

"I brought you a latte. Simon told me that he guessed you would be a latte drinker. I hope that was okay," Olivia said as she pulled a cup from the carrier and handed it to Emily.

"Yes, a latte is perfect, thank you."

Olivia spoke quietly so Henry could not hear her. "I also got Henry something, but I didn't know if he would be allowed."

"Well, I am trying to cut back on his espresso drinking," Emily joked.

Olivia frowned as she seriously told Emily, "Children shouldn't be drinking coffee, Miss White."

Emily laughed heartily and placed her hand on Olivia's elbow for support before composing herself. "I was only kidding. What did you get him?"

"Oh." Olivia frowned—clearly the joke still didn't register with her. "I thought he might like hot chocolate. It soothes me when I'm ill, so I thought he might also appreciate some."

Emily regarded Olivia in wonder for a couple of seconds before turning around to face Henry. "Henry, Miss Lewis has kindly brought you some hot chocolate."

His eyes lit up with excitement, and Emily smiled at seeing some life flood back to the boy.

Olivia was looking at Henry's lunch tray with concern. "I think you should eat a little more lunch," she said.

"I don't like it." Henry sighed grumpily.

"Henry," Emily said in a warning tone.

Olivia picked up the hot chocolate cup and her own cup and walked around the bed to place his drink in front of him on the trolley. "Then what would you like?"

Henry looked up at her in confusion. "What?" Olivia stared at him for a second before he corrected himself. "Pardon?"

Olivia smiled. "If you could have anything, what would you like to eat?"

Emily walked back to her seat on the other side of Henry's bed and carefully sipped at her latte as she watched Henry's face contort thoughtfully. "Macaroni and cheese," Henry eventually said, then grinned. "And chocolate fon ant!"

Olivia nodded and pulled her phone out from her pocket and started to type.

Emily frowned. "What are you doing?"

"Sending Simon out for macaroni and cheese and chocolate fondant." Olivia paused and looked up as if she was afraid she had overstepped her boundaries.

"You don't have to do that." Emily looked at Olivia in surprise. "I'm sure that's not in Simon's job description."

Olivia frowned. "Simon's job is to assist me, to do things for me when I cannot do them myself."

"Yes, but..." Emily struggled to think of how to explain the strangeness of the situation to Olivia, who clearly didn't have a clue what the problem was.

"Mommy, I'd like macaroni and cheese," Henry interrupted with a pleading look. Emily opened her mouth to say something but knew that any further discussion could be saved for another day when he was feeling better. She nodded consent, and Olivia continued to type her text message.

"I'll just take this out," Emily said as she picked up the tray of uneaten food and removed it from the room, returning a moment later.

"I had two operations," Henry told Olivia.

"So I heard," Olivia said as she pocketed her phone. "You've been very brave."

"Who is Simon?" Henry asked as he pushed himself into a more seated position.

"He works for me."

"Like Mommy?"

"No, your mother works for Crown Airlines," Olivia explained. "Simon helps me at my job."

"So Simon helps you be a piggy bank?" Henry asked.

"Yes, sort of." Olivia nodded.

"Miss Lewis came to see you yesterday when you were asleep," Emily said as she opened the door to the bathroom. "She brought some things for you."

Henry's eyes lit up again, and he looked from the giraffe bag that Emily brought into the room to Olivia with excitement. "For me?"

"Yes," Olivia said. Anything else she was going to say was cut off by Henry clamouring forward on the bed. He shrugged out of the bedding and launched himself forward to hug Olivia around her middle.

Olivia looked speechlessly at Emily, who smiled at the two of them before placing the bag of gifts on Henry's bed beside him.

"Please be careful," Olivia said to Henry. Her panicked gaze took in the wires and tubes surrounding the little boy.

Henry maintained his grip on Olivia as he turned around and looked at the bag. "Can I open them now, Mommy?"

"Absolutely," she said with a nod.

He let go of Olivia, knelt in front of the bag, and pointed to the giraffe pictures on the outside of the bag. "Look, Mommy, giraffes."

"Yes, you must have mentioned you liked them," Emily said softly as she rolled her eyes jokingly in Olivia's direction.

Henry picked out a package and pointed at the wrapping paper. "More giraffes!" He turned to look at Olivia and showed her. "More giraffes, Olivia."

Olivia smiled earnestly now and nodded. "Yes, lots of giraffes."

Henry nodded and ripped open the packaging and pulled out a giraffe rucksack. He stared at it with wide and excited eyes. "A bag like a giraffe!"

Emily laughed as she saw it. "Yes, look at that."

Henry sat back on his bottom and looked at the bag in more detail, examining the straps and then putting his hand over the giraffe print exterior. He looked up at Emily with a wide smile.

"Do you want me to put your things in your new bag? Maybe you could drink some of your hot chocolate while I do that," Emily suggested, keen to get Henry to eat or drink at least something.

With a nod, he handed the bag over to her, then reached for the hot chocolate with both hands and very carefully sipped at it through the travel lid. Two sips done, he placed the cup down again, reached into the bag, and pulled out another present before turning to Olivia. "Why did you buy me presents?"

"Because you were so brave," Olivia said softly. She placed her coffee on the table beside Henry's drink and sat gently on the edge of the bed.

"Wow." Henry smiled and then carefully started to open the next present. As the hard rubber giraffe money box came into view, he giggled and pointed to it. "It's a giraffe!"

"Almost," Olivia admitted. "It's something else as well."

Emily was removing things from Henry's tatty, old Iron Man rucksack and putting them into the new giraffe rucksack as she watched the pair interacting. Olivia gently angled the giraffe around and pointed to a slit in the back of the giraffe's neck. "Do you know what that is?" she asked. Henry looked at it for a moment before realisation set in and he smiled. "It's a piggy bank—a *giraffe* bank!"

"Exactly." Olivia smiled.

"I like it, but I don't have any money to put in it."

"Oh, well, how about this?" Olivia reached into her jacket pocket and produced a small handful of coins and held out her palm towards Henry.

"What's this one?" Henry asked as he picked up a silver coin.

"That is fifty pence," Olivia said. "Put it in your money box."

"But it's your money," Henry told her seriously.

"Spare change, you can have it."

Henry nodded and put the fifty-pence piece in the money box and then picked two similar looking silver coins. "What are these?"

"Ten pence," Olivia said and he dropped them both into the money box.

Henry looked at the remaining copper coins. "You can keep them," he said with disinterest, and Olivia laughed out loud.

"Yes, most people don't want these," Olivia admitted and put them back into her pocket.

Henry looked around his crowded bed, and upon discovering there was no space for his money box, handed it over to his mother. Emily took it and smiled at him as he reached into the bag, picked up the final package, and held it up victoriously. "Clothes!"

"How did you know?" Olivia asked as she held her hand out to prevent the overexcited boy from falling backwards.

"He's five," Emily replied softly. "Guessing wrapped presents is in the job description."

Olivia nodded her understanding and looked to Henry again. He was happily ripping open the wrapping paper, and then he looked at the giraffe hoodie like all of his birthdays had arrived at the same time.

"Mommy," he whispered in astonishment as he held up the item of clothing.

"Oh wow," Emily enthused. "Look at that."

"Mommy, look," Henry said as he pulled the hood up and showed Emily the ears and horns.

"Wow," Emily smiled, happy and relieved to see Henry responding so well after his muted behaviour since waking up. "What do you say?"

"Thank you." He turned around to face Olivia. "Thank you, Olivia."

"You're most welcome, Henry," Olivia said with a smile.

"There's one more present," Emily said as she returned to the bathroom and came out with the giraffe balloon.

"Balloon!" Henry cried excitedly as he stood on the bed to get a better view of it. Olivia quickly reached up to steady the boy.

"Sit down, Henry," Emily said softly as she put the weighted feet of the balloon on her chair, so the giraffe was at a height for him to see it better. He flopped backwards with little care or grace, ending up sitting on Olivia's knee. He looked at the balloon before looking up at Olivia's face and giggled.

"Knock, knock." Simon stood in the doorway with two large food takeaway bags. He nodded at Olivia and Emily in greeting.

"Hi." Emily smiled. "Thank you so much."

"No problem." Simon grinned as he entered the room. "You must be Henry."

Simon held out his free hand, and Henry regarded it for a moment before putting his own small hand into Simon's and shaking it, all while nervously pressing closer to Olivia.

"Henry, this is Simon," Olivia introduced.

Simon set the bags down on the table. "I heard that there was a really brave boy who just needed some macaroni and cheese." Henry perked up a little as he saw Simon open one of the bags, remove a polystyrene box and a plastic fork, and place both on the table.

"And?" Olivia asked.

"The *other* thing is here for later." Simon cunningly passed the bag with the chocolate fondant to Emily with a smile. Olivia popped open the macaroni and cheese box and gestured for Henry to sit back up in bed rather than on her knee. "I didn't know if you ladies had eaten, so I popped to Delphine's and got a sandwich platter for you," Simon said as he took a round plastic tray out of the second bag and placed it on the table as well. "Is there anything else?"

"I don't think so," Olivia said as she looked at Emily.

Emily shook her head. "No, that's perfect. Thank you so much."

"Great, enjoy your lunch." Simon smiled and then looked at Henry. "Get well soon, Henry, maybe catch you later." Henry smiled and gave a little wave as Simon left the room.

Olivia stood up and pushed the trolley closer to Henry, so he could easily eat from the tray on top.

"Do you want to watch some TV while you eat?" Emily suggested as she picked up the remote control and turned the wall mounted television on. Brightly coloured cartoons flickered to life. Henry mindlessly ate as he watched the cartoons, and Emily walked around the bed, picking up the sandwiches as she went. She gestured for Olivia to sit on the sofa bed. Olivia sat down and Emily put the sandwich platter between them.

"He'll eat more if he doesn't know he's actually eating," she explained and indicated the television. "The distraction helps."

"I understand." Olivia took the lid off the platter and put it to one side.

"Thank you, for the gifts and the food." Emily smiled. "I'll give you some money, of course."

Olivia frowned. "Why?"

"For the food," Emily explained as she picked up a sandwich.

"I don't need you to do that."

Emily took a bite and seemed to be contemplating her next words. "Miss Lewis," she began.

"Please, call me Olivia."

"Olivia," Emily started again, but quietly so Henry didn't overhear. "I'm really very grateful for the gifts and the food, but what's the story here?"

"I'm sorry, I don't understand."

Emily checked Henry wasn't listening. "Well, you gave me your card to call you, and I explained that I don't have time for someone else in my life right now, which you agreed to and said you understood. Then you turn up at the hospital with presents for my son and start buying lunch. I just…I dunno, I want to know what you're thinking. What are you hoping to achieve with all this? Because I have to tell you that nothing has changed for me. I still have my plate full with Henry. I still don't have time for anything more. If that's what this is about…"

Olivia considered Emily's words. "I know, Henry should absolutely be your priority and I understand that. I'm not hoping to achieve anything untoward. I…I simply felt that he and I connected." Olivia looked at the boy who was still slowly shovelling gooey macaroni into his mouth. "He *is* a special boy, and when I didn't know what had happened, I became very concerned. Maybe I overstepped in coming here, but it was with good intentions and only to ascertain Henry's well-being and certainly not for anything else. You said you didn't know anyone in London, so I'd like to help you if I can. We may not be friends in the traditional sense, but we know of each other, and I cannot imagine the stress you're going through, so if I can help, even to share a coffee, then I'd like to."

"Henry was ecstatic to see you," Emily admitted. "It was like a light switch had been turned on in him. All last night and this morning, he's been very down and very quiet."

A small smile spread across Olivia's face and she picked up a sandwich. "I have also been rather quiet, wondering if he was well or not."

"You two really hit it off, huh?" Emily smiled.

"It seems so," Olivia confessed. "I watched a documentary on giraffes, and I'm seeing the fascination."

"Oh no, not another one!"

"I won't be arriving for work with a giraffe rucksack anytime soon, though," Olivia deadpanned.

Emily laughed, surprised by Olivia's dry wit. "Good, I think you'd be fired."

"Unlikely," Olivia said. "I own the company."

"Oh yes, you're a professional piggy bank," Emily remembered.

Olivia laughed. "Maybe I should reprint the business cards again."

Emily chuckled and regarded Olivia for a few moments. "I'm sorry if I come across a bit standoffish," she said softly. "I'm just used to being cautious."

"Very wise," Olivia agreed. A vibrating from her jacket pocket caused her to frown, and she reached in for her mobile phone. She read the screen with a sigh.

"Problem?" Emily asked.

"I'm afraid I have to go," Olivia said. "Work calls." She picked up a napkin and wiped her fingers.

"Maybe you'd like to come back and see Henry again."

"I'd like that."

"Tomorrow?" Emily asked casually.

"Yes, but I need to look at my schedule."

"Well, come by whenever you can—we'll be here."

"Thank you." Olivia smiled, stood up, and looked at Henry. "Sorry, Henry, but I have to go back to work now."

Henry looked at her with a frown but slowly nodded his head. "Will you come again soon?"

"Hopefully tomorrow." She turned to Emily. "You have my number if you need me. I—I'll see you tomorrow."

"Thanks again, for everything," Emily said with a smile.

Olivia returned a small smile and left.

"I like Olivia," Henry said to his mother as he put a piece of pasta in his mouth and looked up at the television. "And macaroni and cheese."

Emily chuckled. "I'm sure she'll be happy to be in such esteemed company."

CHAPTER FIFTEEN

Hey, Henry, can you pull the blanket down a little bit so we can see those plastic tubes?"

Emily was shocked. "Excuse me?"

The photographer lowered his camera and gave her a cocky grin. "Well, we don't want people to think he's just lounging in bed looking a bit pale. We have to show the readers how life-and-death it was."

Emily glanced at her son, who was looking nervously at the man while hugging Tiny closely to his chest.

"Yeah, that's perfect, hug the giraffe tighter."

"Look, I agreed to a photograph and a little story in the internal magazine, not a sob story photo shoot." Emily folded her arms across her chest and stood protectively beside Henry's bed.

The photographer laughed. "Internal mag? No, love, they're going to push this external. Nice tear-jerker like this, they can rake in good publicity with this one."

"That's *not* what I agreed to."

"What is going on?" Olivia's quiet authoritative voice held an angry tone that Emily had never heard before.

The photographer turned to her. "Who are you?" he asked.

Olivia ignored him and asked Emily. "Are you okay?"

Emily nodded shakily, knowing it was obvious that she was not okay. Olivia turned her attention to the photographer. "Who are you?"

"Rick McCoy." He handed her a business card, which she snatched out of his hand and examined.

"And you're here because…?" Olivia scowled.

"Taking a couple snaps of the kid. Sorry, who are you?" he asked again.

"You intend to use these photographs in the mainstream press?" Olivia asked.

"Yeah," he replied with a sneer. "That's what the airline wants."

"Call your contact at the airline, now."

He mumbled something derogatory about women and stepped into the corridor. Olivia's face softened as she approached Emily. "What is going on?"

Unshed tears threatened to spill down her face as she pulled Olivia away from Henry's bed and whispered, "I was stupid. I made a deal with the devil, and now I have to pay up."

"What do you mean?"

Emily sighed. "Henry needed this operation, and the opportunity came up to get it done in London for free, but I couldn't afford the flight. So I spoke to the airline to see if they could figure out a way to get him here. A way that I could pay the airfare back later. They said they'd let him travel for free, but only if they could put a story into the internal staff magazine, something about how the airline flew Henry to London for his operation. A sort of feel-good story for staff. I didn't really have a choice, so I agreed. But then this guy showed up, and he wants to shine a white light at Henry's face so he looks sicker than he is. And he just told me that they're going to give the story to the press."

"And you don't want that?"

"No," Emily said. "Henry shouldn't have to go through this, but I'm stuck. If I say no, I could lose my job, and I could never afford to get us both home."

"Will you allow me to deal with this?" Olivia looked towards the corridor where she could hear the photographer on his phone. "I have an idea. It's not ideal, but it will give you more control."

Emily looked into Olivia's kind brown eyes and nodded. "You might as well. I don't seem to be doing a very good job of this."

Olivia squeezed her hand and left to talk to the photographer.

"Mommy, I don't want my picture taken any more," Henry whispered.

"I know, baby." Emily sat on the edge of the bed. "But you might have to be a brave boy again for me."

"What's Olivia doing?" Henry asked as he skirted over and cuddled up to her.

"I'm not sure." Emily chuckled. "Trying to fix my mistake, I think."

"But, Mommy, you don't make mistakes." Henry frowned as he burrowed closer.

Emily kissed his hair. "Oh, we all make mistakes."

The muffled sound of Olivia and the photographer arguing filtered through from the corridor, but Emily couldn't make out their words. It was a relief when Olivia finally returned.

"He's gone," Olivia announced.

"But?" Emily could tell that Olivia felt she had bad news to convey.

"I didn't tell them who I was, just that I was a friend. I didn't think you'd want my name brought up." Olivia smiled at Henry, who was wearing his giraffe hoodie and looking at her from within Emily's arms.

"Thank you." Emily nodded her gratitude.

"It seems that your manager sold the idea to the airline based upon an international marketing campaign, generating good publicity for Crown," Olivia informed her. "No mention of just an internal news story."

"Iris." Emily's mouth twisted in distaste.

"However, I think I have come to a suitable compromise," Olivia said. "I hope you'll agree." Emily looked at Olivia expectantly. "The airline doesn't care much how the publicity is generated as long as it is. And Mr. McCoy there had intended to take some staged photographs and sell them to the highest bidder. My advice is to put you in the driver's seat—select journalists you wish to work with, and tell your own story. That way you have final approval on the copy and control over any images *and* you collect any royalties for yourself, rather than them going to that terrible man."

Emily considered this for a moment. "So Crown still gets the publicity it wants?"

"Yes, which is all they want out of the transaction."

"And I get to choose the story and the photos?" Emily continued.

"Exactly. I can put you in touch with a couple of reputable freelance journalists who will take your story and some quotes and photos, and if you're happy, they will then sell it to the press agencies. Of course, you'll get a percentage of any profit made rather than Mr. McCoy getting his hands on everything." Emily hesitated and Olivia continued, "I know it's not about the money, but surely it's better for you to have any profits as a result of this, for Henry."

"Mommy, am I having my picture took?" Henry asked quietly.

"Not today," Emily told him, and the boy nodded his head.

"Is that man coming back?" he questioned.

"No," Olivia said quickly. "He won't be back."

"Good." Henry smiled.

"Henry, could you watch some TV while I talk to Olivia?" At his nod, she switched on the television and sat him up a little, pulling the sheets up to cover him and Tiny. "We'll be right outside," she promised. "Just call if you need me."

"Okay," Henry mumbled, already distracted by the cartoons.

They left the room and walked towards a waiting area. Emily smiled at Olivia softly and said, "Thank you for that. I'm a bit of a mess at the moment. I didn't know what to do."

"I understand."

"No, I don't think you do," Emily said gently. "That's why I wanted to come out here. So I can explain it to you properly."

They sat down, and Olivia crossed her legs and turned towards Emily as they huddled close to avoid the prying ears of passers-by.

"I'm..." Emily sighed. "I'm in debt, as you already know." Olivia blushed and began to apologise, but Emily held her hand up and continued to speak. "Debt isn't an easy thing to talk about, and it's not an easy thing to cope with. It makes you defensive, stressed, and it leads you to make decisions you probably wouldn't have made if you hadn't been in debt. I didn't have a good start in life. I stayed in foster homes, got in with the wrong crowd, made mistakes...you know?"

Olivia nodded and she continued, "Henry is my whole life. When he was six months old, he was so quiet and still that I took him to see a specialist. There were so many tests and so many procedures. The insurance paid for some of it but not all of it. Some of the procedures and medications weren't covered. I couldn't cut off his medication, so I got another credit card and then another and then another. I was working all the time and paying an elderly neighbour to watch Henry while I was out. The only time I saw him was for hospital appointments."

A nurse walked past, and Emily stopped talking until she had gone. She sighed and carried on with her story. "I ended up in a spiral of debt. I couldn't pay the minimum payments on my cards, so I got another one. And then another, and another. That's when I started calling up those ads. You know, the ones that claim to help people in debt but only end up getting them even more in debt? So then I had loans on top of the credit cards I already couldn't afford." Emily shook her head at her own naivete.

"One day, I met this woman at the park," she continued. "Her name was Lucy, and she'd just moved into town with her husband. Henry loved her, and we started to talk, and the pressure of everything just got too much for me. I told her everything, sobbed like a baby on a park bench." Emily laughed sadly at the memory. "We became friends, and after a few months, she convinced me to move in with her and her husband. They had a spare room, and Lucy's husband is a long-haul pilot, so Lucy was lonely and wanted some company in the house."

Emily paused for a moment while she gathered her thoughts. Olivia reached forward and placed her hand awkwardly on Emily's knee before quickly removing it again.

"Tom, Lucy's husband, convinced me to train to be cabin crew. The money was good, and the work was safe. So I did it, and I spent a couple of years working for a low-cost airline. I was still in massive amounts of debt, and bills were stacking up, but I was just about okay, you know? I could cope. I started dating someone—it was kinda casual, but Henry liked her, and she understood my crazy work schedule. But then Henry got worse, and the doctors said he needed an operation that was going to cost more money than I would ever make in my lifetime. They said they'd work out a repayment plan with me." Emily reached into her pocket and pulled out a tissue and gently dabbed at the corners of her eyes.

"As for my ex, well, seems she didn't want that kind of commitment after all, so she left. Dumped me by text, actually." Emily laughed bitterly. "I knew I needed to get more money, so I signed up to long-haul airlines because the pay is better. Tom got me an interview with Crown in first class, and I got the job. I don't know how, but I got it."

Emily felt herself get lost in a memory for a moment before snapping back to the present. "It was just after I saw you in duty free that I had a call from Lucy. Henry had collapsed, and she'd taken him to the hospital. And I was in London, miles away from him and knowing I had to work a shift to get home. Thank God for Dr. Harvey. He saw me lose it in the airport, and he said he knew of a teaching hospital that might take on Henry's case. He made some calls, and they wanted to see Henry right away. It must have been a one-in-a-million chance to get his operation done at a teaching hospital, and one of the best in the world."

Emily sighed and looked at Olivia. "So, here I am. My son is recovering from two massive cardiac operations, I don't have a dollar to my name, and I'm in huge amounts of debt. Henry has more money than me now that you put those coins in his money box."

"You don't need to tell me all this."

"I just think it's right that you know all of this from the outset, and that you know that, as bad as things are, I always manage to get by on my own. I'm very independent, and I don't accept help easily. That probably comes from being a foster kid."

"Thank you for sharing your story with me."

"Thank you for dealing with that sleazy photographer."

"How is Henry doing?" Olivia asked. "He seemed disturbed earlier."

"Aside from not liking the photographer, he's doing a lot better, and he loved the chocolate fondant yesterday, by the way. He has check-ups for another week and then they'll hopefully clear him to fly home."

Olivia nodded and took her phone out of her pocket and expertly typed a message at speed. "I'll get Simon to give you some contact details for freelance journalists. The lady I spoke to at the airline was named Margaret Davison—she works in the marketing department, so you'll have to contact her as well. He can drop by with the information."

"Oh, we're being discharged from here tomorrow morning," Emily explained. "If I can figure out how to get to Kings Cross."

"The Underground," Olivia said with a knitted brow. "From here, it's just a couple of stops. Why are you going there?"

"Henry and I are staying at a hostel there," Emily replied. "We need to give the room up, so we're staying nearby."

"Kings Cross is not a particularly nice area of London," Olivia said seriously. "It used to be the red-light district, and some parts of it are still very run-down."

Emily shrugged. "I checked out the hostel online, and the pictures are good, and the reviews are okay. I don't have much choice."

"You can't trust everything you read online." Olivia sighed as if she was dealing with a child.

Emily bristled at her attitude. "Yes, I know that—I'm not an idiot. But I've done my research, and this hostel is fine. Really."

Olivia shook her head. "Emily, there is no way a hostel in Kings Cross will be suitable for Henry to stay in."

"As I said, I don't have much choice."

"Stay at my hotel," Olivia said, as if it was the simplest thing in the world.

"And what hotel is that?" Emily folded her arms defensively.

"The Hilton, it's two minutes away," Olivia explained. "Henry could easily get back here for his check-ups, and I can vouch for the quality of the rooms and the attentiveness of the staff."

"Have you not heard a word I've said?" Emily groaned in angry exasperation. "I don't have any money."

"But I can help you." Olivia pulled her wallet out of her bag and opened it up.

Emily sprang to her feet in annoyance. "You just don't get it, do you?" She shook her head in disbelief. "I don't want your charity. I can look after my son myself."

"Well, you're doing a tremendously bad job of it." Olivia frowned. "A seedy hostel in Kings Cross is not suitable for a five-year-old boy recovering from surgery. I thought you would know better than that."

"Excuse me." Emily looked at Olivia in shock. "Are you calling me a bad mother?"

Olivia seemed to give her previous statement some consideration before thoughtfully nodding. "Well, yes, I suppose I am."

Emily's jaw fell open. "Okay, that's enough," Emily said when she finally managed to speak. "I want you to go."

"Go?" Olivia frowned. "But what about—"

"I don't want anything from you, Olivia," she said. "I just poured my heart out to you, but you just don't get it. And you just called me a bad mother. I want you to go, and I don't want you to come near Henry ever again. If our paths cross at Crown, then I'll act professionally, but that is it. Goodbye, Olivia."

Emily turned on her heel towards Henry's room, slamming the door behind her.

❖

Twenty minutes later, Olivia stormed into her office and slammed her office door so hard it shook the whole partition wall. She threw her bag under her desk and pulled her coat off and threw it on the coat stand before flopping into her chair. She gave her mouse a good shaking to wake her computer up.

Simon opened the door and stepped in tentatively before closing it behind him. "Is anything wrong?"

"No," Olivia said firmly. "I'm fine."

"Okay," Simon said. "It's just you nearly took the door off its hinges."

"Then we really need more sturdy doors," Olivia told him as she read an email on her screen. "And why does Terry need to see me again? I spoke to him this morning about this."

"I think he wants to meet about something else," Simon said carefully as he took a few steps into the office and sat in a chair in front of her desk.

"Is there something you want?" Olivia glanced at him quickly before glaring back at her screen.

"How's Emily?"

Olivia bristled. "Emily is ridiculous."

"I see. Do you still need me to get those freelance journalists' details over to her?"

Olivia looked at him in confusion. "Of course, why wouldn't I?"

"Because she's ridiculous."

"Even ridiculous people need freelance journalists, Simon."

"Why is she ridiculous?" he asked softly. He picked up a stress ball from her desk and began to squeeze it.

"She wants to take Henry to a nasty little hovel," Olivia declared. "In Kings Cross. In the red-light district!"

"Isn't he a little young for that?" Simon laughed. "What do you mean she's taking him to a hovel?"

"They need to leave the hospital, so she's taking him to some... seedy hostel." Olivia launched herself to her feet and began to pace in front of the large windows overlooking Southampton Row.

"Did she use the words *seedy hostel*?" Simon asked carefully.

"No, but is there any other kind?" Olivia demanded.

"Well, some hostels are okay," Simon admitted. "When I moved here from York, I had to stay in a hostel for a month."

Olivia spun around and stared at him. "A month in a hostel?"

Simon laughed at her horror. "Yes, a month in a hostel. Some of them are actually okay. If you don't mind sharing."

"Sharing?"

"Yeah, hostels aren't like hotels. They are large dormitory-style rooms. It's cheaper that way."

"You sleep in a room with other people?" Olivia was appalled at the thought.

"Yep," Simon said. "Usually between ten and thirty in a single room. They split men and women, of course."

"Oh my God." Olivia put her hand on her heart and leaned heavily against the window. "Poor Henry."

Simon rolled his eyes. "Olivia, he'll be with Emily. They won't put a five-year-old in with the blokes, don't worry."

Olivia let out a sigh of relief. "Okay, good, but still...a hostel."

"Hotels in London are mega expensive, Olivia," he told her. "She might not be able to afford anything else. Although, admittedly, some of Kings Cross is still a bit ropey."

"I had a taxi driver take a shortcut through Kings Cross once," Olivia said. "I saw a man urinating in the street. That was it for me, never went back."

Simon chuckled. "Well, I'm sure that's a rare occurrence."

"I called her a bad mother," Olivia muttered. She turned and leaned her head on the glass and looked down at the street below. In the reflection, she saw Simon briefly close his eyes. That meant she'd done something really bad.

"Did you actually use those words?" he asked.

"No. Well, kind of...yes. I said that she was doing a tremendously bad job of looking after her son. And then she asked me if I was calling her a bad mother, and I said yes."

"And then?"

"And then she told me to go. So I did."

"Did you try to apologise?" Simon asked carefully.

"No, she closed the door on me." Olivia looked away from his reflection and continued to stare out of the window.

"Okay," Simon said. "What happened before that?"

"Before?" Olivia grimaced as she recounted the conversation. "She told me she was in debt. Henry's hospital bills. Oh, and that she was a foster child."

"Anything else?" Simon pressed.

"I don't know. I'm upset." Olivia sulked and turned to face Simon.

"Olivia, some people are very sensitive about money issues. You telling her the hostel was a dive probably upset her," Simon pointed out.

"She got annoyed when I tried to help her," Olivia said. "I got my wallet out to give her my spare hotel room key."

Simon frowned. "You...why?"

"They have to leave the hospital tomorrow, and since tomorrow I go back to New York, I thought they could stay in my suite while I was away."

"Jesus," Simon whispered and then spoke up. "Did you explain that to her?"

"What do you mean?"

"Did you say, *I have a hotel room you can use while I am away*? Or did you just flash your purse about while telling her the hostel was seedy?"

"I..." Olivia thought for a moment before realising her mistake. "Oh."

Simon let out a heavy sigh.

Olivia turned back to the window and softly banged her forehead on the glass. "I'm so tired of it, Simon."

"Tired of what?" Simon gently asked.

"Trying to understand people. Struggling to get them to understand me. It's exhausting. I'm trying to do the right thing, but I just don't seem to be able to." Olivia sighed before pushing herself away from the window. "Provide Miss White with the journalists' details," she said formally, then sniffed and sat down in her chair again. "Tell her I send my apologies and that I won't bother her or her son again."

"Olivia…" Simon started.

"Thank you, Simon." Olivia dismissed him and returned her attention to the screen.

Simon looked at her for a moment before he returned the stress ball to her desk and quickly and quietly exited the room.

Chapter Sixteen

On Friday morning, Simon arrived at the hospital bright and early. Emily stood by Henry's bed, folding clothes into a small travel bag. She looked at him in exasperation.

"Here we go," she mumbled. "So, she sent you?"

"I bring freelance journalist details, as requested." He held up a sealed envelope.

"Oh, I completely forgot about them." Emily felt herself blush. "I'm sorry, Simon, come in."

Henry yelled, "Pasta man!"

Simon grinned, and Emily shook her head in mortification at her son's manners.

"Yep, Henry, that's me, Mr. Pasta. Or Simon, if you prefer."

"Simon." Henry grinned. "Olivia's Simon."

"Yep." Simon smiled. "Good to see you looking better. And what a nice giraffe hoodie you have there."

Henry grinned proudly. "Olivia got it me."

"Olivia got it *for* you," Emily gently corrected.

"She apologises, by the way," Simon said quietly to Emily.

"Did she tell you why she needed to apologise?"

"In her own way," Simon said. "She is genuinely sorry and didn't mean it like that at all. But she said she understands and respects your wishes and will leave you and Henry alone from now on."

"Good," Emily grumbled as she folded some of Henry's clothes into his new rucksack. "Because I don't need her charity."

"If you say so." Simon shrugged.

"What's that supposed to mean?" Emily spun around and stared at him.

"She told me you were in debt. She didn't go into all the details, but she told me that much," Simon said as he started to help her pack Henry's clothes.

"Did she tell you she called me a bad mother?" Emily replied with a bark of laughter.

"That she did. But I don't think she realised that she'd said it exactly, not until she got back to the office."

"This social awkwardness thing doesn't excuse her from her behaviour," Emily argued quietly.

"If you say so," Simon repeated.

Emily folded her arms, glancing over to where Henry was reading a book to Tiny, before looking back at Simon. "Go on, say what you want to say."

Simon shrugged. "It's up to you, but I just think we should judge people on their intentions. Like, when I came in here, your son shouted pasta at me. Now, I took into account that he is five, and I laughed it off. I could have taken it personally, but I didn't because I know that he's still learning social skills. Olivia is the same—social awkwardness, on the spectrum, just plain crappy childhood, whatever you might want to call it or blame it on…I dunno. But the honest truth is that she struggles to make herself understood. She says the wrong things and accidentally hurts people, and that hurts her. But I can see that you're a very proud woman, and there's nothing wrong with that—it's just an observation. So I'm not going to come in here and defend Olivia to you because there's no point. What's done is done, and I think you and she are always going to clash."

"How many meanings can there be to *You're a bad mother, let me pay to fix your mess*?" Emily questioned quietly, more sad than angry now.

"You know, I can't figure out if you have a problem with accepting help or accepting help from her."

"What do you mean?" Emily asked.

"Okay, let's say that a very kind, rich old man, picture a Father Christmas type, right? Let's say he's Lord Richard the Rich of Richshire, and he's walking through the corridors of the hospital, and he sees Henry and gives you a cheque for a thousand pounds, dollars, whatever. Would you turn it down?" Simon asked.

"I…" Emily hesitated.

"See? You hesitated, because you are thinking of all the things that a thousand whatevers could do to help your son, and it's right of you to do that. It is absolutely right. Sometimes we need to accept help from others, lock our pride away," Simon said. "And, for your information, Olivia wasn't planning to give you money. She was planning to give you the spare key card to her hotel suite."

Emily opened her mouth but no words came out.

"She's gone back to New York today," Simon continued, "and she figured that you and Henry could stay in her suite until you got something sorted out. At least she could save you some money," he said. "She has been staying at the hotel every week for years, so she has a permanent suite. It's empty on the weekend, so she lets whoever needs it use it. Sometimes *I* use it if I have family down from York or something."

"She has a permanent suite at the Hilton?" Emily said in shock. "Why doesn't she just own property?"

"You remember what I said about Olivia and logic?" Simon laughed. "She stayed there when she was a kid visiting her father in London. His new wife didn't want Olivia or her mother staying at her home. And later, Olivia just kept on doing it. I think she likes it because she can see the office from her hotel window. She likes symmetry in things. Anyway, not that it matters, but that's what she was going to do. Not shower you in fistfuls of fifties."

"Okay." Emily sighed. "Okay, I admit I'm a bit sensitive when it comes to accepting help and especially so when it's from Olivia. I don't know why. I suppose I just find her intimidating or something."

"I know she's not easy to talk to sometimes," Simon admitted. "It took me a while to figure her out."

A moment of silence passed as they packed up the last few items. "Isn't this the part where you tell me to forgive her?" Emily asked, folding a small sweater.

Simon shook his head. "No, I didn't come here to fix things. As I said, you two might always clash. I'm here to help you, if you want any help."

"I think we'll be okay." Emily shrugged as she looked at the packed bags.

"Sure, you'll be absolutely fine going to a busy London Underground station with a suitcase, three bags, and a sick child all on your own. The long escalators and staircases will be the best bit."

Emily smiled and shook her head. "Fine, thank you, Simon. I'd love some help. How's that?"

"Better." Simon grinned.

"Shouldn't you be working?"

"Yeah, but she's"—Simon looked at his watch—"just checking in at the airport, so I won't hear from her again until later this evening."

Emily walked into the en-suite bathroom and picked up Henry's toiletry bag. "What did you mean when you said we might always clash? Olivia and me, I mean."

Simon laughed. "Are you sure you want to go down this route?"

Emily laughed along with him. "Go on, hit me with it."

Simon blew out a breath. "Olivia…is Olivia. She won't change. Not that she doesn't want to, she just can't. If she could choose to not be socially awkward, then she would obviously choose that. And she can't learn from all her mistakes, or she would stop making them. But she doesn't—she does the same things again and again. So in my opinion, that's that. She's fixed the way she is, and it's up to those around her to accept who she is and change their way of interacting with her. I'm not saying that's easy," Simon said. "I've wanted to throttle her many times, but when I realised that her actions don't always match her intentions, I started to change the way I communicated with her. Ask for clarification, don't fly off the handle, and always assume the best in her. But it's not always easy."

Emily nodded. "But she's your boss, so you had to find a way to deal with her."

"She's my friend too," Simon confessed. "She may be a mess when she's in here calling you a bad mother and critiquing your choice in hostel. But she is one of the best financial brains there is. She's an expert on taxation law in every country in the world, she can quote investment returns across hundreds of funds, she brokers impossible deals. I have learnt more from her and her way of doing business than I would have working my whole career at another firm." Simon folded his arms and smiled at Emily. "As awkward as she is in her personal life, she's completely different in her work life. Analytical, sharp, and shrewd. It's like she's a different person, like the corporate world just clicks with her. And because of that she gets things done. For example, without Olivia, your son would not be in this room today."

"How do you mean?"

"She worked with the Great Ormond Street charitable trust for years. When they came to her with the redevelopment plan, she was the person who convinced investment banks to part with their profit margins to fund the construction of this new wing."

Emily looked around the room as realisation began to sink in.

"Anyway, before you accuse me of being a one-man Olivia Lewis appreciation society, where are we heading? If you still want help, that is," Simon said.

"She's lucky to have you, Simon," she said seriously as she picked up her handwritten notes and looked through them.

"Yeah, I know. If you ever speak to her again, tell her I need a raise." Simon grinned as Emily handed him a page with the hostel address.

Simon gave it a curious look. "I know the road but not the actual hostel. Look, I have a travel allowance—let's just grab a taxi. It will be better than fighting against the morning commuter crush."

Emily opened her mouth to complain but quickly closed it again. "Well, I'm opening myself up to the idea of accepting help, so whatever you think is best."

They signed Henry out of the hospital and collected his medication and schedule for check-ups. Then Emily, Henry, and Simon hailed a black London taxi to take them to Kings Cross.

Henry was ecstatic to be in the London icon and spoke animatedly with the chatty driver. He looked out of the window and pointed out everything to Emily, from red double-decker buses to other taxis.

At the hostel, Simon paid the driver and looked up at the old Victorian building with a tilt of the head. "Hopefully it's better on the inside," he said.

Emily nodded with a frown. "Yeah, the pictures online looked okay."

They made their way down a dark and narrow passage to a large metal door that looked like it wouldn't be out of place at a maximum security prison. Simon pressed the bell, and they waited. "Don't come down here at night," Simon warned Emily quietly.

Emily looked around the dank passageway and at the metal door, which was obviously there to keep undesirables out. "No, I won't," she agreed, holding Henry's hand a little tighter.

Several heavy metal bolts slammed, and the door creaked open to reveal an older man who looked as run-down as the building.

"What?" he growled at them.

Emily blinked at the rudeness and spoke up. "Um, my name is Emily White. I made a reservation by telephone the other day."

"Come in," the man said, taking in Simon's suit and tie with a roll of the eyes.

They stepped into the cramped reception area. Henry pressed close against her and clutched Tiny to his chest. Emily looked at the people in the lobby and wondered who the metal door was supposed to keep out if these were the people they let in.

"You okay?" Simon checked with her, and she gave a half-hearted nod. He looked down at Henry whose eyes were darting about the room in panic and back at Emily. "Is this what you were expecting?"

"Nope." Emily shook her head.

"Excuse me," Simon called out to the old man. "Can we just have a minute?"

The man looked at Simon and then Emily and walked away into, presumably, an office.

Simon turned to Emily and spoke quietly. "This place is a dive. Are you sure you want to stay here? I'd offer you a bed at my place, but I share a house, and we're at full capacity. I'm sleeping on the sofa at the minute because my sister is visiting."

The sound of a fight breaking out around the corner made Emily jump, and she took a hesitant step backwards. Henry pressed himself into her leg. "Mommy, I don't like it."

"I know, Henry," she said as she looked around the lobby.

"Look," Simon said calmly, "you can't stay here. Let's go back to the office. You can sit down and use the internet to find something else. At least it will be warm and safe and...not here."

"I can't take up more of your time." Emily shook her head.

"Look, Olivia will skin me alive if she ever found out I left you and Henry here," Simon pointed out. "Come on, let's go. London's got other places to stay. I'll help you find something else."

"Mommy." Henry squeezed Emily's leg tightly as a woman in the corner give him a wave. Emily wondered distractedly if she was a sex worker by the way she was dressed, or rather underdressed.

Mind made up, she looked at Simon. "Let's go."

He nodded and called out to the old man to open the door again. He told him they'd changed their minds, and before long, they were in a taxi again, making their way back towards Bloomsbury. The difference between the two London districts was like night and day, despite the short distance.

"Maybe I am a bad mother," Emily muttered as Henry chatted to the new taxi driver. "God, that place." She shuddered at the thought.

"You know what would make you a good mother?" Simon said with a serious face.

"What?"

"Swallowing your pride and letting Henry stay at the Hilton for a few days," Simon told her. "You'll have the suite to yourself, and there's no metal security door in the lobby. Olivia won't be back until Monday evening, so if you don't want to see her, you have until then to organise something else."

"I think she's probably retracted that offer by now."

"No." Simon shook his head. "She's not like that. She'd want you and Henry to have somewhere safe to stay, no matter what was said yesterday."

Emily remained silent as her brain struggled to think of another option. She really didn't want to take Henry to Olivia's office while she looked for somewhere new, and she already knew the options were pretty slim in her price range.

"Is this silence a yes?" Simon pulled her from her thoughts.

Emily gave him a small smile. "It might have to be."

"Wow, we wore you down." Simon chuckled before speaking up to the driver. "Change of plan, mate, can you take us to the Hilton on Southampton Row?"

❖

Simon spoke to the hotel staff at the reception desk and obtained a new key card. Then all three made their way to Olivia's suite on the fourth floor. Henry was the first to walk hesitantly into the suite while Simon held the door open for him. He clutched Tiny to his chest and looked around at the plush surroundings with an awed expression.

"Who lives here, Mommy?" he asked.

Emily came in behind him and stood with her mouth open as she took it all in. "Well, this is where Olivia lives when she's in London," she explained softly.

"Is Olivia here?" Henry asked excitedly, his face beaming as he wandered off to look for Olivia.

"No, Henry, do you remember I told you yesterday that Olivia is very busy, and we may not see her again for a long time?" Emily said.

Simon wheeled the large suitcase into the room. "I'll pretend I didn't hear that."

Emily flushed with guilt.

"So," he continued, pointing out various doors and hallways, "this is obviously the sitting room, and through there is the kitchen and dining room, and over there are the bedrooms." He opened a door that led to a small hallway. "On the left is the spare room and the main bathroom, and on the right is Olivia's room and in there is her en suite."

"Okay." Emily nodded and watched as Henry flopped on a comfortable looking sofa and stared up the ceiling while whispering to Tiny about the taxi adventures. "Are you sure she'll be okay with this?" Emily asked again.

"Positive," Simon said with a serious nod. "If it makes you feel better, I can call her on the flight. But I know she sometimes sleeps."

Emily shook her head quickly. "No, I don't want to disturb her." She looked around. "It's big, isn't it?"

Simon laughed. "Yeah, it's massive, but then she does live here."

Emily looked around again and sighed. "It just feels weird to be here, you know? I feel like I'm trespassing."

"Well, I think you better settle in." Simon indicated Henry with a nod of his head. "Because it looks like someone is exhausted from all the excitement today."

Emily looked over at her son, who had fallen asleep on the sofa, Tiny wrapped in the crook of his arm and his thumb firmly in his mouth.

"Look, I need to get back to the office to do some stuff," Simon said. "Feel free to use the Wi-Fi, and Olivia's iPad is on the coffee table if you need it. I'll pop back after work, and we can call Olivia then and tell her what's going on, so you feel less like a squatter."

Emily laughed. "Thanks, I think."

"Seriously, though." Simon smiled. "Chill out, watch some TV, call those journalists, whatever. But don't worry about Olivia—she'll be fine."

Simon handed her the key card, and she took it with a grateful smile. "Thank you so much, Simon. I really don't know what we would have done without you."

"See? Sometimes accepting help is a good thing. I'll come by again around five o'clock. If you need anything, feel free to give me a call. Do you still have my card?"

Emily nodded, and Simon said goodbye as he headed over to the door and showed himself out. Emily turned and looked around the large suite and shook her head as she whispered to herself, "Oh, White, what are you getting yourself into?"

Chapter Seventeen

Emily had to begrudgingly admit that the hotel was amazing. The room had a perfect view of Southampton Row below, as well as the Applewood Financial offices across the road, but large netted curtains maintained the privacy of her suite.

Henry spent hours looking out of the window watching people below, calling out every time he saw a black taxi or a red bus, as well as providing frequent weather updates whenever it started to rain. When Henry had commented that he could see Simon, Emily had initially assumed that he was walking in the street, getting lunch or running errands, but when Henry pointed directly opposite, she realised they could see straight into the offices from their lounge.

Emily looked out of the window herself and saw Simon sitting in a small office next door to a larger executive office. He scribbled down a note and walked into the larger office, which Emily now took to be Olivia's. The room was spacious with ceiling-to-floor windows that stretched across the entire office. Emily squinted to pick out the details in Olivia's office in an attempt to discover more about her, but when she realised what she was doing, she stepped back and shook her head. She gently pulled Henry away from the window and reminded him that snooping on people wasn't very nice and told him to play with his toys instead.

After a while Emily had given up using her phone to look for other hostels and picked up the iPad. The screen on the phone was too small to properly see the pictures of the rooms, and this time she wanted to scrutinise them, to be sure of what she was getting herself into. She sat on the sofa with Henry, who watched television and drifted in and out of sleep, Tiny held tight in his arms, and a blanket wrapped around him. Eventually he fell into a deep sleep, and Emily carried him into the second bedroom, now their bedroom, and put him to bed. She drew the curtains and closed the door before heading back into the living room.

Just after five o'clock, there came a knock on the door. Emily checked the peephole to see Simon standing in the hallway with paperwork under his arm, his phone in his hand, and a pen in his mouth. She opened the door, and he walked in and quickly placed the files on the coffee table.

"Evening." He took the pen from his mouth and gave her his familiar cheeky grin. "Everything okay?"

"Yes, we're all good. Henry's asleep at the moment. How are you doing?"

"Busy, we've just been given instructions for a major restructuring." Simon started to open up files and take out pieces of paperwork. "When Olivia calls, I'm going to have to brief her on all of this."

"Do you need me to leave you to it?"

"Nah." He shook his head. "Nothing too confidential. Just wanted to warn you that I need to talk to her about all of this, and then I'll tell her about you guys staying here."

Emily nodded, still nervous about the conversation. "I spent hours looking online for other places to stay, but they're either booked up, too far away, in a bad area, or out of my price range."

Simon sat on the sofa as he organised pieces of paperwork. "Tell me about it. After I graduated in York, I decided to come to London, you know, to make my fortune in the city. I didn't really think it through and certainly didn't do any research. I stayed in a cheap hotel on the first night, making appointments for a week in advance just to speak with recruitment companies. So I realised I needed somewhere else to stay, and quickly, until I got a job. Everything I could afford was too far out of London. What I was saving in accommodation costs, I would end up paying in travel instead."

"What did you do?"

"I ended up staying in a hostel," he said. "First night was a bit scary. It was a big dorm room, but I met a bunch of guys, and they seemed nice enough. I got a bit lax, a bit naive I suppose, and on the third night they stole my wallet, and I had to ring my dad and beg for him to send some money." Simon laughed at the memory, but Emily was horrified.

"That's terrible!"

"Yep," Simon agreed. "But I didn't let it stop me. I chalked it up to a bad experience, and then I found a new hostel and stayed there. I was a bit more cautious with my belongings and who I trusted, though. I ended up staying there for a month while I got some temporary work."

"Maybe I could stay there," Emily suggested.

"It's a male-only place," Simon said apologetically. "But not in that way, though—I'm straight," he joked.

She laughed. "Okay there, macho," she replied with a wink.

Simon grinned. "Just wanted to clear that up. I know the intense personal grooming, snappy dress sense, and well-spoken manner can sometimes confuse people."

"I did wonder."

He rolled his eyes. "I wish I was gay, I really do. I think I'd really be hot stuff on the gay scene but, sadly, no."

"No girlfriend?" Emily quizzed.

"No," Simon said with a shake of the head. "There's this girl, but I don't think she knows I'm interested in her. Mainly because every time I'm around her, I panic and become incapable of speech."

"But you seem so chatty!"

"I am," he agreed. "People have to frequently tell me to shut up, but when I see this girl, I just forget how to talk, and if I do say anything, it's always something stupid. Like, last week I asked her if she likes Frisbees."

"Frisbees?" She blinked for a second before laughing.

"I know. Stupid." Simon laughed. "Why would a sensible person say that?"

"Why did you say that?"

"I play in a Frisbee team. I thought we'd get into a discussion about Frisbees, and I could tell her about my awesome Frisbee skills." Simon waggled his eyebrows. "But then, as I said it, I realised that only a very odd person would ask something like that."

Their laughter was interrupted by Simon's phone ringing. "It's Olivia, I need to put her on speakerphone so I can make notes."

He answered the phone. "Evening, boss," he said with a smile.

"Good afternoon, Simon," Olivia replied—it was five hours earlier in New York.

"Just letting you know that you're on speaker. Have you checked your emails?" Simon asked.

"I got as far as your email that said to call you urgently," Olivia said, over the background noise of a busy airport.

"Cool," Simon said. "TCA Engineering is on the brink of insolvency, and Peters and Co. want us to do an emergency restructure to try to rescue the business."

"I see," Olivia said. "Well, this was what we expected after their last set of accounts were delayed."

"I've sent you all the accounts we have, plus the debtors and creditors lists. There's some interesting reading," Simon said.

"What figures are we looking at?" Olivia asked.

"Debts of around four hundred and twenty million at the last count." Simon winced as he read out the figure.

"Any property?" Olivia asked. "Equipment?"

"Six warehouses"—Simon picked up a piece of paper—"valued at a combined thirty-four million. Equipment in the region of seventy-two million, vehicles totalling twenty-three million."

"Contracts?" Olivia asked, not missing a beat.

"Three majors, two are agreed at fifty-one million and seventeen million respectively, and the third is shaky but provisionally agreed at forty-seven million."

"Okay," Olivia said. "So we just need the other one hundred and seventy-six million."

Simon nodded and grinned at Emily who was raising her eyebrows, impressed at Olivia's mental calculations while on the go, not to mention the way she dealt with such enormous amounts of money with such ease.

"What kind of salary bill are we looking at?" Olivia asked.

"Let me double-check that." Simon looked through some papers. "One hundred and fifteen million, and we need that by Tuesday."

Olivia sighed. "Okay, how many employees?"

"Five hundred and eighty-three," Simon replied.

"I'll draft a statement this afternoon, but in the meantime, it's the usual message. We'll do what we can, no forced redundancies, et cetera, et cetera," Olivia said. "Is the managing director still that awful man?"

Simon laughed at Olivia's question. "Yes, Frederick Stokes."

"I don't think he likes me," Olivia commented.

"No, he doesn't," Simon agreed. "When he called up this afternoon to speak to you, he called you *the uptight bitch.*"

Emily's eyes snapped up and she frowned at Simon.

"Charming," Olivia replied without missing a beat. "Well, no one likes the restructurers."

"No," Simon agreed, looking over at Emily as he continued to speak. "But then I don't think they understand that you're trying to protect jobs by making the hard decisions for them, rather than just in it for the money."

"Quite right. As I always say, it's business, not a popularity contest. I'll call him when I've reviewed the files for myself."

"He's expecting your call."

"Thank you, Simon. Is there anything else?"

"Yes, one other thing," Simon looked at the phone lying on the table as he spoke. "I invited Emily and Henry White to stay in the suite. I assume that's okay?"

There was a brief pause on the phone, barely long enough to be detectable. "Of course, yes. It would remain unused if they didn't."

"Yep, thought so, Emily wanted me to check with you, though," Simon explained.

"I see. Did you pass on my apologies?" Olivia's voice had changed from that of the confident financial executive to a more hesitant tone.

"I did," Simon said simply.

"Oh." Sorrow that the apology had been dismissed was palpable in Olivia's tone.

Emily looked guiltily at Simon, wishing she could speak and clear the air.

"The hostel wasn't suitable," Simon explained. "I suggested the suite while Emily looks for somewhere else."

"Of course." Olivia understood. "Oh, and did you pass on the journalists' information?"

"I did that too," Simon said. A moment's silence passed before Simon spoke again. "I'm actually at the suite. Would you like to speak with Emily yourself?"

"I don't think she wants to speak with me again."

In the same moment Emily held out her hand for the phone. "I think she does." Simon smiled. "I'll hand you over now." Simon took the phone off speaker and handed it to Emily, who stood up and walked over to the window.

"Hello, Olivia."

"Emily." Olivia's voice sounded hesitant and small. "I'm very sorry for what I said. I think it came across wro—"

"I know." Emily cut off the apology, not wanting Olivia to tie herself in further knots over the incident.

"How is Henry?" Olivia asked softly.

Emily smiled. Olivia's genuine concern for her son was heart-warming. "He's sleeping but doing really well. Enjoying the suite. Thank you for letting us stay here. I promise we'll be out of here when you get back on Monday."

"You don't have to run away from me," Olivia said quietly. "I understand if you don't want to see me again, but I would like to have a chance to apologise properly, if I may? Face to face."

"I—I'd like that." Emily looked at Simon's reflection in the window and saw him engrossed in paperwork. "I mean, to see you again, not to hear you apologise again. I realise I was as much to blame for that as you. We miscommunicated. Simple as that."

"Story of my life." Olivia sighed.

"Maybe we could have lunch when you're back in London," Emily said. "Maybe on Monday?" Olivia hesitated for a moment and Emily quickly added, "I know that Henry would love to see you again. He didn't get to talk to you last time you visited him."

"Yes, meeting for lunch on Monday would be lovely. I'll need to be close to the office, in case I'm needed."

"How about here? It feels weird to invite you to lunch in your own suite, but I could set up something before we leave. Think of it as my way of apologising to you." Emily smiled as she turned to Simon, who was fiddling with his paperwork but clearly listening in.

"W-why are you apologising to me?" Olivia stuttered.

"For flying off the handle," Emily said. "I realise I didn't give you a chance to explain, and you've told me you're prone to miscalculations, and I need to allow for that."

Simon threw his hands up in the air and silently mouthed, "Yeah!"

"That…that sounds lovely," Olivia admitted. "I must go—I have lots of calls to make. I hope you enjoy the suite. The breakfast is divine, and I'm sure Henry will enjoy the pancakes."

"Yes, I bet he will. Thank you, Olivia. See you on Monday."

"See you on Monday," Olivia confirmed, and Emily handed the phone back to Simon.

"Hi," Simon said and quickly jotted down some instructions from Olivia. "No problem, I'll probably speak with you tomorrow."

He hung up the phone and looked apologetically at Emily. "I'm sorry for the subterfuge and having her on speaker. I know it sounds awful, but sometimes you have to push Olivia into social situations and conversations."

"I did wonder," Emily confessed.

"So. Lunch, eh?"

"Just lunch." Emily smiled nonchalantly but knew she was blushing.

"Mm-hmm." Simon started to gather pieces of paper together.

Emily broke down and laughed. "Okay, so I'm seeing another side to her, thanks to you," she admitted. "It doesn't mean anything. I just… Henry likes her."

"Yeah, Henry likes her." Simon nodded vigorously. "That's it."

"He does!"

"I know, I'm agreeing with you," Simon said with a wide grin.

"You're a brat." She laughed as Simon gathered his papers and stood up.

"Yep, a brat who's going home because he's going to have to work this weekend. Fancy having lunch with me tomorrow? I can come over to see you and giraffe man."

"Sure, as long as you don't talk about Frisbees."

Simon pouted, and she laughed as she walked him to the door and patted him on the shoulder kindly.

❖

The weekend passed quickly for Emily, despite spending most of it cooped up in the hotel suite with a convalescing Henry. True to his word, Simon came by for lunch on both Saturday and Sunday. Henry started to develop a friendship with the man who made him laugh with funny voices and stories about the open-top tourist buses with no roofs so the giraffes could sit on the top deck.

While Henry stared out of the window waiting for open-top buses with giraffe passengers, Simon told Emily about the woman he was hopelessly trying to flirt with, a barista at a local coffee shop. Emily laughed as he told her stories about his awkward attempts to converse with the woman. Apparently, Olivia's caffeine intake was going through the roof with his frequent trips to the coffee shop.

Outside of Simon's visits, Henry slept a lot, which the doctor assured her was completely normal for the small boy while on medication and still recovering from his operations. While browsing websites, Emily had found a couple of good hostels which she could afford by stretching her budget a little. She knew it would be tight, but it would be worthwhile to ensure that Henry was somewhere safe and clean for the last few days of his stay in London.

After a conversation with a friendly freelance journalist, she managed to agree to an article that would also highlight the great work at Great Ormond Street Hospital. She also agreed for a photograph of Henry to be taken at the hospital with his doctor and a couple of his favourite nurses. The tone of the article was one that Emily was much happier with, and she felt relieved that she could give something back. The publicity would help the hospital with future fundraising.

Margaret Davison from the marketing department of Crown Airlines seemed very happy with the arrangement too and promised to get in touch with Emily before anything was actually published.

Finally, she'd spoken with Iris Winter, who luckily seemed unaware of any hiccups concerning the article. Iris was very happy to hear that Henry was recovering well. It looked likely that he would be cleared to fly on Thursday, and Emily asked if she could have her usual shift on the Friday morning flight. She might as well be earning some money while taking Henry back home. Neither could she ignore the happy coincidence that it would be Olivia's usual flight.

Emily had been thinking about Olivia all weekend. She didn't know if it was because she was staying in her hotel suite or because of the telephone call, but she was struggling to get Olivia out of her mind. The woman frustrated and intrigued her in equal measure. Olivia processed thoughts and speech in a different way to everyone else, and Emily had to admit she found it captivating. She'd never known anyone with Olivia's social awkwardness before and found herself researching the condition online. Despite not having much information to go on, she found many interesting sites and forums that seemed to accurately describe Olivia's behaviour pattern. Simon's words about intention versus action had struck a chord with her. How would she deal with Henry if he ever exhibited any of those behaviours? She was terrified that she would react to him as badly as she had to Olivia.

She considered what Simon had told her—that it was really down to Emily to change her approach towards Olivia, as Olivia couldn't.

Having so much time for reflection allowed her to revisit her interactions with Olivia and analyse them with a more critical eye. As she thought about the way Olivia acted, what she said, and the way she said things, Emily realised she could detect patterns and could easily see that the intent was genuine. Emily began to better understand the hesitation in Olivia's manner and how she seemed to genuinely struggle with what to say and how to say it.

Even though she didn't know exactly what would happen between them, she knew that she would be seeing Olivia regularly at work and, if Henry had his way, probably socially as well. Once he'd realised he was in Olivia's suite and could see Olivia's office straight across the street, he became a fully paid-up member of the Olivia Lewis fan club and wouldn't stop talking about his new best friend, a friendship sealed by his beloved giraffe hoodie, which he refused to take off, forcing Emily to use the hotel laundry facilities in the dead of night to wash and dry it for the next day's wear.

Henry's excited scream of *Olivia!* indicated he had seen her arrive for work on Monday morning from his window. Emily stood behind him and watched with a smile as Olivia settled at her desk and spoke with Simon. After a while, she realised she too was snooping and quickly told Henry that it wasn't polite to watch people without their knowledge. A brief discussion ensued, which was quickly resolved by Emily playing the overriding because-I'm-your-mother card. Henry returned to watching television, though he did occasionally sit up on the sofa and look over at Olivia with a huge grin.

Mid-morning, Emily took Henry out to a local store to buy some things for lunch. Henry excitedly bounced around the store, asking her what Olivia liked, and she used her knowledge of Olivia's airline menu preferences to choose what to buy.

When they returned to the suite, Henry was exhausted, and Emily put him down for a nap. She anxiously set up lunch and paced the room, occasionally looking nervously over at Olivia in her office.

CHAPTER EIGHTEEN

Emily examined the table with a tilt of her head. She genuinely wanted to thank Olivia, and she wanted to apologise now that she had a better understanding of her. But she also didn't want to look like she was trying too hard. She didn't want Olivia to get the wrong impression and think that the lunch was anything other than a meal shared between new friends.

However, she did mentally gloss over the fact that she had changed clothes three times that morning, telling herself that it was nothing more than wanting to be presentable and not appear too out of place when Olivia arrived in her impeccable clothes and perfect make-up. She heard the door to the suite open and belatedly remembered that Olivia had a key and would obviously let herself in rather than knock. With one last, quick breath to calm her nerves, she headed for the door. The sound of Henry screaming Olivia's name as he ran to greet her told Emily that she would be the second in line to meet their host.

In nothing but his underpants and vest, Henry excitedly tore past his mother, heading for the door, his uneven running causing him to sound like a herd of small elephants. He launched himself at Olivia, grasping her around her thighs and holding on tightly. The look on Olivia's face was absolutely priceless. She was effectively imprisoned between a five-year-old and a door. She was wearing a light grey skirt suit with a crisp white shirt, stockings, and heels, and Emily smiled as she realised how much she had missed her.

She watched as Olivia hesitantly placed her hands on Henry's shoulders, clearly still concerned about the appropriate rules of engagement when it came to touching him, especially in his current state of undress.

Brown eyes flicked up to meet Emily who smiled back warmly, trying to express herself with her body language to let Olivia know that all was okay.

"Olivia! We've been staying at your house," Henry said, his voice muffled against Olivia's hip.

"So I hear." Olivia smiled and gently touched the boy's hair. "I can't tell you how happy I am to see you feeling better, Henry."

"Why can't you?" Henry pulled back to look up at Olivia.

"It's an expression," Emily filled in. "But I think you need to get dressed now. Do you need some help?"

Henry released Olivia and looked at Emily like she was an enemy. "No, Mommy, of course not." He stomped past her to their bedroom to dress himself, and Emily briefly wondered what mash-up of clothing he would return in before she turned her attention to Olivia.

"Hi," Emily said, breaking the ice.

"Hello." Olivia nodded with a tight smile, clearly nervous.

Emily took a breath and took the first step for them both. "I'm sorry for overreacting."

Olivia raised her hand, waving away Emily's apology. "No, I'm the one who should be apologising. I was completely out of line. I've thought about it a lot, and I—I can't explain what I...why I..."

"How about we agree that we were both wrong and we are both sorry and put it to one side? Just have lunch, without the awkwardness."

"I'd like that." Olivia followed Emily through to the dining room.

"I just got a few light foods," Emily explained. "Salad, chicken slices, some bread, some pasta salad."

"This is wonderful," Olivia said, and Emily gestured for her to sit down at the head of the table and took a seat beside her.

A moment later, Henry came tearing back into the room wearing his giraffe pyjama bottoms, his giraffe hoodie on backwards with LEGO characters in the hood, and a Darth Vader mask. Emily sighed.

"Henry..."

Henry breathed deeply in his own impersonation of the Dark Lord. "Mommy...I am your son!"

Olivia laughed.

"Don't encourage him—he thinks he's funny enough as it is."

"I am funny," Henry stated.

"Henry, mask off, LEGO out of your hood, please," Emily instructed, and he begrudgingly complied with her wishes. "How is work? I noticed that Simon was working all weekend," Emily asked Olivia conversationally.

Olivia sighed. "We're struggling to keep a firm from insolvency," she said.

"Yes, he said something, but it went over my head," Emily said. Henry sat opposite her, next to Olivia, and Emily started to plate up some food for him, passing Olivia another plate.

"We need to either find someone to buy the business or convince the companies who are owed money to take less or wipe the debt entirely," Olivia explained. "That's the real issue. And we're up against a deadline of tomorrow."

"Why tomorrow?" Emily asked, pouring Olivia a glass of water from the jug on the table, not needing to ask Olivia's beverage of choice.

"Tomorrow is when the staff payroll is due to be finalised," Olivia explained.

"And the business can't pay?"

"No, they've been surviving on bank loans, and they have now been cut off." Olivia picked out a few lettuce leaves and added them to her plate.

"Sounds familiar," Emily said under her breath.

"Indeed," Olivia said softly, lining up her drink coaster at a precise angle.

"So, what happens if you can't find someone to buy or reduce the debts?" Emily asked.

"Insolvency, the business will cease to trade." Olivia sighed, a weight seeming to come over her. "But I don't want to talk about that," she added quickly and, changing the subject, asked, "How is Darth here doing?"

Emily laughed. "He is doing well—very tired but that's to be expected. He's recovering on schedule, and the doctors are pleased with him. We're hoping he can fly home on Friday morning."

Olivia looked up with a hopeful face. "On my flight?"

"Hopefully." Emily grinned.

"Can I sit with Olivia again?" Henry's eyes lit up.

"We don't know where you'll be sitting, Henry," Emily explained. "There may not be room where Olivia sits."

Henry looked disappointed but didn't say anything else.

"Have you enjoyed the hotel, Henry?" Olivia asked in an obvious attempt to change the subject and cheer the boy up.

"The bed is soft," he said. "But there are no giraffes on the buses."

Olivia blinked in surprise, her fork suspended inches from her lips.

"Simon said that there are buses without roofs so the giraffes can sit on them. Because they can't get taxis," Henry explained.

"Oh, I see," Olivia said, looking at Emily blankly.

Emily smiled. "Henry's been looking out of the window religiously, but he hasn't seen any yet. We think that maybe there aren't any giraffes who work around here."

Olivia seemed to catch on that it was a joke of some sort and nodded. Emily watched her thinking about the statement and could see the wheels turning in her mind.

"Quite right," Olivia said tentatively. "They work around St Paul's Cathedral."

Emily smiled at Olivia's playing along. "Oh, that makes sense, because St Paul's has high ceilings," she said.

Henry looked at both of them in awe at the idea of the cathedral being filled with giraffes busily working. "Mommy, can we go?" Henry asked.

"Not now," Emily answered easily. "They're all on vacation at the moment."

"In Madagascar?"

"Yes, in Madagascar," Emily confirmed.

Henry nodded thoughtfully at the information before turning back to his lunch.

"We found a hostel, a good one this time," Emily said lightly.

"Oh." Olivia frowned. "But I thought you liked it here."

Emily was confused. "Well, yes, of course we do but you're back now."

"Oh," Olivia said, looking down at her plate and scrutinising a crouton.

"What are you thinking?" Emily asked softly.

Olivia picked up her fork and speared more salad. "I had made a foolish assumption—it's quite all right."

"What assumption?" Emily pressed.

Olivia hesitated for a moment, a thoughtful frown covering her face, before she finally spoke. "I didn't think you had need for a hostel," she said.

Emily considered this for a moment before realisation hit. "Oh! I see. We couldn't intrude. You've been so kind as it is."

"No intrusion," Olivia said. "It's a large suite."

Emily looked at her thoughtfully for a moment. In truth, she had already been in close quarters with Olivia, preparing her airline bed, seeing her in her pyjamas and without make-up. And Olivia was clearly good for Henry's well-being, not to mention the fact that while the hostel was undoubtedly good, it was also expensive. Emily considered what Simon would advise and knew immediately he would tell her to stay in the suite, enjoy the luxurious surroundings, and save the money. Besides, it was only four more nights.

"Are you absolutely sure?" Emily asked. "It wouldn't put you out in any way?"

Olivia shrugged. "I had already, mistakenly, assumed that was the plan. It seems silly that you would uproot yourself again, never mind spend money you can't afford to waste."

Emily took a deep breath and held it in for a second as she attempted to calm herself from Olivia's bluntness. Silently, she counted to five in her head and pushed down the rising anger, reminding herself that Olivia didn't mean to call her silly.

"What's *soltancee*?" Henry suddenly asked. He looked angrily at a small leaf of lettuce that had fallen onto the table near his plate.

Emily could see that Olivia was confused as to what Henry meant. "Insolvency," she translated for Olivia's sake before sounding the word out for Henry, who repeated it back.

Olivia paused, and Emily assumed that she was considering exactly how to explain the complexities of business insolvency to a five-year-old with his giraffe hoodie on backwards.

"It's when a business doesn't have any money and can't be a business any more," Olivia finally said.

"Why?" Henry asked.

"Why do they not have any money, or why can they not be a business any more?" Olivia replied.

"Both." Henry shrugged.

"Well, they don't have any money because they made mistakes or people didn't pay them money. And they can't be a business any more because they need money to be a business," Olivia said.

"Why?" Henry asked.

"Because they need to pay their bills," Olivia replied.

"What are bills?" he probed.

"Bills are requests for money."

"Why do we need businesses anyway?" Henry asked with a dramatic sigh.

"So people have jobs."

Emily looked up from her lunch in surprise. She had felt for sure Olivia was going to say that businesses were needed to make money.

"Why do people need jobs?" Henry asked.

"People need jobs, so they can pay for places to live and food to eat," Olivia explained. "Businesses give them jobs, so they have money to pay for things. If we don't have businesses, we don't have jobs, and then people don't have money."

"And then they have no house and no food," Henry said with some basic understanding.

"Exactly. Which is why I need to try to save this business. Because if I don't, then a lot of people won't have jobs."

Emily picked over her lunch thoughtfully. She knew that jobs would be at stake if the company was declared bankrupt, but she hadn't considered the human side of the issue.

"Save the business, Olivia," Henry cried out excitedly.

"I will try my best." She smiled at him.

"Mommy, can I look for the giraffes again?" Henry asked as he fidgeted on his chair.

Emily looked at what he had eaten and nodded. "Okay, Henry."

Henry rushed off, and Olivia watched him go. Emily noticed that the pensive look was back on her face. She stood to clear the table, and as she picked up Henry's plate she noticed Olivia was pinching the skin between her thumb and forefinger.

"What are you thinking?" she asked.

"Oh, it's nothing," Olivia said, far too quickly for it to be true.

"Nice try. What are you thinking?"

Olivia hesitated a moment before placing her hands flat on the table. "Why are we lying to Henry?"

Emily blinked and laughed. "About what?"

"About giraffes on buses? And working at St Paul's?" Olivia looked confused.

"It's just a joke," Emily pointed out.

"You're making him look silly," Olivia replied.

"No," Emily said gently. "It's playing and imagination. Henry is five years old—he thinks a thousand unbelievable things every day. It's an important part of his growth and development."

While Olivia took that in, Emily continued, "Making things up, joking around, playing with his imagination is good for him. I'm not trying to trick him."

Olivia nodded in realisation. "So he wouldn't be annoyed if he went to St Paul's and there were no giraffes?"

"No," Emily smiled. "He'll probably forget about that by tomorrow, not to mention that he won't be going there on his own anytime soon."

"I see," Olivia replied, and Emily could see her filing away the information for later.

"Didn't you ever imagine wondrous things when you were a child?" Emily asked.

Olivia chuckled. "No, when I was a child I was preoccupied with organising my teddy bear's life."

Emily put the plates on the kitchen worktop and smiled. "Oh yes?"

"Yes." Olivia smiled at the memory. "He had a job at the factory, and then he came home and went shopping to get groceries."

"And how is that different from Henry's giraffe buses?"

Olivia paused as she thought about it. "Well, my teddy bear was being practical. He had a job. And a family."

"The giraffes are going to work," Emily pointed out. "It's just as practical. And just as ridiculous. What was your teddy bear's name?"

"Edward Bear," Olivia replied and Emily laughed.

"Okay, so maybe Henry is a little more imaginative than you were when you were a child, but it's the same principle."

"At least I didn't call him Teddy."

Emily cleared the rest of the plates away and asked Olivia if she wanted anything else.

"No, thank you. It was delicious."

"You're welcome. And thank you for letting us stay here," Emily said.

Olivia's hands disappeared from the table and fell into her lap. A nervous expression washed over her face, but she remained silent.

"Olivia? Is something else on your mind?"

"We didn't confirm the situation with your accommodation," Olivia pointed out.

"Oh, right." Emily realised that Olivia was clearly uncomfortable with the uncertainty. "Well, you're right. It would be simpler to stay here, but I just want to make sure that you're absolutely okay with that."

Olivia nodded. "Yes, I wouldn't have said it otherwise."

Emily smiled wryly. "No, I suppose you wouldn't have."

"So you'll stay?" Olivia pressed.

"Yes, we'll stay, but you have to promise that if we become a nuisance, you'll tell me immediately," Emily said seriously.

"Why would you be a nuisance?" Olivia looked confused.

"Well, I hope we won't be. But five-year-olds are noisy and boisterous. Henry can be a handful."

"Well, sadly, I don't think I'll be seeing a lot of either of you," she said as she looked at her watch. "In fact, I need to be getting back to the office."

"Saving the business?"

"Hopefully." Olivia sighed and stood up. "Thank you for agreeing to see me again. I felt terrible about the way things were left."

"So did I," Emily admitted. "I'm glad we're past that now."

Olivia smiled at the acknowledgement that the argument was now truly behind them. "Me too. And thank you again for lunch. I'm sorry I can't stay longer."

"It's okay, I understand," Emily said as she walked with Olivia to the sitting room. "Henry, Olivia is going back to work now."

He looked up from the coffee table where he was drawing on a sheet of paper. "Wait," he said as he hurriedly picked up another colour and quickly ran it across the page.

"No, Henry," Emily said softly. "Olivia has to go now."

"It's okay." Olivia paused as he raced to finish his drawing before jumping to his feet. He dashed over and pushed the paper into Olivia's hand. She perused it thoughtfully before looking at Emily with pleading eyes.

"Right," Emily said as she looked at the drawing. "So…this is Olivia?"

"Yes." Henry nodded. "And that's the business that she's gonna save." He pointed to a large squiggle.

"And that's a giraffe." Olivia pointed to a random scribble next to the stick figure of herself.

"Yes." Henry walked away to look out of the window again.

"It's a metaphorical business," Emily whispered.

"Good." Olivia nodded. "Because if it looks like that, then I'm afraid it's in worse shape than I thought." They shared a laugh before Olivia nodded towards the door. "I have to…"

"Yes, go, and thank you again. I suppose I'll see you tonight."

Olivia nodded and smiled. "Yes, though I may be late."

"I'll be up," Emily assured her.

"Olivia, go and save the business," Henry called out from his spot by the window.

Olivia laughed. "Okay, I'm going."

They exchanged quick goodbyes. Emily closed the door behind Olivia and gently leaned her forehead on it and bit her lip.

"Mommy?"

"Yes, Henry?" Emily turned to face her son.

"Will she be back soon?"

Emily rolled her eyes, realising it was going to be a very long afternoon.

CHAPTER NINETEEN

Emily sat in the hotel suite sitting room with the lights off, trying to convince herself that she wasn't spying on the Applewood Financial offices across the road. After dinner and some television, Henry had started to drop off to sleep, despite his valiant attempts to stay awake for Olivia's return. Emily put him to bed and started to clean the lounge area of various toys and giraffe paraphernalia to ensure that the room would be clear for when Olivia did finally return.

That had been several hours ago, and the busy hum of the street below had turned silent as the evening drew on. Emily had read, browsed the internet, and watched some television, but she was too distracted to truly concentrate on anything as she waited for Olivia. At first, she would occasionally stand up and peek through the closed curtains to see Olivia and Simon busily working. On the twentieth visit to the curtains, Emily knew it was useless trying to kid herself that she was doing anything other than spying and decided to turn the lights off and open the curtains so she could see without getting up from the sofa every few minutes.

At ten o'clock Simon left the office, but Olivia remained on. Emily watched as she made telephone calls and typed on her computer for the next hour until finally she stood and started to pace her office.

With a frown, Emily wondered if Olivia was avoiding her, avoiding the awkwardness of returning to the suite, knowing that they were there. She nervously chewed her lower lip as she thought back to the conversation over lunch. Olivia hadn't seemed at all hesitant then, and she didn't seem to even understand why Emily thought it might be a problem. But she watched Olivia slowly pace the office until she stopped by the huge glass windows and looked down at the street below. With just a short distance between them, Emily could see sadness in Olivia's expression.

Realisation struck that she knew hardly anything about Olivia. She travelled a lot, she worked in financial services, and Emily knew she was gay or maybe bi, but that was it. She decided to make a concerted effort to find out more. They were going to share living space for the next few days, and after that Emily would be seeing her twice a week at work. She also suspected that Henry was already planning ways to spend more time with his new best friend, and if Olivia was willing, then Emily certainly wasn't going to prevent it from happening.

Emily had spent most of the afternoon and evening thinking about Olivia, kidding herself that she was only thinking about her because of her kindness regarding their current situation. What she *couldn't* kid herself about was that her feelings were purely platonic. That didn't change the fact that her son had to remain her top priority. She didn't have time for a relationship, and she couldn't put Henry through the pain of another separation.

Emily looked over to Applewood Financial, and much to her surprise and relief, the lights were off in Olivia's office. Finally, she had called it a day and was on her way home. Emily watched her exit the building and make her way across the quiet street towards the hotel.

Quickly, she drew the curtains and turned on a couple of table lamps so it wasn't obvious that she'd been sitting in the dark. She picked up her book and tried to look relaxed while she waited for Olivia. Ten minutes later, she heard the key card in the lock, and the door opened. She looked up with a smile.

Olivia paused in surprise. "I didn't think you'd still be up," she commented, her tone low and tired.

"I don't need a lot of sleep," Emily replied softly. "You're back late."

"Yes." Olivia nodded in agreement as she removed her coat and hung it in the closet by the door.

Emily smiled to herself and made a mental note that Olivia hadn't caught on to the question in her tone, only the words she had spoken. She didn't know if this was because Olivia was tired or distracted, but she filed the information away for later.

"Why are you back so late?" Emily tried again. She closed her book, a finger marking her page.

Olivia put her laptop bag and handbag on the coffee table and sat heavily on sofa, still maintaining more grace than Emily thought she would in a similar situation.

"I was attempting to make a last-minute deal," Olivia explained. "But I couldn't. The debts are too large."

"Oh." Emily found that she was surprised by Olivia's defeat. She had somehow suspected the woman could do the impossible. "So what happens now?" Emily asked.

"We sell off any assets to pay outstanding bills," Olivia said. "But more immediately we file a press report, speak to the directors of the company, and then advise the staff."

Emily started to understand Olivia's sombre appearance. "Are you going straight to bed, or would you like a drink?"

Olivia looked up at her and gave a small smile. "I think I'll be staying up, but you don't need to serve me."

"It's not a problem. I was going to make a drink anyway. Tea, coffee, juice?" Emily joked, repeating verbatim her standard speech while at work.

Olivia grinned with understanding. "Coffee, please, if it's not too much trouble. I didn't offer you a place to stay so you'd end up serving me beverages."

"Might as well make myself useful." Emily smiled as she went to the kitchen and filled the kettle.

When she came back into the room, Olivia was waiting for the laptop to start up.

"You're not planning to do more work, are you?" Emily asked in surprise.

Olivia turned to face her. "I'm afraid I must. There are a lot of people who need to be informed that a deal couldn't be brokered."

"It's past midnight," Emily said with a look at her watch.

"Would you be asleep if your livelihood was on the line?" Olivia questioned, though not unkindly.

"No, I suppose I wouldn't," Emily agreed.

Olivia's smartphone started to vibrate on the coffee table. She picked it up. "Stuart, thank you for calling me back."

Emily felt that she was intruding, so she returned to the kitchen to finish making the coffee. Olivia's side of the conversation was audible from the kitchen.

"Yes, I understand that, but really it is your place—" Olivia appeared to get cut off. "I know you're upset but…" Olivia paused, presumably listening to Stuart, before saying, "Of course, yes…I can certainly understand your point of view. But I assure you that we have done all we can."

Emily slowly and quietly made the coffee, knowing that eavesdropping was impolite but not being able to stop herself.

"Well, your opinion of me is, quite frankly, irrelevant," Olivia said firmly, and Emily could tell by the change in volume that Olivia was now pacing the room as she softly spoke. "Of course if you don't feel you can do it, then it will fall to my team."

Emily had delayed all she could and entered the room with two mugs of coffee, silently placed them on the coffee table, and sat on the sofa.

"That's…disappointing," Olivia said, and Emily could hear an angry man shouting down the phone. Olivia held the phone to her ear with one hand while pulling back the curtain to look out of the window with the other. "Very well, yes, well, you leave me with no option."

Emily heard the man shouting some more, and Olivia sighed and said, "Of course, yes, we'll make the calls in the morning." She hung up and closed her eyes for a moment as she gripped the phone in her hand tightly.

"Are you okay?" Emily asked softly. Olivia's eyes flew open. Either she was surprised that someone was there or surprised that someone cared enough to ask, Emily wasn't certain.

"Yes, that was the owner of TCA Engineering." She indicated the phone as she crossed the room and sat back down. "He refuses to take any responsibility. He claims we're making him into a scapegoat for our own failings."

"That's crazy," Emily declared. "You wouldn't have been brought in unless there were serious problems."

Olivia smiled. "Precisely, but he doesn't see it that way. We have cascaded a message to the employees not to go to work tomorrow, but we still need to speak to them all individually, explain the situation, and advise them of their legal rights. He's refusing to help or to instruct his own Human Resources department to do it."

"So what happens now?"

"We do it," Olivia said with a sigh. "This news will obviously be difficult for people to accept, but it would have been slightly less hurtful if the message was at least conveyed by someone they knew, like a colleague who worked with them and found themselves in the same situation. Now I will need to divide the names of five hundred and eighty-three people between my staff, and we have to call each one of them."

Emily's jaw fell open. "Five hundred and eighty-three calls?"

"Yes. Well, five hundred and eighty-two, as the owner is obviously aware of the situation."

"How will you do that?" Emily asked, still in shock at the scale of the job.

"If I have the two other partners, their assistants, seven members of the insolvencies team, two members of the restructuring team, Simon, and myself making calls, that makes fifteen of us, so around thirty-eight calls each. Say, five minutes per call? Although allowing for some to be unavailable and the others who will not wish to speak to us, it will take about three hours." Olivia picked up the steaming coffee mug and held it in her hands.

"Sounds tough," Emily said sympathetically. "But you'll be making calls yourself?"

"Yes." Olivia took a sip of her beverage. "I won't give jobs out to my staff that I wouldn't do myself. Besides, they need an extra person to make the calls. It's a necessary evil."

Emily regarded the tired woman in front of her. She was surprised at Olivia's hands-on approach, but then everything she had seen about Olivia so far led her to believe that she wasn't a stereotypical boss.

"Do you want something to eat?" Emily asked. "There's some food in the fridge."

"I was going to call down to the kitchen."

"I thought they'd be closed, but special treatment for you, right?" Emily chuckled.

"Yes," Olivia admitted. "They know my habit of skipping dinner."

"Wait, what?" Emily looked up. "You skipped dinner?"

Olivia looked like she had been caught underage drinking by strict parents. "Well, I didn't have time. There was so much to do."

"You haven't eaten for twelve hours?" Emily shook her head at the thought. "I'm making you something to eat. The hotel will take ages, and you need to eat now." Emily hurried into the kitchen, and Olivia followed her with her drink in her hand and watched as Emily pulled out various ingredients from the fridge. "How about a sandwich, or do you want something hot?"

"Um…" Olivia paused, clearly torn between wanting to eat and not wanting Emily to feel obliged to serve her. Apparently hunger overcome her concerns. "May I have a sandwich? I don't want anything too heavy."

"Of course, chicken salad?"

Olivia's eyes lit up and she nodded. "Thank you, you don't need to do that, I can—"

"You flew a night flight into London, went straight to the office, where you've been working all day, literally, and most of the night too. I've been drawing giraffe pictures most of the afternoon."

Olivia leaned against the counter and sipped her coffee. "Where did the giraffe obsession come from?"

"I'm not sure." Emily smiled as she started to make sandwiches. "One day about two years ago the television was on, and there was a news report about a baby giraffe being born in some zoo. Henry literally ran for the screen and was staring at it like it was the most amazing thing he had ever seen. I showed him some photographs online, and he was giggling at how ridiculous they looked. From then on, everything has been giraffes."

"Has he ever seen a real giraffe?" Olivia asked.

"No, not in the flesh. But I'll take him to the zoo one day soon, although I doubt I'll ever get him to leave again. By the way, thank you so much for the giraffe hoodie. He absolutely loves it. He claims that he never would have gotten better without it."

"Thank Simon. I asked him to get a few things, and he saw the giraffe hoodie and thought it would be perfect. It seems he was right."

"I have a lot to thank Simon for," Emily said seriously as she opened the fridge. "He's such a nice guy."

"He is," Olivia agreed. "I dread the day he leaves."

"He's thinking of leaving?" Emily asked.

"Not to my knowledge, but the day will come. He's young and probably doesn't want to be a PA for the rest of his life." Olivia sighed. "He'll be impossible to replace."

"Maybe he'll stay for longer than you think."

"Maybe," Olivia allowed, although her tone was clear that she didn't believe it.

"I have to ask." Emily turned around and regarded Olivia with a butter-stained knife in her hand. "Why the hotel?"

Olivia looked confused. "Excuse me?"

"Why live the majority of your life in a hotel rather than buying a place of your own?" Emily clarified as she put a sandwich on a plate and handed it to Olivia.

"Oh." Olivia took the plate. "It's close to the office."

"It definitely is," Emily agreed. "Don't you feel like you want to get away from work sometimes, though?"

"Why?"

"Have a break, do other things?" Emily prompted.

Olivia took a bite and thought for a moment before replying. "I don't think I really have anything else."

"No hobbies or interests?" Emily asked in between bites of her own sandwich.

Olivia considered it for a moment before shaking her head. "I don't have time for anything else."

"So you're in an endless circle. You work all the time because you don't have anything else to do, and you don't have any time to do anything else because you're always working."

Olivia smiled. "I suppose so. What do you do? Outside of work, I mean?"

"Well, outside of work there's Henry, and with my schedule, there's not a lot of time for much else. But if I wasn't working, then I have plenty of hobbies I'd be getting involved with. I love reading and writing. I play sports, love yoga, I used to play the piano but I'm a little rusty these days, and I bake." Emily laughed as she picked up her coffee mug and clasped it. "If I didn't work, I'd be able to fill the day with hobbies."

"If I didn't work, I don't know what I'd do."

"Do you love what you do?" Emily asked.

Olivia thought about it for a moment. "I enjoy it—I don't know if I would say I love it. There are days when…" She trailed off, and her expression changed to one of distant reflection.

"When?" Emily prompted.

Olivia blinked. "Sorry, there are days when I don't know what the purpose is."

"I think the purpose is to fill your time with things you enjoy. Sure, we all have to do things we don't like, but the rest of the time, you should be enjoying living your life."

Olivia opened her mouth to speak but the sound of her phone vibrating on the coffee table in the sitting room stopped her, and she went to answer it. "Olivia Lewis."

Emily cleared away some things in the kitchen while she overheard Olivia speaking with someone and advising them that a deal hadn't been brokered. She unloaded the dishwasher, which had recently finished, and quietly restacked it again with the used dishes and cups. She realised a mug was missing and returned to the living room where Olivia was off the phone and typing on her laptop.

"Do you want anything else?" Emily asked as she picked up the empty coffee mug.

"No, thank you." Olivia stifled a yawn. "I'm just sending these reports over to the bank, and then I need to draft an email to the solicitor, and then I need to divide up the employee list."

Emily regarded her for a couple of seconds before she nodded and returned to the kitchen, understanding that it wasn't her place to tell Olivia when she should stop working.

The sound of Henry crying pulled Emily from her thoughts, and she rushed to the bedroom to check on him. Although the boy often slept through the night, there were still times when he woke in the middle of the night with bad dreams.

She climbed into bed and pulled a very sleepy Henry into her arms and cuddled him. Softly she sang a lullaby and swayed him gently to encourage him back to sleep. After a few minutes, he fell back into a deep sleep, and she quietly left the room. Back in the living room, she grinned at the sight of Olivia slumped on the sofa fast asleep.

Emily was well-versed in the art of waking sleeping passengers. She had even undergone a two-hour training course on it when she enrolled with Crown Airlines. She stood by the arm of the chair and gently put her hand on Olivia's shoulder. "Olivia," she said softly, "Olivia, wake up."

Olivia's eyes fluttered open, and Emily smiled at her. "I fell asleep." Olivia started to get her bearings.

"So I see, and I'd only been gone a few minutes." She took the phone out of Olivia's hand and placed it on the table in front of her. "Turn the computer off," she commanded gently. "You need to sleep."

Olivia didn't argue. She saved her work and shut down the computer. She stood up and silently walked towards the bedrooms. At the door to her room, she turned to face Emily and gave a sleepy smile. "Thank you."

"You're welcome, now go to bed," she commanded lightly.

Olivia slowly nodded her head, entered her bedroom, and closed the door behind her.

CHAPTER TWENTY

Emily awoke the next morning and quietly slid out of the king-size bed, trying not to disturb Henry, who had spread out during the night and was taking up much more room than a five-year-old should technically require. She grinned at the sight of her son sprawled out. She dressed in tight jeans and a white tank top, desperate for her first coffee of the day.

As she exited the bedroom, she could hear Olivia in the kitchen on her phone and glanced at her watch to see it was seven thirty. Entering the kitchen, she saw paper strewn all over the dining table. Olivia was sitting at the table with her phone pressed to her ear. She was dressed in a white shirt and black trousers, her hair and make-up, as always, completed to perfection.

"As I say, Miss Dorchester, a letter will be with you shortly so…" Olivia paused as a female voice on the other end of the telephone began shouting. Looking over at Emily, she smiled ruefully before lowering her head onto her hand and closing her eyes at the stream of hatred that was being hurled at her down the line. Then the shouting stopped, and apparently realising she had been hung up on, Olivia lowered the phone to the table. "I'm sorry, I'll clean up the mess."

"No, it's fine, it's your kitchen," Emily said as she looked around the disarray. "How long have you been up?"

Olivia looked at the clock on the wall and calculated. "Two hours?"

Emily nodded but remained silent as she knew it wasn't her place to say anything about Olivia's working schedule. "So, you started the calls?" She opened the dishwasher and started to gather the dirty mugs that lined the worktop.

"Well, I started with paperwork until it was a reasonable hour to call people. That was the third. The first was out, the second cried, and the third...Well, she wasn't happy. Understandably."

"Let me make you some breakfast. What would you like?"

Olivia shook her head as she attempted to straighten some of the papers on the dining room table. "I'm not hungry."

Emily frowned. "Have you eaten anything since the sandwich I made you last night?"

Olivia shook her head as she moved papers around, making the haphazard pile worse rather than better.

Emily watched her thoughtfully for a moment before folding her arms. "Olivia, while I did agree to stay here, I think you also need to understand that this has to be a suitable environment for a child, yes?"

Olivia looked up at Emily in concern. "Well, yes, of course."

"Breakfast is the most important meal of the day," Emily lectured. "And I don't want Henry to think that he can get away without having breakfast, especially when he's recovering from surgery. If he sees you are skipping meals, then he will want to do the same—you must know how he looks up to you."

Olivia looked slightly ashamed. "Oh yes, of course...Well. Maybe I can eat something small? Just to set a good example."

"Good, thank you." Emily turned around to fill the kettle, a smile forming on her face. "Henry usually doesn't get up for another half an hour, so we can all eat breakfast together then. If you'll still be here, that is."

"I will. I'm going to work from home this morning," Olivia said. "I'd rather make these calls here."

"Okay, if you want some peace and quiet, let me know. More coffee? Or should I be cutting you off?"

Olivia looked at her seriously. "More coffee."

Emily laughed and set about making it. "So, three down, how many left to go?"

"Thirty-five." Olivia picked up her phone and began to dial a number. "Wish me luck."

Emily quietly got everything ready to make the coffee and listened to Olivia's opening spiel.

"Good morning, may I speak with Roger Lincoln?" Pause. "Hello, Mr. Lincoln, my name is Olivia Lewis, and I'm calling from Applewood Financial. We are the administrators for TCA Engineering."

Emily could hear the man on the other end of the phone erupt with anger, and Olivia attempted to calm him down and explain the situation, but it was no good and he continued to rant and rave. At one point Emily could hear him demanding Olivia tell him how much money she was making from the insolvency. Over and over he asked the question while Olivia continued to calmly attempt to provide him with pertinent information.

Eventually the call was over. Olivia took a deep breath and ticked a name on her spreadsheet, making a short note before dialling the next number, and the cycle continued.

"Good morning, may I speak with Stephen Walker? Thank you." As Olivia waited, Emily approached with the coffee and placed it on the only space available on the table in front of Olivia. She returned to the worktop and finished making her own drink.

"Oh, hello, Mr. Walker, my name is Olivia Lewis, and I'm calling from Applewood Financial. We are the administrators for TCA Engineering." Emily couldn't hear the other side of the conversation, and Olivia managed to get through everything that she had to say. She apologised for the situation and explained what had happened, what they had done, and what was happening now. She advised him that the company was in the process of selling off assets, and when that was complete, they might be able to pay him the redundancy package they were required to provide by law, but in the event that the sum required was not raised, he had the right to go to court. Olivia answered some questions, and soon the call was over.

"If they were all like him, that would be a lot easier," Olivia commented as she ticked another line on her spreadsheet and made another note.

The sound of Henry padding through the suite made them both look up. He appeared in the doorway in his giraffe pyjamas and stopped dead when he saw Olivia. He looked around for Emily, and the second he saw her he rushed towards her and threw his arms up to be lifted.

"Morning, sweetheart," Emily said as she put her coffee down and lifted him up. His legs wrapped around her waist, and his head burrowed into the crook of her neck as she folded her arms around him.

She softly threaded her hand through his hair. "Henry's a little shy when he wakes up, aren't you, sweetheart?" she told Olivia, who was watching with raised eyebrows. Henry tuned his face away and nuzzled into his mother, so Olivia wasn't able to see his face.

"Should I…?" Olivia pointed to another room, clearly worried she was upsetting Henry.

"No." Emily shook her head. "He'll be okay soon—he just needs to wake up a little." She sat down on a chair, and Henry tilted his head slightly and squinted sideways at Olivia. Olivia smiled at him, and he regarded her sombrely.

"So, will you be joining us for lunch again today?" Emily asked Olivia. "I told Henry that if the weather is good, we might have a little picnic in the park by the hospital before his appointment."

"I wouldn't want to intrude," Olivia said. She pensively watched Henry, clearly worried that she had somehow fallen out of favour with the boy.

"Henry, do you want Olivia to come with us on our picnic?" Emily asked softly as she kissed his hair. Henry continued to silently watch Olivia as if evaluating her and wondering what she was going to do, before slowly nodding his head. "There you have it," Emily said. "Henry at his most grumpy still wants you to come with us—if you have time, of course."

Olivia sipped her coffee and distractedly made some notes on a piece of paper. After a while, Henry started to fidget, and Emily whispered in his ear to go and get dressed while she made him breakfast. Slowly, he slid off her knee and went back to their bedroom.

"He seemed scared of me," Olivia said the second he was gone.

"He'd just woken up. It takes him a while to get with it. He always wants to sit with me and cuddle when he first wakes up, even at home with Lucy, who he adores. It's just a kid thing—don't take offence."

"So he's like that every morning?" Olivia asked.

"Yep, he tears out of his bedroom, bleary-eyed and half asleep, and no matter what I'm doing, I have to stop everything and hold him for a while. Then he goes to get dressed and he wakes up a bit more. When I'm not at home, apparently he runs downstairs and looks around before running back upstairs and hugging Tiny for a while until he's ready to get up."

"It must be hard for him when you're not there."

Emily took a deep breath and mentally counted to five before replying. "Yes, it's hard for both of us."

"But as a child, he doesn't understand why and—" Olivia continued.

"Olivia," Emily said, cutting her off, "I get it. Now, what would you like for breakfast? Toast? Cereal?"

Olivia hesitated for a moment, as if unsure whether she was in Emily's bad graces. "Toast, please."

Emily smiled but it was mainly for show. She could see Olivia struggled with the understanding that she had been insensitive and relented a little. Henry returned wearing pull-up jeans and his giraffe hoodie, which never seemed to be out of his sight. Tiny was under his arm, and he was sucking his thumb. He looked from Olivia to Emily with uncertainty.

Olivia looked back to her laptop, perhaps to give him some space and time to acclimatise to the new day, company, and surroundings. Emily watched as Henry regarded Olivia thoughtfully and then ran over to her. He pulled Olivia's arm out of the way and silently struggled to climb into her lap, Tiny still clutched to his side.

"Henry, Olivia's busy," Emily said.

"Do you want to sit on my lap?" Olivia asked.

At his insistent nod, she lifted him onto her knee, Tiny included. Emily smiled as Henry adjusted himself to sit sideways and tucked his head under Olivia's chin while she worked around him.

Soon the toast was ready. Emily placed butter and jams on the table and told Henry, "Time to eat. Go sit on your own chair."

"I don't mind," Olivia said softly.

"He'll cover you in butter and jam." Emily pulled out a chair and looked at Henry.

He shook his head and burrowed in closer, turning away from Emily and wrapping his arms around Olivia as he pressed his face into her chest. Olivia dropped her pen and slowly looked down at Henry in surprise, before putting her arms around him. Emily smiled and went to get him some milk from the fridge. She hadn't missed the panicked look in Olivia's eyes that told she had never interacted with a child this closely before. Taking her time, Emily allowed Olivia to get used to the contact. She fussed over cleaning the kitchen worktop for as long as she could before placing Henry's glass of milk on the table.

"Henry?" she said in a lightly warning tone. This only caused the boy to tighten his hold on Olivia. "Henry, if you don't eat your breakfast, then you won't be able to watch the morning cartoons." Carefully he slid off Olivia's lap and climbed onto the chair that had been pulled out for him.

"Thank you," Emily said and prepared him a slice of toast with butter and jam while he drank some milk. She looked over at Olivia. "Toast?"

Olivia shook herself out of her daze and nodded as she picked up a slice of toast from the rack that Emily held towards her. They all continued to eat breakfast in comfortable silence, both of them regarding the sleepy boy fondly. When Henry had eaten as much as he could manage, he looked at his mother with big pleading eyes and Emily laughed. "Go on, then."

He quickly slid off his chair and ran towards the sitting room, and a few moments later, the muted sound of cartoons could be heard.

Olivia smiled. "He's a curious thing in the morning."

"Yep, he's shy in the morning," Emily said. "In fact, he usually doesn't take to people as quickly as he has to you."

Olivia gave Emily a surprised look. "Really?"

"Really," Emily confirmed. "He obviously has good taste." She stood up and cleared away the breakfast things while Olivia sat silently in thought.

"Well, back to it, I suppose." She picked up the phone and started to make more calls.

Emily opted to wash the dirty dishes in the sink rather than stack the dishwasher as it allowed her to spend more time in the kitchen and listen in.

She fumed over the next twenty minutes as she overheard call after call where Olivia apologetically and politely explained to people what had happened, only to receive abuse back. She occasionally glanced at Olivia and saw her changing expressions, from businesslike perseverance to hurt, etched on her face. As Olivia was shouted at yet again, she hung up and lowered the phone to the table, taking a deep breath as she ticked another line off the spreadsheet. With a swallow, she began to dial another number.

Emily stepped forward and snatched the phone out of her hand. "No way, you need a break."

Olivia looked surprised that Emily was holding her phone to ransom. "But I have to make these calls."

"I know," Emily agreed. "But no one deserves to listen to thirty-odd people spewing abuse at them one after the other. Take a break."

"I don't have time for a break," Olivia said as Emily pulled over the paperwork and started to dial the next number. "What are you doing?"

"I've listened to your patter enough to know the routine. If they're just going to be insulting and shout, then it doesn't matter who's making the calls." Emily shrugged as she put the phone to her ear. Olivia watched in amazement as Emily started the call. "Good morning, may I speak with Zara Blake?"

Emily waited as Blake came to the phone, then said, "Hello, Miss Blake, I'm calling from Applewood Financial. We are the administrators for TCA Engineering." The woman immediately began blaming the administrators for not helping the little people and ended with calling Emily an expletive before hanging up. Emily took the pen from Olivia's hand and ticked Zara Blake from the list and made a note by the side.

"You don't need to do this," Olivia said softly. "I can manage."

"I know you can," Emily said as she dialled the next number. "But it doesn't mean that you have to. Does it really matter which one of us is being shouted at? Your job is to try to make people aware of the situation. If they don't want to know, you can't make them listen. I'll do the next one and then you can do one, and we'll share the rest of the list, okay?"

Over the next half hour, they raced through the calls. Some were simple hang-ups, some were abusive, and some people were upset but sensibly wanted to hear what Olivia had to say. If Emily made a call to someone who wanted more information, she handed the phone to Olivia, who would go through the technical and legal details with them. It was obvious to Emily that Olivia was exhausted from the lack of sleep and the emotional toll the whole insolvency case was having on her.

With just three more calls to go, Emily looked at Olivia and said, "I'll take these next three. Would you mind sitting with Henry for a bit and check that he's okay? If I need you, I'll come in."

Olivia hesitated. "Are you sure?"

"Yes, I'm kinda enjoying it. I've not done anything work-related for nearly two weeks. I'm feeling like a grown-up again."

Olivia paused in thought and then nodded her agreement. "Okay, I'll sit with Henry."

Emily stretched to release some of the pressure in her neck before picking up the phone and making the next call. She was pleasantly surprised by the man's nice manner. He asked a few questions, which she knew the answers to from listening to Olivia. The conversation lasted longer than most of them, but Emily was happy to have had a decent discussion rather than rabid shouting, which, while understandable, was tiresome. The next call was also productive, and Emily wondered if the list had been split up by departments as she was now talking to more rational people. Referring to the spreadsheets of data, she read some figures and answered some questions and was taken aback when she was even thanked at the end of the call.

She dialled the final number on the sheet and waited while the phone rang out until, eventually, a voicemail service kicked in. She left a message and, with a relieved sigh, made some final notes on the spreadsheet before standing up and stretching her back out. It had been a long time since she'd had a job where she was on the phone all day, and while she knew how hard it could be, she was still surprised by how exhausted she was in just two hours.

She walked into the living room. "Well, the last three weren't too bad—"

"Shush, Mommy," Henry hissed. Olivia lay on the sofa, fast asleep. He had put a hand towel from the bathroom over her as a blanket and tucked Tiny in with her. He now sat on the floor in front of the sofa, watching the television on its lowest volume, guarding the sleeping woman.

Emily felt her heart instantly melt. It was a relief that Olivia was finally resting. Emily sat in the armchair beside the sofa, picked up her book from the coffee table, and quietly read while she gave Olivia some time to rest.

CHAPTER TWENTY-ONE

An hour passed, and Emily kept a watchful eye over an exhausted Olivia while half-heartedly reading her book. Henry sat in front of the sleeping Olivia, playing with toy soldiers and watching television.

As the characters on the screen gathered for their goodbye, Henry got up onto his knees and leaned his face close to Olivia's and whispered, "You're missing the singing."

Emily tried to stop him, but it was too late. Olivia's eyes flickered open, and she regarded Henry in confusion as he smiled at her before turning back to the television. Olivia blinked a few times before sitting up and looking in bewilderment at the towel covering her.

"Henry didn't want you to get cold," Emily said.

"I…" Olivia started, clearly still half asleep.

"Fell asleep. Yes, I noticed." Emily grinned.

"I'm sorry," Olivia said as she checked her hair and straightened out her clothes.

"No need to apologise," Emily replied. "You were clearly exhausted."

"I suppose I must have been." Olivia watched Henry happily bouncing along to the song on the television.

"Tuesday naps, you might start a trend."

"Excuse me?"

"Tuesday naps—" Emily began to repeat her statement.

"It's Tuesday!" Olivia interrupted with sudden realisation. She looked at her watch and sighed.

"Oh, I'm sorry. Should I have woken you? Do you have a meeting or something?" Emily asked, instantly feeling guilty for allowing Olivia to sleep for an hour in the middle of the day when she was clearly so busy.

"No, it's okay," Olivia said. "But I can't do lunch, I'm afraid."

"Oh." Much to her chagrin, the disappointment was clear in her voice.

"I meet someone for lunch every Tuesday and Thursday," Olivia explained. "She'll be on her way now, and it would be rude to cancel at this point."

"Of course," Emily said. "I understand. Maybe another day?"

"Yes." Olivia nodded as she stood up and pointed to her bedroom. "I'm just going to freshen up a little."

Henry watched as Olivia left and then looked at Emily thoughtfully. "Will you play with me, Mommy?"

"Of course. What would you like to play?"

"Jigsaw."

"Okay, go and get it from your bag."

On the sixth time Emily and Henry completed the twelve-piece giraffe jigsaw, Olivia emerged from her room in a tailored light grey dress. Emily tried to focus on the jigsaw as Olivia moved around the suite, packing her laptop bag and handbag for work, but she found herself hopelessly distracted.

"Mommy, that doesn't go there," said Henry with a sigh. He pulled the piece out of her hand and fit it into the jigsaw correctly.

Olivia stood in the sitting room with her bags in one hand and her coat draped over her arm. "I'm sorry, again, about lunch."

"Oh, it's fine," Emily said kindly. "I understand."

"I'll see you this evening, hopefully not as late as last night," Olivia said apologetically.

"No problem, I'll be up late."

They said their goodbyes, and Olivia left the suite.

"She works hard," Henry said as he turned a jigsaw piece over and over in his hand.

"Yes, she does."

"Like you," Henry added.

"Yes, a little like me."

"Did Olivia save the business?" Henry asked as he forced two pieces together that clearly didn't match.

"No," Emily said as she took the pieces apart again and turned them over so they would fit. "It was very hard, and it couldn't be done."

He nodded and changed the subject to talk about the disturbing lack of giraffes on buses outside the window.

❖

Her lunch companion was looking at her with surprise. "So you went from never seeing each other again to living together?" Nicole asked.

"It's not like that," Olivia huffed.

"When you called me last, you said you'd called her a bad mother, and she kicked you out. Now she's staying in your suite, helping you with work, and making you sandwiches. Sounds like you're married."

"I would hope for more than sandwiches from a wife," Olivia said in a low tone, keen to not be overheard in the busy restaurant.

"Ah." Nicole nodded her understanding. "So you're no further with her in that regard?"

"No," Olivia admitted. "And I don't know what the situation is. I can't get a read on whether she's being nice or whether she's interested in me."

"Have you tried asking her?"

Olivia shook her head. "I don't want to make things uncomfortable. Everything is going so well. It…it's not awkward, as it has a tendency to be when I'm involved. I'm pretty sure I said something wrong this morning, but she appeared to gloss over it."

"Well, that's good. She's clearly making allowances for you being…well, you." Nicole winked and Olivia let out a small laugh.

"Which I appreciate," Olivia said. "But it doesn't help me to figure out our relationship."

"And you don't want to make assumptions."

A waiter placed two plates on the table. They voiced their thanks, and he left them in peace again.

"I want more," Olivia stated.

"You haven't even eaten that yet," Nicole said as she poured dressing onto her salad.

"I'm not talking about lunch."

Nicole grinned knowingly. "Oh, I see. It's like that, is it?"

"I'd like to see if it could be."

"Then you have to go for it." Nicole shrugged. "You can either wait and see what happens, which might be nothing, or you test the waters."

"But how do I test the waters?"

"Come on, Olivia"—Nicole looked up from her salad—"it's not your first date. You've asked women out before, you've dated, you've… you know."

Olivia sighed. "But this feels different. I don't want to…" She drifted off as she considered what she was about to say.

"You don't want to…?"

"I don't want anyone to get hurt," Olivia admitted. "Emily, Henry, or me. Not to mention I have to fly with her twice a week. Any kind of falling out between us could mean I'd have to change my schedule."

"Perish the thought."

"You know what I mean." Olivia sighed. "I don't want there to be any awkwardness."

"Yes, I can understand that. But clearly you have feelings for this woman, or you're starting to develop them. Isn't it worth the potential fallout?"

"I don't know." Olivia grumpily stabbed a piece of cucumber and then looked at it fondly, remembering Henry's first foray into green foods.

"Olivia." Nicole sighed. "You've always dated the same kind of women, vacuous airheads with killer bodies who you don't have to talk to. This woman seems different, very different. And I think that's good for you. I think you need someone in your life who you can converse with. Someone who makes sure you eat breakfast and almost makes you forget about long-long-standing lunch engagements with your best friend in the world."

"It's just easier to date those women," Olivia pointed out.

"I know you think it is."

Olivia was confused. "Of course it is. I date them because it's easier. They don't ask about my complicated work, they don't want to talk, they don't care when I'm not paying them enough attention, or when I say something wrong—"

"They don't care about *you*," Nicole added. "They just want you to wine and dine them and take them to great parties or to the theatre.

You don't care about them either—you just want an escort to the aforementioned parties and productions. And to, well, to warm your bed, if we're going to be plain about it." Nicole chewed a mouthful of chicken thoughtfully, then added, "But the real reason you date those women is because you're afraid of getting hurt. You can deny it all you like, but you know it's true. You think that if you date a certain kind of woman, you won't care when it's all over because you never invested that much into it in the first place."

Olivia fiddled with her cutlery and avoided Nicole's gaze.

"Emily White seems to be different. She has a brain *and* a child," Nicole pointed out. "She's a mature, responsible adult. There's a chance that if you fall for her, you could get hurt."

Olivia angrily chased a crouton around her plate.

"Am I close?" Nicole pushed.

"Maybe," Olivia admitted. "But I'm concerned she just sees me as…" She struggled for the word for a moment. "That she sees me as simple. I'm being extra careful in what I say to her, so I don't offend her, and I think it's coming across as insecurity and looking…simple."

"Yes, I noticed your hand," Nicole said, her gaze dropping to Olivia's left hand.

Olivia noticed the beginning of a bruise on the skin between her thumb and index finger. "It helps," she said softly.

"I know," Nicole said. "I was just saying that I'd noticed it. Anyway, I'm sure she doesn't think you're simple, but if you're worried about it, then you need to prove otherwise."

"How?"

"By being brave," Nicole said. "You need to talk with her. You need to get to know her. And let her get to know you. And yes, there is a chance that you will say the wrong thing, but, Olivia, darling, that is a part of who you are, and she needs to know that. Have you spoken to her about it?"

"No." Olivia quickly shook her head.

"Maybe you should," Nicole offered. "Better to have these conversations now. That way you'll know sooner whether you have a chance with her or not. Before anyone develops strong feelings."

"You're just fed up with going on double dates with me."

"No, I love some of the women you bring along," Nicole deadpanned. "My favourite was the one who thought that tuna was part of a dolphin rather than a fish in its own right. Or maybe the one that didn't understand why there was so much singing at the opera. No, no, actually the one who thought that the Middle East was a country—she was my favourite."

Olivia picked up a crouton and threw it.

❖

Olivia entered the Applewood Financial reception and walked down the corridor towards her office.

"Simon," she called. He got up from his desk and followed her in. "Get Bob to have another look at those final figures for the property in Wales. I'm sure we're a little out on that." She hung her coat on the coat stand. "And speak with the mailing house and ensure that all the employee letters will definitely go first-class post today. Then can you cancel my meeting with Vanessa Ludgate? I've been looking for an excuse to move that, and the insolvency is perfect."

"No problem," Simon said as he made notes in a tatty notebook. "Anything else?"

"Yes, I'll be leaving the office at five this evening, so please make sure that my calls are held fifteen minutes beforehand. I don't want to get caught in some endless conversation," Olivia said as she sat down at her desk and moved her mouse to wake her computer.

"Will do. I was thinking, should I change your car on Friday morning to a larger vehicle?" Olivia frowned at him in confusion. "I assume you'll be travelling to the airport with Emily and Henry plus luggage," Simon explained.

"Oh." Olivia suddenly realised her usual car would be too small for the luggage. "Yes, please—well done, Simon."

"No problem. Anything else?"

"Yes." Olivia nodded as a thought abruptly occurred to her. "Do you know what day the journalist is due to take Henry's story?"

"I do. Thursday morning," Simon replied. "Henry has his last check-up then and hopefully will be given the all-clear to fly that day too."

"Clear my schedule for the afternoon, and contact Tom Perthshire from ZSL," Olivia instructed as she looked at her emails.

"The Zoological Society of London?" Simon grinned knowingly.

"Yes, Simon." Olivia looked up at him. "ZSL."

Simon wrote in his notebook and smiled. "Any particular reason why you want to speak to London Zoo?"

"To find *you* a suitable home with the monkeys. Oh, and contact the airline. I want to book another seat for Friday."

"Tell me you're not actually going to buy a giraffe and fly it to New York first class, because it ain't gonna fit."

Olivia rolled her eyes. "I've checked, and personal giraffe ownership is frowned upon. No, I want to ensure that Henry has a seat in with me. The return journey can sometimes become rather busy. He was only in first class on the way over because of an empty seat. We cannot take the risk that they'll put him in economy."

"Heaven forbid."

"He'll be away from his mother," Olivia explained.

"Or you could go and sit with him in economy," Simon suggested with a wry grin.

"Please, Simon, we're not savages." She dismissed him with a small smile.

"Of course." Simon paused at the door on his way out. "Can I get you a coffee?"

❖

At four o'clock, Olivia picked up her office phone, dialled the hotel suite, and nervously fidgeted with the stress ball on her desk until Emily answered. "It's Olivia, I was wondering what you and Henry have planned for dinner?" Olivia got straight to the point, hoping she sounded more confident than she felt.

"Oh." Emily sounded momentarily flustered. "I hadn't really considered it."

"I was wondering if you'd both like to join me at an Italian restaurant just down the road."

Emily paused for a moment. "Yes, that sounds really nice, but I warn you that someone has been a bit of a handful this afternoon, so I can't guarantee good behaviour."

"I'm sure I'll find a way to keep you in order, Miss White."

"Ha ha. I meant Henry, as you well know. I'm perfectly well behaved *all* the time."

Olivia swallowed at the flirty comment before finding her stride again. "Well, as it happens, I might just have some good bribery material where he is concerned, but I wanted to run it by you first."

"Okay?"

"I've spoken with an acquaintance at London Zoo, and he's arranged for Henry to visit the giraffes, to feed them, and all that." Olivia rushed over the details as she nervously waited on Emily's reaction.

"Oh my God, really?" Emily squeaked. "That's amazing, he'd love it!"

"Obviously we'll accompany him and make sure he doesn't overexert himself," Olivia added quickly.

"Olivia, thank you so much. That's…that's amazing."

"So that's a yes?"

"Yes, it's absolutely a yes."

"Good." Olivia breathed a sigh of relief. "I thought we might go on Thursday afternoon, once he's had his final appointment."

"That sounds great," Emily said, her wide smile detectable through the phone. "Oh, but don't you have to work?"

"No, I'm taking the afternoon off. What's the point of being in charge if you can't take an afternoon off to feed giraffes now and then?"

"Absolutely! Well, he's going to be over the moon when you tell him."

"Me?"

"Of course. It's your gift—you should tell him," Emily explained. "Just don't do it when he's holding anything breakable. Or eating. Or drinking."

"I'll confirm with you regarding timing. What time is dinner usually for you two?"

"Around five thirty or six," Emily said. "So Henry can get to bed at a decent time."

"Understandable. I'll be back around five."

"Looking forward to it," Emily replied.

Olivia hung up and pressed the intercom button on her desk for Simon to come into her office.

"Yes, Olivia?"

"Did you get the other ticket for Friday?" Olivia asked as she typed on her keyboard.

"Yes, seat 10K, as you requested. I had to have the airline move someone, but it's all sorted now," Simon said.

"Good, and the car?" Olivia asked.

"Booked, however it will be an earlier departure than usual."

Olivia frowned as she looked up at him. "Why?" She was extremely fussy about her schedule.

"Because Emily will need to be there earlier than you for briefings and such. You have a two-hour check in, but she probably needs to be there an hour before that."

"Oh, I see. Very well. Thank you for looking into that."

"No problem," Simon said with a smile. "It's my job."

Olivia opened up her top desk drawer and took out an envelope. "Simon, I have these tickets to that show you were talking about. They were for tonight, but I have other plans."

Simon's eyes lit up as he saw the proffered envelope. "*Book of Mormon?*"

"That's the one." Olivia held the envelope out of reach as he went to take it. "Do my caffeine levels a favour—go to the coffee shop, and ask whoever it is in there you're so enamoured with to go along with you."

Chapter Twenty-two

As Olivia travelled up in the elevator towards the suite, she smiled to herself. Everything was going so well. She felt rejuvenated following her lunchtime discussion with Nicole and ready to go after what she wanted, damn the consequences. She spent far too much time living in fear of what might be rather than just living her life and trying to allow good things to happen. Emily had agreed to dinner, albeit one where Henry would be present, so Olivia was fairly certain she couldn't count it as a date, but it was certainly a step in the right direction.

She opened the door, but as she entered the room, the smile fell from her face. Henry was bawling in the middle of the floor. Tears streaked down his red cheeks with an inconceivable amount of mucus precariously balanced on the end of his nose, either to be sniffed up or about to fall onto his chest. Olivia closed the door quickly, so other guests at the hotel didn't assume a murder was taking place, and stared at the normally sweet little boy in horror.

Emily sat on the sofa, facing away from Henry, casually flicking through a magazine as if nothing was happening. Olivia looked from Henry to Emily and back, as she wondered what was going on. Why was Emily ignoring her extremely distressed son? Meanwhile, Henry looked at Olivia as if she was a lifeline that had been thrown to him. He shakily stood up, crying loudly with his arms held out.

"Henry White, don't you dare," Emily told him firmly without even looking up. He turned and looked at his mother with venom as he half-screamed, half-cried something that was completely unintelligible to Olivia.

"Sit. Down," Emily ordered. He stared at Emily for a couple of seconds in defiance, and she said calmly, but firmly, "Sit down, right now."

A standoff was forming before Olivia's very eyes as she looked hesitantly from one to another.

With a loud scream, Henry began bawling, flopped to the floor as if he had been shot, and lay there crying. Olivia put her bags down and walked further into the sitting room, giving the boy a wide berth.

"How was your day?" Emily smiled at Olivia as if nothing was happening.

Olivia blinked in surprise. "Well, it...yes." She looked at Henry and then back at Emily. "It was...What on earth happened here?"

Emily looked over at Henry, who was still flailing about on the floor. "Well, first he was moody with the doctor and tried to hit him when he took his blood pressure, then he threw his afternoon snack on the floor, then he pushed a chair over, and then he refused to have a bath. Now he's refusing to get dressed," she casually explained.

"He's crying," Olivia pointed out as if Emily wasn't aware.

"Yes, he has been for some time," Emily agreed. "And if he would apologise and come talk to me and tell me what's wrong, we could fix it. But he's refusing, so we're having a time out."

"Time out?" Olivia questioned.

"Yes," Emily replied as she indicated a dining room chair that had been placed in the sitting room facing the wall. "He's not doing a very good job of it because he refuses to stay on his time out chair."

Henry sat up and sniffed as he looked at them and fought down some tears while sucking in big gulps of breath.

"Henry, please go and sit on your time out chair," Emily said softly. With a swallow, he looked at Olivia before crawling towards the chair, taking far longer than necessary to get there, before slowly pulling himself up and dragging his body over it. "Sit nicely, Henry. Five minutes, please," Emily said calmly.

He fidgeted on the chair for a while before sitting up and folding his arms while pouting, craning his neck around so he could still see them both.

Olivia sat down beside Emily and whispered, "What is time out?"

"When he gets very upset, it's impossible to get through to him," Emily explained in a whisper, so Henry couldn't hear. "He acts out more and more, so I put him into a time out. He has to sit on the chair with no interaction with anyone, no TV, no toys, for five minutes. By the end of the five minutes, he's usually calmed down enough that he can tell me what's bothering him, if he knows himself."

Olivia nodded. "I understand. So now he just sits there?"

"Yep," Emily said. "Don't look at him. He'll act out for you or will try to make you feel sorry for him."

Olivia averted her eyes from Henry and looked at Emily instead. "I do feel sorry for him, all those tears. I thought he was dying."

"What would you have done?" Emily asked with interest.

"I'm not a mother," Olivia answered. "But I would have probably given in and given him whatever he wanted, which I know is wrong."

Emily chuckled. "It's hard to be the bad guy, but I keep telling myself it's what's best for him."

"You do a remarkable job with him," Olivia said, struggling to maintain eye contact with Emily, knowing she shouldn't look over at Henry. "Do you know why he's acting out?"

Emily thought for a moment. "He's been through a lot, and I think he's a bit fed up with the doctors and being cooped up in here. I think he just wants to go home, sleep in his own bed, and play with his toys, you know?"

"Understandable," Olivia agreed.

Emily frowned at Olivia's hand. "Can I ask why you do that?"

Olivia followed Emily's gaze and noticed that she had been absentmindedly pinching the skin between her thumb and index finger.

"Oh. Well…" Olivia felt heat in her cheeks.

"You don't have to tell me. I've just noticed that you do it sometimes when we talk." Emily pointed at the bruise. "And it looks painful. I think you're starting to bruise there."

Olivia let out a quiet breath. "Maybe I can explain tonight, after dinner."

Emily nodded and gently separated Olivia's hands.

"How was Henry's appointment? Aside from hitting the doctor," Olivia asked, unsuccessfully holding back a smile.

"It's not funny." Emily chuckled. "He's doing well. They're pleased with his progress. Looks likely that we'll be flying home on Friday."

Olivia nodded. "That is good news."

"Mommy, I'm thirsty," Henry whined.

Emily looked at her watch. "Three more minutes."

Olivia look at her in horror at the unexpected cruelty.

Emily whispered, "He's not really thirsty—he's trying to get around me."

Olivia shook her head. "Devious. Should we cancel our dinner plans?"

"No, he'll come around soon. He just needs to calm down. Oh, and let's keep the surprise from him until his mood has stabilised."

Olivia nodded. "Well, I'm going to have a quick shower and get changed."

"Okay, we should be ready when you come back out. Don't worry, he won't be like this at the restaurant."

Olivia walked past Henry on her way to her bedroom and only just managed to avoid eye contact with the pleading boy.

❖

Three quarters of an hour later, Olivia entered the lounge, having spent far too long choosing an outfit for what was supposed to be a simple dinner. She had eventually decided on a simple red top with a black pencil skirt. She had also opted to take her high heels down a notch for the sake of comfort, though still high enough to make her equal to Emily's height.

In the sitting room, Henry knelt by the coffee table dressed in smart-looking dark blue jeans, a white button-down shirt, and a blue and grey argyle sweater. He was humming a tune to himself while colouring on some pieces of blank paper, and Olivia was surprised at the dramatic turnaround.

"Hello, Henry, you're looking very smart," Olivia told him.

He looked up at her and smiled a toothy grin. "I'm a big boy."

"Yes, you are." She smiled, wondering how the child had managed to worm his way into her heart so quickly.

"And big boys are allowed to go to nice restaurants," Emily's voice floated from the bedroom as she stepped out. Olivia turned around, and her voice caught in her throat at the sight of Emily in a tight purple pencil skirt with a silky white blouse. She was putting on one of her earrings, and her just-curled hair fell beautifully around her face.

"I hope you don't mind me repurposing my work uniform," Emily said with a soft smile. "I didn't bring anything special, but it's nice to dress up. Without the jacket, the skirt doesn't look too worky, does it?"

"You look lovely." Olivia managed to not sound too distracted as Emily walked past her.

"Henry, shoes, please," Emily said as she slipped on her own high heels, causing Olivia to wish that she had kept with her higher heels after all.

Henry dashed past on his way to the bedroom, and Olivia looked at Emily appreciatively while her back was turned.

A few moments later, they exited the hotel and began the short walk up the road to the Italian restaurant, Henry holding both of their hands and chatting animatedly.

"I'm going to have macaroni and cheese," Henry exclaimed loudly.

"Don't you want to try something else?" Olivia asked him as they weaved around people.

"Why?" Henry asked.

"To see if you like other things," Olivia answered.

"What if I don't?"

"What if you do?"

"But what if I don't?" Henry argued.

Emily laughed and looked over at Olivia. "You'll not win this argument, I'm afraid."

"We'll see." Olivia grinned. "Henry, if I order you a small tasting plate, will you try new things?"

"No." Henry shook his head and grinned.

Olivia paused walking and knelt down to look at Henry, face to face. "Please, for me?"

Henry looked at her curiously for a few seconds before asking, "But what if I don't like it?"

"Okay," Olivia negotiated, "what if I order you a small tasting plate as well as your highly boring usual of macaroni and cheese? Then you can eat that if you don't like what's on your tasting plate, which I think you will like."

Henry made a thoughtful face and then nodded. She stood up again, pleased with her victory, and they continued walking. She was very aware of the glances Emily was throwing her way.

The eatery was cosy and welcoming and Emily breathed a sigh of relief. "Thank goodness it's not a high-end establishment."

"I didn't think Henry would appreciate anything more highbrow." But before Emily could answer, an older Italian man who appeared to be the manager came over and kissed Olivia on both cheeks, welcoming her in Italian. Olivia replied comfortably, also in Italian, and they were escorted to their table. It was tucked away in the corner away from the other diners and set for three with a seat booster on one of the chairs.

"So, you've been here before, I take it?" Emily took in the decor.

"Oh yes." Olivia nodded as a menu was handed to her by their waiter. "I take all my flight attendants here."

Emily raised her eyebrows and gave her a pointed stare, though a smile played across her lips. The waiter handed Emily a menu and walked away.

"Mommy, look." Henry pointed at the cutlery set in front of him.

Emily burst out laughing. "Giraffe cutlery? Really?"

"While I would love to take credit for that, it was Simon who booked the table and presumably arranged the cutlery." Olivia smiled, happy Simon's suggestion had worked so well.

"He really wants that raise."

"If it makes you happy, then maybe he deserves it." Olivia studied her menu intently, indicating she was not going to be drawn into further conversation about it.

The waiter came over and addressed Emily. "Good evening, miss. We have pencils and paper if you would like me to fetch some for your son."

Henry's head snapped up and Emily laughed. "Yes, please."

The waiter returned with some activity sheets and colouring pencils and placed them in front of Henry with a wink.

"Thank you," said Henry as he picked up a pencil and started to colour.

"So, how did the rest of the day go?" Emily glanced over her menu at Olivia.

During the meal Olivia spoke about her day in the office and how the insolvency was going. She also told Emily about her suspicion of a love interest in the coffee shop. They laughed over Simon's sudden desire for highly complicated caffeine-based drinks that took an age to make, just so he could spend a little more time in the coffee shop.

Occasionally, Henry dabbled in conversation in between his drawing, talking about giraffes as well as outer space, in which he had recently became interested. But he mainly focused on his excitement about going home on Friday.

"Just remember," Emily said with a warning tone, "you'll probably be sitting on your own on the way back."

"I know," Henry said with a sigh, his understanding of the potential seating arrangement clearly disappointing him.

"Actually"—Olivia swirled the red wine in her glass and decided this was the best time to broach the subject—"he'll be sitting with me."

Emily looked up. "What do you mean?"

"I bought him a ticket, 10K, right where he was last time."

Henry cheered happily, and Emily stared hard at Olivia. "You did what?"

Olivia faltered for a moment, torn between celebrating the good news with Henry and wondering why Emily suddenly looked furious, apparent even to Olivia's untrained eye.

A heavy silence fell over the table as a waiter came and cleared their plates away. As soon as he was gone Olivia spoke again.

"I...I bought him a ticket. I thought you'd be pleased. It means he'll be sitting up front where you and I can keep an eye on him."

Emily took a deep breath and clenched her jaw for a moment before picking her napkin up from her lap and placing it on the table.

"I'm going to the bathroom, please watch Henry." She abruptly left.

Olivia watched her storm away before turning to face Henry in confusion.

"You're in trouble," he sing-songed with a little laugh to himself.

"Why?" Olivia asked him.

Henry shrugged. "I dunno, I'm five."

"I bet you're quick to play that card when it suits you." Olivia reached into her handbag and pulled out her phone. She scrolled through her contacts before pressing her thumb to the screen and holding the phone to her ear.

"Nicole, I need advice," she whispered tersely as soon as the call was answered, looking around to check she wasn't being overheard.

"Aren't you on a date?"

"Yes, but I've done something wrong, and she's stormed off to the loo." Olivia's eyes flicked up to see if Emily was returning.

"What happened?" Nicole sighed.

"I told her I bought Henry a ticket home, and she seemed angry."

"Didn't he have a ticket home?" Nicole asked.

"Yes, but they'll place him wherever they can—there's no guarantee he'll be in first class with me," Olivia explained.

"So you bought a first-class ticket," Nicole asked, "for the son of the woman in debt, who was so proud she nearly stayed in a grimy hostel rather than accept help?"

"Shi—" Olivia looked at Henry. "Shield. Shield software is the... name of the company."

"Smooth," Nicole drawled. "I take it the munchkin is there?"

"Yes."

"And you know what you did wrong now?" Nicole pushed.

"Yes, what do I do?" Olivia asked in a panic.

"You need to figure that one out between you," Nicole said. "Sorry, darling."

Olivia saw Emily returning with a face like thunder. "Nicole, Nicole! Nicole!" Olivia looked at the phone, shocked to find that Nicole had hung up on her. Then Emily was opposite her, taking her seat as well as a calming breath, before picking up one of Henry's drawings.

"This is very good, Henry." Emily smiled at her son, who smiled back, pleased with the praise.

"Emily, I..." Olivia started.

"Later," Emily said firmly. "We'll finish our meal and go back to the hotel, and then we'll talk about it."

"But we should—" Olivia tried again.

"Olivia," Emily said. "Think of this as my time out. I need time to calm down. Please."

Olivia felt her chest tighten in fear that her lack of foresight had caused irreparable damage. Emily's hand snaked across the tabletop, took her fingers, and squeezed softly. "It's okay—I know why you did it. I just need some time before we talk about it. But it's okay."

"Ice cream?" Henry said as he watched a waiter walk by with an enormous ice cream sundae.

Olivia looked for permission, and Emily nodded before turning to her son and saying, "Yes, ice cream, but only if you promise to go to bed on time tonight."

Henry silently coloured.

"Henry." Emily sighed. "Do you promise?"

Henry nodded. "Okay, but only if Olivia reads to me."

This time, Emily looked at Olivia for confirmation. Olivia gave a nervous nod in agreement.

"Okay, but remember, you've made a promise," Emily told him as she gently tickled his side.

Olivia watched the pair with a smile, hoping that her miscalculation could be easily ironed out. She was beginning to realise that she wanted a lot of dinners like this in her life.

CHAPTER TWENTY-THREE

Henry ate his ice cream while Emily and Olivia attempted to make polite conversation. They both tried to keep up the facade that Emily was not still angry.

Eventually, the meal was over, and they walked back to the hotel. Henry, again, walked between them, holding both their hands.

"But you liked the lasagne and the dough balls." Olivia laughed at Henry who had turned his nose up at the idea of his tasting plate.

"Yuck, yuck, yuck," Henry chanted with a smile on his face, obviously having enjoyed more of the new foods than he was willing to let on.

His deliberately drawn-out ice cream eating meant it was time for bed by the time they returned to the suite. Once they arrived, Emily told him to go and get ready for bed. When he asked if Olivia would still read him a bedtime story, Emily looked at Olivia, who nodded with a smile. Henry beamed and ran off to get into his pyjamas, and Olivia looked at Emily.

"Can we talk now?"

"Once Henry is down," Emily said softly as she walked over to a side table and picked up a handful of children's books.

"What do I do?" Olivia took the books that Emily handed her.

"Let him choose a book, but just one. He'll try for more, but only allow him to choose one because it's late," Emily explained.

"And then?"

"Read it to him," Emily said simply.

"Okay." Olivia nodded. "And then?"

Emily smiled. "Say goodnight, turn the light off, and leave the room."

"Right," Olivia said, despite her nervousness.

"It's okay, Olivia—it's just a bedtime story," Emily said kindly.

"I'm not very good with this kind of thing."

"You'll do fine, and don't worry because he'll tell you if you're doing something wrong."

Henry returned to the sitting room wearing his pyjamas and looked excitedly at Olivia.

"Did you brush your teeth?" Emily asked. He opened his mouth for her to see, and she leaned in and gave a small sniff. "I suspect you've just put toothpaste on your tongue again." She smiled. "But I'll get those teeth in the morning!"

Henry squealed with delight as his mother chased him into the bedroom. She picked him up, put him into bed, and quickly lifted his pyjama top to inspect the wound and bandage on his chest. Olivia waited as Emily whispered goodnight to her son and gave him a kiss on the forehead.

"You can't shout out the story from there. You'll get hoarse." Emily looked to Olivia in the doorway.

Olivia swallowed and entered the room. Henry shuffled a little to the side to give Olivia room on the bed. As soon as she sat down, Henry positioned himself against her side to look at the selection of books in her hand.

"All of them," he announced.

"Henry," Emily warned, "just the one." Henry was too tired to argue, so he thoughtfully looked at the selection and picked a book about a cat who had gone to the moon.

"I'll be in the sitting room," Emily said and blew a kiss at Henry as she left.

Olivia placed the other books on the bedside table and opened the selected book to begin reading.

"Olivia?" Henry whispered before she started.

"Yes, Henry?" Olivia asked quietly, the bedtime routine seemingly making speech at a normal volume impossible.

"I'm sorry you couldn't save the business." Henry snuggled closely into her.

"So am I," Olivia said as she placed a light kiss in his hair as she had seen Emily do on so many occasions.

"Is that why Mommy is mad?" Henry asked.

"Oh no, Henry," Olivia assured. "I…I made a mistake."

"Mommy told me that everyone makes mistakes," Henry said through a yawn.

"Yes, they do," Olivia said as she looked at the front page of the book. "Like buying a cat a spacesuit for his birthday."

He giggled, and Olivia read the book in hushed tones, occasionally pausing when Henry slapped his hand on the page to look at a picture in more depth before she moved on. The book was, thankfully, short, and before long, Olivia placed it on the bedside table. She looked at the ridiculous artwork on the front cover and absently wondered at the decisions of the children's literature industry.

Henry burrowed down into the bed, and Olivia stood to go. "Olivia," Henry called, and she turned around and looked at his frowning face. "Goodnight kiss," he told her in a tone that meant business.

Olivia leaned forward with every intention of kissing his forehead, but as she got nearer, he reached up and wrapped his arms around her neck, pulled her down, and kissed her on the lips in a quick, but sloppy, kiss.

"Night night," he whispered, and Olivia turned off the bedroom light and walked in a semi-daze into the sitting room. Emily had made coffee for them both and was sitting on the sofa with a thoughtful expression.

"All okay?" she asked.

"Yes." Olivia sat down on the sofa beside Emily, leaving a lot of space between them.

"I made you coffee," Emily said, indicating the mug in front of Olivia.

"Thank you."

"Olivia." Emily sighed. "We need to talk about the ticket and other things."

Olivia nodded. "I apologise for the ticket. I—"

"I know why you did it," Emily interrupted. "And while I don't necessarily agree with you spending thousands of dollars for a child to sit in first class, I ultimately do understand why, and I appreciate the sentiment."

"Oh." Olivia frowned as her brain tried to capture the increasingly confusing conversation for later playback and analysis.

"The thing is," Emily said, "the airline has a very strict policy on socialising with premium and first-class passengers. And I don't know how I'm supposed to explain how I managed to buy a first-class ticket for Henry when most of my co-workers know I only work the schedule I do because I'm in debt. And when they see you and him together, they're going to put two and two together and assume I'm sleeping with you."

Realisation started to hit Olivia. "Oh!" She mentally kicked herself for not even considering the fact.

"Yeah, and there is an element of pride to it as well," Emily admitted. "But the truth of it is, I could lose my job. My boss is going to be pissed at me as it is now that the interview with Henry didn't go her way. And I get the impression that she's not exactly someone I want to piss off. She's going to take one look at Henry eating lunch at your table and—"

"But," Olivia interrupted, "I'll vouch for you. I'll tell the airline that they can't fire you. I know how much I'm worth to them."

Emily chuckled. "And then I have to work with people who resent me because I broke the rules but managed to stay because you've blackmailed them."

"But I'll protect you," Olivia said. "I made the mistake, so I will fix it."

"And what about when you get bored of me?" Emily asked with a soft smile.

"What do you mean?" Olivia asked hesitantly.

"Olivia, I know your type of woman. I googled you, and there are loads of pictures of you and carbon-copy blondes. A premiere here, a party there, and the dates on those photos don't show any of them being lasting relationships."

Olivia leaned forward and pinched the bridge of her nose against the stress headache that was forming. She'd made a tactical error with the ticket, and even she could see that now. And the knowledge that Emily knew about her love life was mortifying, to say the least. She wanted to explain but didn't know if she had the ability to do so.

"I'd like to explain." She decided to try.

"You don't have to."

"I'd like to. I'd like to try, anyway."

"Okay." Emily nodded.

"I've never had this conversation with anyone before," Olivia admitted. "I've never known what to say." Olivia looked down at her hands in her lap and noticed that she was pinching the skin between her thumb and index finger again and grimaced. "This, this is a good example."

Emily looked at Olivia's bruised skin.

"I…I say the wrong things," Olivia said. "All the time. My thoughts and my actions appear to have no filter. Sometimes, during a conversation that is particularly important to me, I'll worry about saying the wrong thing. Sometimes my brain seems to feed the words straight to my mouth with very little happening in between. The pinching helps. It's a reminder to not blurt out what I want to say. To take a second and to think before I speak."

"When I met you, your hand wasn't bruised like that," Emily pointed out.

"No," Olivia admitted, leaving the word hanging in the air for a few moments while she sorted her thoughts. "My type of woman is… has been…a direct result of my problem. When I was young, I fell in love with a woman. She was the first person in my life to understand me. She laughed off the stupid and thoughtless things I said and did. She tried to explain to me why they were the wrong things to say, but ultimately, I just couldn't understand, and it didn't work out."

Olivia got to her feet and started to walk unhurriedly around the sitting room. "I soon found out that if I wanted any form of relationship, I had to be with someone who didn't care that I said the wrong things. Someone who only wanted me for my money and would suffer the thoughtless behaviour. Women like the ones you saw in the photographs." She paused and leaned on the back of the sofa facing Emily. "I struggle to be understood. I wish I could help it, but I can't. And I do try, Lord knows I try, but time after time, even when I'm convinced I'm doing the right things, I seem to get blindsided."

"Do you know *why* you do the wrong thing?" Emily asked.

"You mean a diagnosis? To be honest I never thought there was much point. I know I'm different, I know I cannot read social situations like other people, so what good would a name do? Would it make it better? No. Would I actively walk around telling people the name of my disorder? No. But maybe I'm wrong again—maybe a diagnosis is what I need. You see, I really don't know. But I do feel that a name will not help me or give me greater understanding. I'm just not capable of that kind of thought process."

Emily nodded her understanding, "I can see your point, especially with these areas where a name isn't a black-and-white diagnosis. Because you have X doesn't mean you'll do Y."

"Precisely." Olivia nodded, pleased that Emily understood her feelings on the subject.

"So what changed? Why did you leave your business card for me? Or didn't it change? Am I another of those women? The airhead flight attendant?"

Olivia balked. "No! Emily, I—I don't see you like that at all. I admit, when I first saw you, I thought you were very attractive, but then as I listened to you and watched your manner, I could see your other qualities. You were intelligent and caring, and I don't know, I just wanted to take the risk. To go out for dinner with someone real, someone I could actually talk to. And then I met Henry, and…he's such a wonderful boy. I saw you together, and I saw more of you that I liked, more of you that I wanted to get to know. Please, don't think that I put you in the same category as my previous dates."

Emily acknowledged her understanding, and Olivia continued.

"I didn't know about the airline policy. If I had, I would have kept my distance," she said. "I'll get Simon to change the name on the ticket, and then the passenger will be a last-minute no-show and Henry will get the seat as it will be vacant. Is that okay?"

"I'm still finding it a little hard to accept. That's a lot of money, Olivia. It's not dinner or tickets to the zoo." Emily stood up and folded her arms as she looked out of the window.

"It's not a lot of money to me," Olivia said quietly. "I'm not the person who created these weird and wonderful rules regarding pride over personal wealth. Not to mention the fact that I don't understand them. I see a problem, and I know I can fix it, so I do."

"I know," Emily said. "I get that, and I totally know why you're doing it, and I appreciate it. But it's still hard, it's…"

Olivia waited for Emily to continue but nothing came. "It's what?"

"I don't want to offend you."

Olivia snorted. "Oh, don't worry about that. Say what's on your mind."

Emily turned to face her. "It's not...normal." She winced as she said the word. "People don't usually spend large amounts of money on people they don't know unless they want something."

Olivia thought about that for a moment before nodding. "Yes, I can understand that. But that's not the case here."

"You know, I kind of believe that."

"Good. You should." After a moment of silence, Olivia quietly asked, "Am I forgiven?"

"Yes," Emily said. "I know you didn't mean any harm. You were just trying to do the right thing. Which could have ended very badly, so you need to talk to me and tell me what you're doing."

"But you wouldn't have accepted it," Olivia commented with a knowing grin.

Emily laughed. "See? You claim to not understand, but you knew I wouldn't have accepted it if you'd approached me first."

"I'm socially inept, not stupid."

"Why do you live in a hotel?" Emily suddenly asked.

Olivia looked around the suite. "I like it."

"You don't feel like you want a home? Someplace you can decorate to your own taste? Change things around?" Emily asked.

Olivia considered this for a moment before honestly replying, "I don't know."

"I suppose you have that in your place in New York?"

Olivia paused and looked at the floor. Emily crossed the room and pulled Olivia's hands gently apart.

"Talk to me—I'm here to listen," Emily said softly as she held Olivia's hands in hers.

Olivia continued to look down at the floor in between them before quietly speaking. "I don't have a place in New York."

Emily spluttered, "Oh my God, you live in a hotel in New York too?"

Olivia's hands clenched in hers.

"I'm sorry, I'm sorry." She softened her tone. "That was judgemental. I'm just really shocked. You spend all your life in hotels?"

Olivia looked up at Emily, feeling shy, and nodded. "It wasn't supposed to be that way—it just happened."

"How long has it been?"

"Six years," Olivia admitted, avoiding eye contact.

"Did something happen?"

"My wife died," Olivia said quietly, her eyes fixed on the floor.

"I am so sorry, Olivia," Emily said quietly.

Olivia nodded her silent gratitude and slightly tightened her hold on Emily's hands, threading their fingers together.

"I don't know what to say," Emily admitted softly.

"There's nothing to say. It was a long time ago."

After a period of silence Olivia finally looked up to Emily's face. As she did so Emily closed her eyes and leaned forward to gently connect their lips in a tender kiss. Olivia felt her mouth quiver, and the smallest tremor of desire shot between them—

"Mommy?"

Emily broke away as if burned. She stepped backwards and stared at Olivia, apparently shocked by her own actions. She turned towards Henry, who stood in the doorway, rubbing his eyes and holding Tiny by a foot.

"Are you okay, sweetheart?" Emily asked.

"I had a bad dream," he whispered. Emily lifted him into her arms, holding him close.

Olivia felt her heartbeat racing. Her lips still tingled at the sensation from the soft kiss.

"Will you read to me?" Henry asked his mother.

Emily turned to look at Olivia, an apologetic look on her face.

"Go," Olivia whispered softly with a small smile.

"I'll be back soon," Emily promised, and with Henry burrowed into her arms, she headed back to the bedroom.

CHAPTER TWENTY-FOUR

A few pages into his favourite story and Henry had fallen back to sleep. Emily sat in the softly lit room with her heart still racing. True, she found Olivia intriguing, kind, and incredibly attractive, but even she hadn't fully understood how deep her feelings ran until she initiated that kiss.

The whole evening had been sparking with emotions—from the debacle with the airline ticket, to the bombshell that Olivia was a widow. Emily found herself wondering about Olivia's wife. She already knew so little about Olivia, and now here was a new layer. Emily felt even more in the dark.

Henry grunted and turned over in his sleep, and she watched over him for a moment. The break-up of her last relationship had been hard on him, and she had been telling herself to keep her distance from Olivia to protect him. But the truth was that it seemed too late for that. Henry was as totally enamoured with Olivia as she was.

She didn't know what to do, but hiding in the bedroom wasn't the answer. She took a deep breath and returned to the living room, where Olivia waited pensively on the sofa.

"Is he okay?" Olivia asked, the concern evident in her voice.

"Yes, he went back to sleep quickly."

"Was it our discussion? Were we disturbing him?" Olivia asked.

"No." Emily shook her head. "He's a kid—they have bad dreams sometimes."

Olivia nodded, seemingly at a loss for further words. "So…"

"So," Emily repeated. Olivia looked stiff and uncomfortable.

Emily joined her on the sofa, curling one leg under herself. After a moment of silence, she let out a chuckle, and Olivia looked at her curiously.

"I'm sorry," Emily said. "I just realised my vocabulary is completely ill-equipped to have the conversation I want to have with you."

"How so?"

"I need to apologise. Kissing you like that, and just after you told me you'd lost your wife." Emily closed her eyes in shame.

"I'll admit I was surprised, but I have no regrets. In fact, I had been hoping…"

"I think we need to take this slowly." Emily opened her eyes and focused on Olivia. "For all of us. I don't want anyone to get hurt here. I mean, we hardly know each other."

"Then let's change that."

"Tell me more about you," Emily requested with a tilt of her head. "Tell me more about…about…"

Olivia frowned. "About?"

Emily sighed in frustration at not having the correct words on hand. "Every word or description I can think of sounds derogatory, and I don't want to use them, and I don't want to use the phrase that you say the wrong thing, because I don't think that's accurate."

"Socially awkward?" Olivia suggested.

Emily made a face. "It feels mean to call you awkward, and that's not accurate either."

"Socially inept?" Olivia tried again.

"No." Emily shook her head. "I don't like it—it's rude."

"It's accurate." Olivia chuckled. "My mother used to call me artless."

Emily frowned. "Well, I don't like it, but it's slightly less cutting than the others."

"I don't mind." Olivia shrugged.

"Okay." Emily nodded in reluctant agreement. "So have you always been artless? Or did it happen over time?"

"Oh, I've always been like this," Olivia answered easily. "As a child it was excused that I didn't know any better, but as I got older and

I upset and alienated the other children, it became a little more difficult for my parents to explain away. Back then there wasn't a lot of interest in diagnosing that kind of behaviour."

"So your mother chose to call you artless instead?" Emily gave a wry smile.

Olivia grinned. "No, she chose to punish me for misbehaving for the longest time. Eventually she came to understand that I wasn't doing it on purpose. I didn't know any better. Then I was promoted from inconsiderate to artless."

"Must have been hard," Emily commented lightly, not wanting to force Olivia to say any more than she was comfortable with.

"It was what it was." Olivia shrugged but Emily could tell there was more to the story.

"But your wife, she understood?" Emily asked, watching Olivia carefully as she skirted around the potentially sensitive subject.

Olivia face lit up at the memory.

"No." She chuckled. "Not at first, anyway. I think I drove her insane at the beginning."

Emily smiled. "Not a good start?"

"The worst. I insulted her mother," Olivia explained with a grin. She turned to mirror Emily's position and shuffled closer until they were facing each other.

"Ouch. Insulting the mother, not good."

"Indeed." Olivia chuckled. "She was rightly annoyed, and she couldn't understand why I didn't see anything wrong with what I'd said. She called me thoughtless and stupid, and I thought that would be it, but fate seemed to conspire to keep throwing us into each other's paths."

"What changed?" Emily asked with interest. She placed her hand over Olivia's, which rested on the back of sofa, and tenderly rubbed circles on the soft skin with her thumb.

"A flight, ironically. As I say, fate kept bringing us together. I had to fly to Paris from London for a Women in Business event that was organised by a company I sometimes worked with. She was invited as well and was seated right next to me."

Emily laughed. "Oh, I bet you both loved that."

"I asked if I could move," Olivia admitted. "But we agreed we were mature enough to sit together for the short flight. We realised we had more in common than we thought. We got to know each other, and I think she started to understand that…" Olivia paused.

Emily squeezed her fingers to encourage her to continue.

"That I'm not insensitive or mean, just artless. After that, things started to fall into place. We still argued, a lot, but she understood me and my limitations when it came to social requirements and rules. She helped me to understand things. If you can believe it, I used to be much worse than I am today."

Emily grinned but remained silent to allow Olivia to carry on her story.

"We fell in love, and before long, we were married. It all happened so fast, but it seemed so right." Olivia smiled at the memory before adding, "It *was* so right."

"How fast?"

"From that flight to our wedding day was exactly six months," Olivia said. "Mother thought I was out of my mind. If she ever thought I was *in* my mind to start with. She did everything she could think of to stop the wedding."

"Why?"

"She didn't think Rebecca was good enough for me," Olivia sighed, clearly remembering the arguments with her mother. "Rebecca was a fitness instructor—she'd established her own business and managed to get a few executive clients. Before long she was being referred to all of the top businesswomen in London, and she had an enormous waiting list. You really had to hope that someone died to be in with a chance of having her as your instructor."

"But that wasn't good enough for your mother?"

"Nothing was ever good enough for my mother," Olivia said grimly before taking a deep breath. "Anyway, she didn't approve, but we did it anyway. Three months later, Rebecca died. Aggressive brain tumour."

Emily blinked in shock at the detached way Olivia relayed the information. "That must have been hard."

"Yes." Olivia nodded noncommittally. "I suppose it was. I don't allow myself to dwell on it. We'd hardly had a chance to start our lives together, and then she was gone." Olivia's gaze travelled over the back of the sofa, and she stared out of the window into the inky darkness outside.

Emily considered her next words carefully. "Henry's dad was killed in a car accident. I was seven months pregnant," she said. "I had just turned twenty-three, and I was young and naive. After I got out of the foster system, I didn't really know what to do, so I moved around a lot, fell in with the wrong crowds. And then suddenly there was Joe, and he promised to care for me, look after me. So I dated him for a while, and we moved in together. He did everything, and I was happy to let him look after me, especially once I got pregnant. It was so nice to have someone. But then he was gone, and I realised I'd become so reliant on him I didn't even know how to pay the rent. I didn't even know who our landlord was, nothing."

"So then you went the other way and became incredibly self-reliant?" Olivia asked.

Emily nodded. "Probably went a little too far, and I ended up pushing people away. I thought I could do everything. More importantly, I started to think that I *should* do everything myself. Especially after Henry was born. I wanted to give him everything and be the best I could possibly be for him."

"You're a wonderful mother," Olivia said with a smile.

Emily laughed bitterly. "Thank you, I'm glad you think so. Sadly, Joe's parents didn't think so. They never wanted anything to do with him. As soon as he was old enough to fend for himself, they tossed him out. Joe's dad was a self-made man, he'd worked hard and made a lot of money, but he was harsh, you know?"

Olivia nodded, taking Emily's other hand and interlacing their fingers.

"So when Joe wanted to join a band and try to become a professional musician, well, that didn't go down too well. They kept trying to force him into the family business, and he kept fighting back. The relationship completely broke down. Things were really bitter between them for years."

"That sounds awful." Olivia looked shocked.

"When I was pregnant, somehow word got back to Joe's parents, and then they suddenly wanted to see him again. They hadn't spoken to him for nearly ten years, and then they turned up at the door one day." Emily stared at their connected fingers, lost in her thoughts for a moment. "It didn't work. Too much time had passed, I guess. When

Joe died," she continued. "I called his father to let him know. He was so…cold, so pragmatic about it. He asked what had happened, and I explained that it was an accident with a drunk driver. He thanked me for letting him know and then hung up the phone."

"Was he in shock?"

"I always hoped so. I can't imagine anyone being that cold. But I didn't hear from them again, not until after Henry was born. Then the letter came, asking for custody of Henry."

"What?" Olivia balked.

"They said I couldn't care for him, that I had no friends, no family, and no chance of giving Henry a good life. They wanted to take him and get full custody. I always thought Joe's mother was the one behind that. Maybe she was trying to make up for how things went with Joe. I don't know. Either way, I won, obviously, and then I never heard from them again."

"Good riddance," Olivia muttered. "You—" Olivia's phone rang, cutting off what she was about to say. She looked apologetically at Emily before reaching into her bag and looking at the screen. "It's the New York office. I have to take this."

Emily nodded, and Olivia took the call in the kitchen. Emily absent-mindedly listened to Olivia giving instructions and relaying information for a while before deciding it was best to give her some privacy, so she reached for the television remote control. She turned the television on and lowered the volume so it wouldn't wake Henry or distract Olivia and sat gazing at the screen, even though her mind was elsewhere, thinking about the kiss earlier.

When she next opened her eyes, Olivia was leaning over her with a pensive look, and Emily realised that she had somehow fallen asleep.

"I thought it best to wake you," Olivia said apologetically, and it was then that she noticed that Olivia was in dark red silk pyjamas, her face devoid of make-up.

"How long was I asleep?" Emily asked as she pushed herself up into a sitting position.

"An hour," Olivia said with a slight blush. "I didn't know what to do. I didn't know if you'd want to keep sleeping, but you would have had a sore neck when you woke up if I left you here."

"You did the right thing," Emily said. "I'm just sorry I fell asleep."

Emily stood up and fussed with her hair for a moment before chuckling. "It must be that sofa," she said with a nod of her head at the offending piece of furniture.

"Absolutely," Olivia agreed with a nervous smile and averted her eyes.

Emily looked down to notice a couple of the buttons on her white blouse had come undone during her sleep and quickly buttoned them up again. "Well, I should…go to bed, properly this time," she said.

"Yes, I should too. I have a client meeting away from the office tomorrow, so I won't be back until later in the evening," Olivia said with a disappointed look.

"I was thinking," Emily said as they walked towards the bedrooms. "Maybe you could meet us after Henry's hospital appointment on Thursday. We can have that lunch in the park and then go on to the zoo."

"I'd like that. Are you going to tell him about the zoo tomorrow?"

"No, you're going to tell him on Thursday during lunch," Emily told her.

"Oh, okay." Olivia nodded with some nervousness. They paused by the doors to their respective bedrooms.

"He'll want to give you a big hug." Emily chuckled.

"Well, that's okay, I guess. Who doesn't like a hug?" Olivia said with a light, nervous laugh.

Emily took a step forward and wrapped her arms around Olivia's shoulders, pulling her into a gentle hug. Olivia returned the embrace.

Emily loosened her grip and leaned back. She gazed into Olivia's eyes for a moment before pinning her to the closed bedroom door. Olivia let out a surprised gasp, which was smothered by Emily's lips.

She threaded her hands through Olivia's thick, dark hair and tilted her head back to trail a kiss along Olivia's jaw and slowly down her exposed neck. Olivia's moan was husky with desire and broke the spell enough to remind Emily what she was doing. She pulled her mouth away from the thrumming pulse point at Olivia's throat.

"I'm sorry," she whispered and leaned her forehead against Olivia's. They both struggled to regain their breath.

"I'm not."

"We shouldn't…"

"I know," Olivia said hoarsely.

They released their hold on each other, and Emily took a step back, smiling shyly.

"Goodnight, Olivia," Emily said softly.

"Goodnight," Olivia whispered back, fumbling for the door handle of her bedroom. When she found it, she almost fell through the door. Emily waited until she closed the door before biting her lip and turning towards her own door.

❖

Emily couldn't concentrate all day Wednesday. She half-heartedly entertained Henry with drawing, games, and television, but her mind was elsewhere. Olivia had left the hotel suite early that morning, and whenever Emily looked out of the window at the empty executive office, she caught herself sighing.

She was going stir-crazy in the hotel and desperately needed someone to talk to. As the end of the day approached, she picked up the hotel phone and dialled the number from a business card and looked across the street.

"Olivia Lewis's office, Simon Fletcher speaking."

"Nice professional greeting you've got there."

"Thank you." Simon chuckled. "Just a little something I've been working on. How are you doing?"

"So bored," Emily admitted.

"Oh, dear, have you been looking for giraffes on buses?" Simon asked seriously.

"Yep," Emily deadpanned. "Like, all day, and there's been none."

"Damn them and their giraffe vacations."

"I was wondering, and feel free to say no, I know you probably have plans," Emily said, "but I was wondering if you wanted to have dinner with me and Henry tonight."

"Is he going to be wearing the most awesome giraffe hoodie ever?" Simon asked.

"Absolutely," Emily said. "I'm surprised you had to ask."

Simon laughed. "In which case, yes, dinner sounds good. What do kids eat? Sushi? Curry?"

"I feel sorry for the barista girl," Emily joked.

"Not sure who you're talking about? Oh, unless you're referring to *my new girlfriend*."

"You asked her out? Oh my God, well done!"

"I know, now we need to get you set up, and we can totally double-date," Simon said in a fake American accent.

"Oh, don't even go there." Emily cleared some of Henry's toys from the sofa.

"Trouble in paradise?"

"No. Well…" Emily flopped on the sofa. "I don't know."

"Oh, this sounds juicy! Do you want me to bring some food over?" Simon asked.

"Hell no," Emily replied. "No, the mission is to get out of here for a couple of hours."

"Does the kid like chicken?" Simon asked.

"It's one of his four primary food groups—chicken, pasta, cheese, and bread."

"Cool, I know just the place. I'll meet you outside the hotel in half an hour, okay?"

❖

The casual dining restaurant was packed, but somehow Simon had negotiated a large round booth in the corner. The food was tapas style, and Simon ordered a number of small plates of various foods for them to share. When Henry got bored with his colouring book, Simon gave him his mobile phone to play some games.

Before long, a couple of flamboyant cocktails were placed on the table at Simon's request, and Emily burst out laughing at the colourful drinks with their little parasols.

"I just don't know why anyone would think you might be gay," Emily joked as Simon removed a slice of orange from the rim of his glass and bit into it.

"I know, right?" Simon laughed with his mouth full of orange.

"So…" Emily stirred her drink with the pink straw. "What's her name?"

"Sophie," Simon said. "She's amazing."

"Ah, young love." Emily grinned.

"She said I'm funny," Simon said and puffed his chest out proudly.

"You are," Emily agreed with a nod.

"We're seeing each other again on Saturday."

"Cool, what's the plan?" Emily asked as she took a sip of her cocktail and was grateful that the alcohol content seemed relatively low.

"We're having a picnic at Greenwich Park, and then we're going to see the Observatory," Simon said. "I'm checking to see if she's as much of a geek as me."

Emily chuckled, and Simon fished out another slice of orange from his glass with his straw.

"So, what's happening with you and"—Simon paused and looked at Henry, who was focused on his games, and then he glanced over at Emily—"O?"

Emily licked her lips nervously and stirred her drink with the straw.

"Come on," Simon said. "I know something's happened. She was all smiley this morning, and then you wanted to talk, and there's cocktails and…I'm basically your gay best friend without the gay. You want to talk—I can see it fighting to get out of you. So spill."

Emily laughed and looked at Henry to check he was occupied before leaning closer to Simon. "We kind of…kissed."

Simon raised his hand. "Up high."

Emily rolled her eyes. "I am not high-fiving you."

Simon smiled while lowering his hand. "Fine, your loss. So? What happened?"

Emily shrugged. "Nothing happened."

Simon pouted. "Oh, that's boring."

Emily snorted a laugh. "Sorry to disappoint you."

"She likes you," Simon said simply. "Like, really likes you."

Emily rolled her eyes. "Do not tell me she told you to say that—this isn't high school."

Simon grinned. "No, she didn't tell me to say that. In fact, she's been very cagey about it, which is why I know she likes you."

"Well, it doesn't matter," Emily said. "It can't happen."

Simon gasped and put his hand to his chest. "You're secretly married?"

"No." Emily chuckled.

"Seeing someone? Given up romance for Lent? Straight?" Simon guessed in quick succession.

"No, no, and no." Emily laughed. "If you must know…I like her but there's other things to think about, you know?"

"This is about her really mean streak when it comes to online Scrabble, isn't it." Simon shook his head. "So competitive."

Emily threw her cocktail umbrella at him. "No! It's…it's work." She sighed. "I can't get involved with a passenger. I'll lose my job. Not to mention a billion other reasons."

"A billion, huh?" Simon smiled.

Emily sighed and indicated her head towards Henry, who was busy slicing up fruit on Simon's touchscreen phone. "*Some people* are already very attached. I don't want him to think of her as part of his life if she's not going to hang around. He is my number one priority."

"Why do you think she won't hang around?" Simon asked.

"Because I know the kind of woman she usually dates," Emily said pointedly.

"What, like *that* kind?"

Emily looked over to where Simon was indicating with the tip of his cocktail umbrella and saw a buxom blond waitress carrying a tray of drinks to a table.

"Exactly," Emily said as she turned back to face Simon.

"Fair enough. I have a question for you, though. Do you think she's the kind of person who would get involved with someone with a kid when she could get what she wants from women like her over there?" Simon asked.

"Well, no," Emily admitted.

"So maybe she's a bit more serious about it than you think." Simon shrugged.

"You have all the answers, don't you?" Emily shook her head at him with a wry grin.

"I dunno, I might have. What are the other reasons?"

"Well, I might lose my job. That's a pretty big one."

"True, but isn't sneaking around fun?" Simon waggled his eyebrows.

"Oh my God, did I actually ask you for advice?" Emily snorted.

"Come on, you're adults. You can keep it professional at work,"

Simon said in a theatrically serious way. "And then fool around on terra firma."

"Simon!" Emily balked and then burst out laughing.

"What?" Simon giggled.

"I'm cutting you off if this is what you're like after one multi-coloured cocktail." She shook her head.

"You like her," Simon said with an accusatory stare, pointing with the end of his umbrella.

"Give me that." Emily snatched the umbrella out of his hand and put it beside her, out of his reach.

"You do!" Simon's eyes went wide and he grinned. "You like her."

"Of course I like her," Emily hissed back quietly. "She's gorgeous and smart and kind and funny and great with Henry."

"What?" Henry looked up at his name.

"Nothing, sweetheart." Emily smiled, and he went back to his game.

"So, who kissed who?" Simon asked with an excited grin.

Emily felt her cheeks begin to flush, and Simon snickered.

"Well, the first time we were interrupted—"

"Whoa, wait up." Simon held up his hand. "The first time?"

Emily ducked her head. "It happened twice."

"And who instigated it the second time?"

Emily raised her eyebrows and looked pointedly at him. Simon let out a small laugh and grinned.

Emily rolled her eyes. "Whatever you're thinking, don't."

"Oh, I'm not going to do anything," Simon said. "You'll do it yourselves. You don't need any help from me."

"Oops." Henry looked up at Simon with wide eyes as he held the phone out.

Simon looked at the phone's screen and smiled knowingly. "Looks like you answered a call with all your mad fruit-destroying skills. You better say hello."

Henry nervously held the phone with two hands to his ear and said, "Lo?" His face lit up with a smile. "Olivia!"

Simon looked at Emily and said quietly, "Did you ever consider that your number one priority might think it's worth taking a chance?"

Emily glanced over to where Henry was animatedly speaking with Olivia.

"I had an omelette, but Simon said it was a tortoise."

"Tortilla," Simon added helpfully.

"And then I ate a shrimp!" Henry fidgeted in his seat as his excitement grew. "But it was yuck, so I spit it into Mommy's hand. But I liked the ham and the cheese in the crunchy things. And the bread."

Simon smiled at Henry's enthusiasm. "Yeah, the shrimp in the hand was a personal highlight for me."

"Just wait, you'll have children one day," Emily said.

"They put everything in tiny bowls," Henry continued his conversation with Olivia. "It was okay—I'd give it a seven and a half."

With a sigh, Emily lowered her head to the table.

CHAPTER TWENTY-FIVE

Olivia was sitting on the sofa reading a book when Emily and Henry returned to the suite. She clipped a magnetic bookmark in place and set the book aside. "Did you have a nice dinner?"

Henry shrugged out of his coat and let it drop to the floor for his mother to pick up as he dashed across the room and climbed up onto the sofa beside Olivia.

"I splatted fruit!"

Emily picked up Henry's coat and smiled at Olivia. "On a game on Simon's phone."

"Do you have games on your phone?" Henry asked Olivia as he crawled closer and examined the book she was reading.

"No, my phone isn't like Simon's," Olivia told him.

"I ate chickpeas," Henry told Olivia as he lay on his back and put his head in her lap. "They look funny."

Emily looked at the sweet scene before her and desperately tried to fight the small amount of alcohol she had imbibed.

"They do," Olivia agreed as she regarded the boy, who was making himself comfortable.

"Can you draw giraffes?" Henry asked her with a thoughtful frown.

"Henry, Olivia is busy," Emily said as she hung the coats in the closet.

"No, I'm not," Olivia told Emily before smiling down at Henry. "I don't know. I don't remember ever trying to draw a giraffe before."

Henry looked shocked and slid off the sofa to run towards the bedroom. Olivia stared curiously after him and then at Emily with a questioning rise of her eyebrow.

"He either needs the bathroom, or you're about to draw a giraffe, or both. I'm going to get a drink. Can I get you anything?"

"Could I have some water?"

"Sure," Emily said as Henry came running back towards the sitting room with some loose sheets of paper and his pencil case.

Emily smiled at Olivia's flustered look and called out as she walked into the kitchen, "Focus on the head and work your way down."

Emily returned a moment later with a small glass of milk for Henry and a full tumbler of water for Olivia and placed them on the table.

Henry slapped the paper onto the coffee table, knelt in front of it, and patted the floor beside him as he opened his pencil case. When Olivia didn't move, he looked up at her and patted the floor beside him again.

"Come here, Olivia," he told her. Olivia nodded and knelt on the floor, adjusting her knee length skirt as she sat on the carpeted floor.

He handed her a green pencil. "Draw the body," he ordered.

Olivia took the green pencil and frowned. "This is green."

Henry stared at her as he struggled to see her point.

"Giraffes are brown and yellow," Olivia told him.

"Draw the body," Henry repeated, clearly not understanding Olivia's concern.

"Don't let him boss you about," Emily said.

Henry was fidgeting anxiously from side to side, and Emily looked at him. "Henry, do you need the bathroom?"

"No," he whispered.

"Henry, go to the bathroom. We'll be right here when you get back," Emily said, trying again.

"Draw the body," Henry told Olivia as he got up and ran towards the bathroom. "Please," he added as an afterthought.

"Remember to wash your hands!" Emily called out.

Olivia held the green pencil in her hand and was poised over the paper.

"Is this your first time drawing giraffes?" Emily sat beside her on the floor.

"I'm finding I can't even remember what a giraffe looks like," Olivia said with a nervous smile.

Emily regarded Olivia casually. "Want a hand?"

Olivia nodded, and Emily shuffled closer and took the pencil from Olivia's hand and quickly sketched out a giraffe body in a few seconds before sliding the paper towards Olivia.

Olivia looked impressed. "I can see you've done this before."

"On and off, about fifty times a day for the last six months."

Olivia smiled as she sat waiting for Henry's return. "I'm sorry I disrupted your meal."

"You didn't," Emily replied. "We were getting ready to leave anyway."

"Oh." Olivia nodded and gave a tight smile as her hands drifted together in her lap.

Henry came running back, and Emily looked up at him. "Henry, hands!"

The boy grumbled as he turned around and ran back towards the bathroom again.

"May I read Henry his bedtime story tonight? If he wants me to, that is," Olivia asked while staring intently at the piece of paper in front of her, seemingly avoiding eye contact with Emily.

"He'd love that, and yeah, you're more than welcome to do it."

Olivia smiled. "I'm enjoying his company. The suite is usually very quiet."

Emily understood and nodded. She looked up as Henry ran back into the room and excitedly skidded to a halt by the coffee table. He fell heavily onto the floor and grabbed the paper from Olivia. A heavy silence filled the room while Henry assessed the drawing before he nodded and picked up another blank piece of paper, putting it in front of Olivia. "Draw another one."

Henry started to colour the giraffe outline Olivia had provided for him.

"Henry," Emily warned.

"Draw another one, please. Sorry, Mommy."

"We're working on demands," Emily explained to Olivia. She noticed Olivia's panicked look at the blank paper in front of her.

"Can Olivia and I just do some general colouring by ourselves?" Emily asked as she reached across the table for a piece of paper and a pencil.

"Okay," Henry agreed.

She and Olivia set about doodling random drawings with different colours. As they did so, Olivia told Emily about the eccentric client she had visited that day.

"So, he's completely obsessed with pig ornaments?" Emily chuckled. She reached across to pick up another colour pencil, making sure to brush her hand against Olivia's as she did.

Olivia caught the movement and grinned. "Yes, every time I go to visit him, I make an effort to get a new, cheesy pig ornament for his collection."

Olivia changed her position so she was sitting closer to Emily, their arms brushing against each other as they doodled on their respective pieces of paper.

"A millionaire pig farmer who likes cheap pig ornaments, wow. You must meet some characters."

"I do." Olivia nodded her agreement. "But Michael is the one I enjoy spending time with the most. We see eye to eye on a lot of things. He likes that I cut to the chase."

"I suppose you told him how ridiculous it is for a man who spends his life"—Emily looked towards Henry before whispering—"slaying pigs to collect pig ornaments?"

"Yes, the first time I met him," Olivia acknowledged. "Actually he was driving me from his farm to his father's farm, and he stopped the car to show me some piglets in a field and how cute they were."

"I can picture your reaction."

Emily looked at the cartoon pigs that Olivia was drawing, reached over, and drew a crown on the top of one of the pigs' heads. Olivia stared open-mouthed at Emily as she joked, "You dare to deface my pig?"

"I was improving your pig," Emily corrected with a wink.

"What's terra ferra?" Henry suddenly asked while adding pink spots to his girl giraffe.

Olivia and Emily looked at each other in confusion. Emily tried to figure out what they had been talking about that might have a similar word.

"Where did you hear that?" Olivia asked.

"Simon said it," he said without looking up. "To mommy."

Emily's eyes flew wide open as she realised he had been listening to their conversation, clearly picking up on Simon's suggestion that she and Olivia fool around on terra firma.

"Um, nothing, sweetheart, don't worry about it," Emily said.

"But Simon said you should fool—" Henry started.

"Drink your milk, Henry," Emily said quickly, cutting him off mid-sentence.

"Fool terra ferra?" Olivia looked at Emily with a chuckle. "I thought you said you had one cocktail."

"I did," Emily agreed. "But clearly our private talk about adult things was being overheard by someone with big ears."

"Oh." Olivia frowned before quietly whispering, "What were you talking about?"

Emily grinned. "I *so* cannot tell you."

Olivia looked at Emily with interest. "Why do I get the feeling I really want to know?"

Emily regarded Olivia seriously for a moment before leaning in close and positioning her mouth next to Olivia's ear, softly whispering, "There was a suggestion that you and I could fool around on terra firma."

"And…?" Olivia coughed to get her voice back to a normal tone. "What did you conclude?"

Emily smiled, picked up a pencil, and continued to colour on her piece of paper. "Well, there wasn't any conclusion exactly. But I find myself warming to the idea more and more."

Olivia grinned. "I see."

"Henry, ten minutes until bedtime," Emily announced. "You might want to finish up."

"Okay," he said distractedly as he ran the coloured pencils wildly across the paper.

"Do you want Olivia to read to you tonight?" Emily asked with a sideways glance at him.

His eyes flicked up and he grinned as he looked from Emily to Olivia and nodded.

"Not the cat that went to space," Olivia said as she put some finishing flourishes to the calligraphy lettering she had been fine-tuning since her pig was ruined. "That was just ridiculous."

"Okay," Henry shrugged.

"If you think that's ridiculous, just wait until you read about Nibbles the hamster running for president," Emily said.

"Nibbles!" Henry cried out with excitement.

"Ah, yes, President Nibbles," Olivia laughed to herself.

"You know Nibbles?" Emily asked incredulously.

"Not personally," Olivia admitted with a grin. "When we were on the plane, I asked Henry who lived in the White House, and he told me Nibbles did."

"Ah," Emily said knowingly.

"And now it all becomes clear," Olivia replied.

As it turned out, Emily allowed Henry an extra five minutes of colouring time while she permitted Olivia to giggle at her admittedly bad attempts at drawing a number of other zoo animals. It was eventually declared that, while an expert giraffe drawer, Emily was not so talented when it came to any other animals, causing much amusement as Olivia and Henry attempted to guess what the various four-legged blobs Emily had created actually were.

Noticing the time, Emily stood up and told Henry that she would be supervising his getting ready for bed procedure that evening as she was convinced he was not correctly brushing his teeth.

The dramatic sigh and lowering of his head indicated that Henry knew he was busted as he dragged himself to the bedroom.

❖

Olivia looked into the bedroom and saw Emily sitting on the edge of the bed, whispering soft words to Henry that Olivia couldn't make out. As Henry's eyes drifted towards Olivia, Emily turned and smiled. She stood up, gestured to the edge of the bed, and handed Olivia a large book with a hamster in a suit on the front cover. Olivia fought hard to prevent herself from rolling her eyes as she looked at the book.

Emily headed for the door. "I'll put the coffee machine on," she told Olivia before blowing Henry a kiss and drawing the door closed behind her.

Olivia sat on the bed and pushed herself up against the headboard, stretching her legs out in front of her, and was surprised when Henry nuzzled up to her.

"Olivia?" Henry asked as he cuddled into her side.

"Yes?"

"I don't wanna go home," he whispered.

"Why not?" Olivia frowned.

"I wanna stay here with you and Mommy, forever," he said as he wrapped an arm around her middle and held her tightly.

Olivia looked up at the closed door and swallowed as she debated what to say to that. "I'm...sorry, Henry. It's just not possible."

"Why?" Henry asked as he strengthened his grip around her.

"Because, well, because you need to go home to your own room and your own bed. You miss your own bed, don't you?"

Henry gave a small nod.

"And your toys? Don't you miss them?" Olivia said, remembering what Emily had told her and hoping that it would ring true.

"We can bring them here," he told her.

"But your mother has to work," Olivia said gently. "And so do I. And that means you have to be at home where Lucy can look after you."

"But what if I never see you again?"

Olivia paused. She knew it was a real possibility that she might never see Henry again if she and Emily had a disagreement. She also knew that this was exactly what Emily had been worried about when it came to potentially dating someone. Now, when she could see the sadness in Henry's expressive eyes, she could palpably feel Emily's fears.

"I...don't think that will happen," Olivia said carefully. "But we really must read about Nibbles now."

Henry's face remained gloomy as he slowly turned his head to face the book Olivia held in front of them. She opened the front cover and waited as Henry analysed the page. Once he nodded his approval, she began reading.

Olivia soon got into the ludicrous idea of Nibbles becoming president. As she finished the book, she realised that Henry's body had become heavy against her, and that he had fallen asleep.

She placed the book on the bedside table before gently manoeuvring off the bed. Henry was slumped onto the pillow, and she wondered how to lift him and put him into bed properly. She'd always been very careful about how she had touched Henry, as she was very sensitive about strangers touching her.

She knew that Henry didn't regard her as a stranger these days, but she still felt she had to be cautious, and with a nod to her own ingenuity she pulled the bedcovers aside and gently dragged him down the bed by his ankles. His arms flopped above his head, and she placed them by his sides before realising how stiff and uncomfortable he looked, so she placed one on his stomach and the other to his side. She sighed as she looked at the ridiculous pose before she noticed Tiny on the other end of the bed. She leaned over and grabbed the cuddly toy and wrapped Henry's arm around it before nodding her approval and replacing the bedcovers. After a moment's hesitation, she placed a small kiss on his forehead and left the bedroom, turning off the light as she went.

Emily was flipping through television channels with a mug of coffee in her hand. Emily heard her approach and looked up. "Everything okay?"

"Yes." Olivia took a seat in the armchair beside the sofa.

Emily looked at Olivia with a small smile. "Not very convincing. Do you want to try that again?"

"He said he didn't want to go home."

"Ah." Emily nodded her understanding and took a deep breath. "And?"

"He said he wanted to stay here with you and me forever," Olivia said. "But I told him he couldn't and that he had to go home to his own bed and his own toys. I said we both had to work."

Emily narrowed her eyes as she looked at Olivia.

"And then?" Emily asked when nothing else was forthcoming.

"He was worried about never seeing me again," Olivia said. "I'm sorry, I realise this was what you wanted to avoid."

Emily chewed her lip and looked into the dark coffee in her cup. "I want to avoid him getting hurt," she said quietly.

"I know," Olivia nodded. "What do I do to fix this?"

Emily looked up at Olivia's nervous expression. "Well, that depends on a few things."

Olivia nodded, anxious to smooth over any rough patches she might have caused.

"Henry has clearly become attached to you," Emily explained delicately. "We can't go back now. You are, in some way, a part of his life. If you want to be, that is."

"Yes," Olivia said quickly and then shook her head. "I mean…I'd like to…well, I…"

Emily's smile was comforting. "Just say what you want to say. Don't worry about it coming out wrong. We'll get there together."

Olivia looked at Emily with utter relief as she nodded. "I…I like Henry. He's become very special to me, and I would like to spend more time with him. Though I'm not sure if a thirty-seven-year-old woman should necessarily be saying she wishes to spend time with a boy of five."

Emily laughed. "Well, as long as you don't take him with you to strip clubs and casinos, and use him to pick up chicks, then I think we're okay."

Olivia smiled and let out a small sigh of relief. "I'd still like to take you out for that drink sometime."

Emily bit her lip before replying. "I'd like to go out for that drink sometime too."

"You would?"

"Yes, but there needs to be some ground rules."

"Of course," Olivia said, quickly agreeing.

"Firstly, Henry is always going to be my priority. There may be times when I can't be there for you because I need to be there for him. I need that to be absolutely clear from the outset," Emily said seriously.

"I understand."

"Secondly, I need my job. If we're to explore this, then we have to be very careful that we are completely professional while I'm at work. No one at Crown can know."

"That makes perfect sense too."

"Lastly, I need to get Henry home and safely settled before whatever might happen between us…happens. I'm only just kinda keeping it together at the minute with all the stress of his operation and his recovery, the ongoing care and the doctors. It's a lot to deal with right now."

Olivia nodded, deciding to remain silent in case she said the wrong thing.

"What about you?" Emily asked. "Any ground rules from your side? I don't want to be laying down the law here."

Olivia's hands instinctively drifted together and she started to pinch her hand. "I…" She stumbled to say what she wanted to say.

Emily leaned forward and put her hand on Olivia's to stop what she was doing. "Say what you're thinking."

Olivia separated her hands and held Emily's. "I would like you to…try."

"Try what?" Emily frowned.

"Try to…hear me out," Olivia said. "I will say the wrong thing…I will make mistakes. I will probably hurt you. And Henry. But I don't mean to. So I'd like you to try to give me a chance when I do."

"I can promise you that I will definitely try," Emily said sincerely. "And I will try my best."

Olivia took a deep breath and chuckled. "If we don't change the subject, I'm going to break your third rule by kissing you right now."

Emily blushed and sat back with a smile. "Shall we watch a movie, then?"

"Yes," Olivia agreed quickly. "Yes, let's do that."

Emily found a movie channel, and they mindlessly stared at the screen.

CHAPTER TWENTY-SIX

Olivia left for work early on Thursday morning, leaving a note for Emily to call her with a time to meet in the park for lunch. Once in the office, she raced through her workload.

She looked at an email that popped into her mailbox, flagged with the obligatory and overly dramatic red exclamation mark that always accompanied a communication from Marcus Hind, one of the long-serving senior partners at the firm.

She read, then reread, the email before pressing the button on her desk that alerted Simon that his presence was required. A moment later he walked into the room with a smile and a raised eyebrow. She swung her monitor around one hundred and eighty degrees so he could read the email for himself. With a roll of his eyes Simon shook his head and said, "Dick."

"Agreed, but I'll have to attend. Can you call Emily and advise her that I won't be able to make lunch?"

Simon straightened up and nodded. "Sure, but are you really going to let him summon you like that?"

Olivia shrugged. "If I let him stew all weekend, he'll be unmanageable next week. No, I can take a quick journey upstairs and smooth his ruffled feathers."

"What's he so stressed about?" Simon asked. "I thought that stuff with TD Medical was all sorted, and he was happy."

"Oh, it is. This is because I gave James and Stuart the engineering insolvency without consulting with him first." Olivia sighed as she got a compact mirror from her bag and analysed her make-up and fluffed her hair. "You know how he hates it when I trample on his fragile masculine pride."

"But you're the boss."

"And he is a senior partner with a say in how this business is run," Olivia replied. "Always make sure your stakeholders are happy, Simon. Even if they happen to be dicks."

"I'll call Emily and tell her you'll be delayed."

An hour and a half meeting with Marcus Hind left Olivia with a headache and a bad mood as she marched through the office. Members of the staff hurried to get out of her way. Taking the stairwell rather than the elevator, she clomped down each step, mentally counting them as she always did. She thrust the door open to her floor and walked towards her office. She scrolled through the messages on her mobile phone and angrily tapped out one word replies where needed, until she heard a familiar noise that was out of place in her workplace.

Entering her office, she was surprised to see Simon standing in the middle of the room holding Henry around the middle and spinning him around while Henry giggled loudly. She was confused to see a red and white checked cloth placed on the meeting table and Emily in the process of laying out food and drinks.

"*Oliviaaaaaaaaa!*" Henry cried out through a laugh as Simon spun him around.

Emily looked up and smiled. "Hi," she said and indicated the table. "Simon said you couldn't come to us for lunch, so we came to you. Inside picnic!"

Olivia stepped further into the room. "You…came to me?"

Simon stopped spinning Henry and placed his feet on the floor, and the two staggered around with dizziness.

"Yes." Emily stepped around the two stumbling males and approached Olivia. "That is okay, isn't it?"

"Yes," Olivia said quickly. "Yes, sorry, I just had a difficult meeting."

"Simon told me about the jerk," Emily whispered. "He also told me you like potato salad."

"I do." Olivia smiled as Emily took her hand and pulled her towards the table and pulled out a chair for her.

"Henry, come and sit down," Emily said as she and Olivia looked at the boy, who was still giggling loudly as Simon pretended to fall to the floor.

"Simon, would you like to join us?" Emily asked him as Henry tried to help him to his feet.

"Thanks, but I better get on with some things," Simon said as he got up.

"Join us," Olivia said with a smile. "You clearly played a part in this set-up, so you should enjoy it too."

"Sure, okay, if you don't mind." Simon scooped Henry up into his arms and carried him to the table before taking a seat next to him.

Emily pointed out the different foods available at the indoor picnic and served Henry some breaded chicken bites. Olivia absent-mindedly stared out of the window as the others served themselves food and started to talk. After a while Emily placed her hand on Olivia's forearm. She turned to see Emily watching her with concern on her face.

"Are you okay? You looked miles away."

"Yes, I'm fine." Olivia began serve herself food. "I'm sorry, I was just distracted. How did Henry's appointment go?"

"Really well. He's cleared to fly tomorrow. All the medical files are being sent over to his doctor in the States, and he was discharged from follow-up care at Great Ormond Street."

Olivia could see the relief and joy etched on her face. It was completely infectious and she smiled too. "That's wonderful news."

As they ate, they spoke about Simon's girlfriend and his looming date with her. Olivia and Emily both jokingly provided him with terrible advice on how to behave. All of which he laughed at and said he would ignore.

Emily told of her relief to be going home, knowing that Henry was recovering well, and that hopefully this chapter of their lives would be over. As she began to get teary-eyed, Simon reached across the table and comforted her, and they shared a smile. Olivia sneaked a peek at Henry, clearly just as confused as she was as to why Emily was crying, and they gave each other a miniscule shrug as they continued to eat their lunch.

When Henry finished eating, he slid from his chair and walked over to the window and looked down at the street below with interest while the three adults continued to talk. After a while, Olivia stood with Henry and listened as he pointed out each and every red double-decker bus and black taxi that he could see. Suddenly, he waved straight ahead, and Olivia looked curiously as she followed his line of vision.

"Who are you waving at, Henry?" Olivia asked him as she looked across the street at the net-curtained window.

"Tiny," Henry said. "He's by the window where Mommy always sits."

"Oh, really?" Olivia turned to look at Emily with a raised eyebrow. "And what does she do when she sits there?" she asked him.

"Sometimes she reads but mostly she watches you and Simon," Henry said with a shrug before looking down at the street and pointing. "Bus!"

Emily lowered her head to the table and gently thumped it on the wood as Simon laughed.

"You little spy!" he accused.

Emily sat up. "I don't spy—it's just…boring, and the window faces right over here. It's hard *not* to look."

Olivia chuckled. "That is true. Which is why I have this," she said as she pointed to a little button by the window.

"What's that?" Emily asked.

"Henry," Olivia said, "could you press that button for me?"

He reached up and pressed it, and in a flash, all the windows became frosted.

"Wow," Henry said as he jumped back in shock.

Emily and Henry looked at the large windows in surprise as the view disappeared and was replaced with an opaque cloud.

"That's impressive," Emily said. She stood and approached the glass to see if she could see out of it at all.

"Privacy glass," Simon said. "Privacy at the flick of a switch without the loss of light."

"Olivia, can I press it again?" Henry tugged on her sleeve.

"Of course," Olivia said, and Henry tentatively reached out his index finger and pressed the button. He jumped back when the windows became transparent again.

"The best thing ever," Henry announced with a big grin and pressed the button again.

"Actually, that's not quite the best thing ever," Emily told Henry with a smile before looking meaningfully at Olivia.

"Oh," Olivia said as she realised her moment had arrived, and she was expected to tell Henry the good news about their afternoon trip. She paused for a moment as she considered how to tell him. Henry looked from Emily to Olivia with a questioning gaze before finally following his mother's pointed finger and focusing on Olivia.

"Henry," Olivia said as she folded and then unfolded her arms and held them loosely by her side. "Um, you like giraffes, right?"

Henry nodded and smiled up at Olivia.

"Well, I thought that…I thought that…" Olivia suddenly had a flash of inspiration. "As you have been so good with your operations, and getting well, and the doctors' appointments and everything, maybe you would like to meet a giraffe."

Henry frowned, her words not immediately sinking in. Then slowly his mouth dropped open and he stared at her with shock. "A *real* one?"

Olivia nodded. "Yes. Several, in fact."

Henry slowly turned around to look at his mother to get confirmation that such a thing was even possible. At Emily's smile, he quickly spun back and launched himself at Olivia's legs and pulled her into a surprisingly tight hug. Olivia put one hand to his head and one hand behind her to steady herself on the edge of her desk and smiled down at the happy boy.

"When?" he asked.

"Well, soon," Olivia said. She quickly calculated what she needed to do in order to leave.

Henry's face fell. "Oh," he said as he took a step back.

"Not my soon," Emily said with a smile, understanding Henry's fear that soon meant weeks or even months. "Olivia means soon as in within the next hour or so."

A smile took over Henry's face again as he looked from Olivia to Emily excitedly. "Really?"

"Really." Olivia walked around her desk and started to tidy up some final items.

It only took Olivia, Emily, and Simon fifteen minutes to clear the lunch items and finish up some last pieces of work, but clearly Henry thought it was taking far too long. He spun around in Olivia's office chair, making an indistinguishable noise similar to a siren.

"So…" Simon said once they had cleared everything away.

Emily made a sad face. "I suppose this is goodbye."

"For now, at least." Simon stepped forward and hugged Emily. "Keep in touch or else."

Emily laughed. "I will. I need to know what happens on your date."

Simon stepped back and looked down at Henry. "Henry, it's been a pleasure." Simon held out his hand formally, and Henry took it with a giggle.

"You're silly," Henry told him.

"And you have an awesome giraffe hoodie that I'm extremely jealous of." Simon shook Henry's hand and winked. "Right, I'm going to do some of that work stuff that keeps appearing on my desk. Have fun at the zoo." Simon paused in the doorway and turned to Emily one last time. "Take care of yourself. Remember all the wise things I said."

"I will, I promise."

They stepped out into the busy London street, and Olivia raised her hand. Seemingly out of nowhere a black London taxi performed a U-turn in the road and came to a stop in front of them. Olivia opened the back door and indicated for Emily and Henry to get in before climbing in herself. "London Zoo, please."

Henry looked excitedly out of the window as the driver pulled into traffic. Olivia attempted to distract herself from the heat building where her thigh pressed against Emily's.

"Are you sure you're okay?" Emily said softly. Her lips were close to Olivia's ear, and her breath stirred her hair. Olivia shivered with delight.

She opened her mouth but found she couldn't think of anything to say, so she simply smiled, though she knew it was unconvincing.

"After your meeting," Emily clarified, still leaning in close, her hand gently resting on Olivia's thigh, "you seemed very distracted. Is everything okay?"

"Yes," Olivia said. "The senior partner, he…he is hard work. He knew my father and didn't think I should have been given the London office. Now we have frequent battles. I find him very difficult to read."

Emily nodded her understanding. "So there's a bit of a power struggle."

"Yes, I suppose you could say that. I'm sorry if I seemed off."

"It's okay." Emily squeezed Olivia's thigh and then removed her hand. "We all have those times when work gets to us."

"Rebecca said I worked too hard," Olivia said with a soft smile. She turned her head away to look out of the window. "I work more now than I did then."

"How come?"

Olivia shrugged. "Because it's there."

"What do you mean?"

Olivia let out a breath, gathering her thoughts. "I do it because I don't know what else to do. I go to the office every day because it's there. I do the work because it's on my desk. My father instilled a strong work ethic in me. I work until there is no more work to do, or until I must rest." She smiled, realising now that she had verbalised it, how it must sound. "In order to do more work."

"If something else was there, would you maybe work less?" Emily asked.

She looked at Emily warily.

"No expectations," Emily explained. "And I'm not referring to me or him." She indicated Henry, who was busy chatting to himself about everything outside on the street. "I'm just asking if you found other things that you enjoyed in life, would you work less? Are you in a position to be able to work less?"

Olivia considered the possibility. "Yes, I think I would work less."

"Maybe you should explore that," Emily said casually as she looked towards Henry. "We only get one life, so you need to make the most of it and enjoy it while you can."

"We're going to see giraffes!" Henry shouted excitedly to the driver.

"Giraffes? That sounds like fun," the taxi driver called back.

"Yes, it's amazing," Henry agreed before turning his attention back outside.

A few minutes later, the taxi pulled up by the Regent's Park zoo entrance. Olivia paid the driver and told him to keep the change. The driver seemed very pleased and wished them well before driving away.

Henry was looking at Emily with a very serious expression. "Are we sure they will be in?"

"Um, yes, I think so. Why do you ask?"

"Because all the other giraffes are on vacation, and I don't want to come all this way for nothing," he said with a sigh.

Olivia and Emily laughed and Olivia led them to a small building beside the gate. There, a staff member checked a clipboard before opening up the gate for them.

Inside the zoo, Henry looked around in awe at all the exhibits and animals that they could see on the way to the giraffe house. Olivia led the way, explaining to Emily that the zoo ran a lot of night-time events, and that was why she was so familiar with the layout and not, as Emily joked, that she secretly spent all her spare time in the zoo.

Walking with a five-year-old seemed to take five times longer than walking on her own, which would normally annoy Olivia, but seeing Henry's reaction to the animals made up for it. However, she was anxious to get to the giraffe enclosure, so she could see his expression when he finally came face to kneecap with his idols.

They finally rounded the final corner and started walking towards the giraffe house. The outside area seemed to be empty of the majestic animals until, suddenly, a giraffe stepped through the arched gateway that led into the high-ceilinged house. It walked slowly into the outside enclosure, and Olivia turned around to see the look on Henry's face.

What she saw was not at all what she expected. She had expected smiles and excitement, even happy laughter. Instead, Henry came to a skidding halt before the enormous animal. A look Olivia could only describe as fear flitted across his face, and he burst into tears.

Emily scooped him up and held him tight. "Shush, it's okay, Henry," she whispered.

Olivia looked on in complete bewilderment, looking from Henry to the giraffe and back again. She had no idea what had gone wrong. Emily walked away from the enclosure and sat Henry on a nearby bench. Olivia followed and sat beside her as Henry continued to cry and hold on to his mother with terror.

"Everything is okay," Emily whispered into his hair as she cuddled him closely.

"I-I don't like th-them," Henry stuttered between tears.

"But it's a giraffe." Olivia pointed to the animal that could be seen in the distance. "You love giraffes!"

Emily gently rocked the upset boy as she said, "Henry has only ever seen cartoon giraffes, giraffes in books, giraffes on television, giraffe balloons, giraffes on hoodies." She tickled his tummy gently as she said the last point. "He's never seen a real one, and I think he's a little surprised at how big they are. Is that right, Henry?"

Henry snivelled and sniffed as he agreed with a nod.

"But he knows they're big," Olivia whispered. "He knows everything about them."

Emily looked at Olivia seriously. "He's five. He doesn't know what facts and figures mean. Besides, that giraffe is like, fifteen feet tall, and Henry is just over three feet. He's never seen an animal that big."

"I want to go home," Henry said, looking at his mother with a red and puffy face.

"Okay," Emily said as she brushed the mussed hair from his forehead. "But I'm a little tired at the moment. Can we stay here a little while? Just until I feel better?"

Henry looked at her hesitantly and nodded.

"Thank you." Emily smiled at him. "We'll just ignore that big old giraffe over there. He's all locked away in his enclosure anyway, so he can't come over here and steal our ice cream."

Henry sniffled and ran the back of his hand across his nose. "We're having ice cream?"

"I think so," Emily said. "That's what people do when they go to the zoo, I think. Don't they, Olivia?"

"Oh yes, that's right," Olivia replied, watching the interaction between them with fascination and a little confusion.

"Would you like ice cream?" Emily asked Henry. "We'll have to eat it here."

Henry angled his head around to see the large giraffe in its enclosure and analysed the safety of the situation before slowly nodding.

"Okay, can you stay here with Olivia, and I'll get some," Emily said. She was already transferring him from her lap to Olivia's. "You want anything?"

Olivia took hold of Henry as he was deposited on her knee and shook her head. "No, thank you."

"Okay, back soon." Emily smiled as she headed off.

Henry turned around to watch her leave and then regarded the giraffe with a furrowed brow. Olivia gently held him in place.

"I'm sorry you don't like the giraffe," Olivia said. "I thought you would."

Henry remained silent as he looked at the giraffe enclosure, checking that the animal wasn't about to get any closer. Olivia realised she had little else to say and decided to also remain silent until she saw Emily return with two ice cream cones.

"Can you sit on the bench, Henry?" Emily requested, and he climbed off Olivia and sat beside her with his hands outstretched and his eyes focused on the ice cream.

Emily handed him the cone and then sat on the other side of Olivia as she ate hers.

"Why are we eating ice cream?" Olivia suddenly asked, fed up with not understanding what was unfolding around her.

"To give him some time to adjust," Emily said quietly so only she could hear.

"And then we're going to leave?" Olivia whispered back with confusion. "I thought he would like the giraffes."

"He will. He just wasn't expecting them to be so big and so real. Sometimes kids imagine things, and then when they see them for real, it's so different that it's a little scary."

"So...we're not leaving?"

"We'll see how he gets on," Emily said. "He'll come around."

"I upset him," Olivia said quietly, angry at herself.

"He's a child," Emily replied. "He's unpredictable, and sometimes he gets upset. Sometimes about silly stuff. Sometimes about nothing."

"I wanted to do something nice for him," Olivia said with a sigh. "But I terrified him."

"You didn't terrify him—the giraffe did. And, as I said, he's a child. These things happen."

"But I wanted to do the right thing."

"And you did," Emily replied. "Things may not always go the way you think they will, but it's the intention that matters. Besides"—she grinned—"look."

Olivia turned around to see Henry had left the bench. He was slowly walking towards the giraffe enclosure with a curious tilt of the head, steadily licking his ice cream. Olivia smiled.

"Ten bucks says he'll cry when we tell him it's time to go home," Emily said.

Olivia was about to reply when Henry turned around, looked at them, and giggled. "A giraffe! Look!"

CHAPTER TWENTY-SEVEN

"Help!" Henry giggled. He held the leafy branch with both hands and looked over at Olivia with a smile.

Olivia wrapped her arms around him and held him tightly while the giraffe reached forward and roughly pulled a mouthful of leaves off the branch.

Emily was filming the moment on her mobile phone through fits of giggles as she watched the large animal easily pull both Henry and Olivia forward in its exuberance to eat the leaves.

"I had no idea they were so strong," Olivia said, looking over at Emily filming them.

"My money is totally on the giraffe." Emily laughed. The zookeeper prepared another branch as Henry finally gave up and let go of the one in his hands. It was immediately whisked away by the adult male giraffe.

A smaller, though still quite enormous, giraffe quickly took its place, and Henry anxiously proffered the new branch for it to munch.

The young female keeper smiled at Henry. "As you're so good with the giraffes, maybe you would like to come and see inside the giraffe house."

Of course, Olivia had already discussed with the managers of the zoo what special access she could obtain for Henry that would be both safe and educational for him. He looked at the keeper with amazement and managed to nod in agreement. The keeper smiled and held out her hand. "Come on then, your mummy can finish feeding the giraffe."

Olivia was about to state that she was not Henry's mother when he thrust the branch at her and took the keeper's hand.

"We'll be just over there." The girl smiled before heading off with Henry through the doors of the giraffe house.

Emily came over to where a distracted Olivia stood watching them walk away.

"I know they have long necks, but you have to help them out a little." Emily indicated the giraffe, who was straining to reach the branch in Olivia's hand.

"Oh." Olivia lifted the branch for the giraffe to eat. It pulled hard, and she was dragged forward, much to Emily's amusement.

"It looks easier than it is," Olivia said as she played an impromptu game of tug of war with the giraffe, causing Emily to laugh even more. The giraffe tugged, and Olivia surged forward. Emily grabbed for her, and they fought to stand their ground. They both giggled at the ridiculousness of the situation, and eventually Emily suggested, "Let go on the count of three. One…two…three!"

The giraffe moved away with its prize. From the viewing platform, they could see down into the giraffe house where Henry was watching a keeper clean the enclosure while his companion explained things to him.

"I can't believe the change in him," Olivia said with a smile.

"Kids are resilient."

"He was terrified before, and now he is happily feeding them."

"You'll come to realise that kids can be like that about a lot of things."

"Erratic and unreliable?" Olivia questioned grumpily, still not over the shock that her perfect surprise for Henry had caused the boy to cry in fear.

"Yes, I suppose that's one way to describe it."

"She thought I was Henry's mother." Olivia indicated the keeper with a nod of her head.

"Yes, she did." Emily nodded, watching Henry giggling as the keeper spoke to him.

"I'm sorry," Olivia said quietly.

Emily frowned and turned to look at Olivia. "Why are you sorry?"

"Because you're his mother, and she thought I was. I think it's because Henry and I have the same hair colour," Olivia explained.

"There's nothing to apologise for. If we're all out together, then people will sometimes think that you're his mom or that we're both his moms. It happens—it doesn't matter."

Olivia looked towards Henry with a thoughtful expression.

"Unless it bothers you that someone might think you're his mother?" Emily asked gently.

"No, quite the opposite."

Suddenly, heavy raindrops started to fall, and they hurried towards the door to the giraffe house. Despite only having been out in the rain for a few seconds, they were both soaked by the force of the downpour.

Emily chuckled and pushed strands of long blond hair away from her face and attempted to swipe at some of the damp from her jacket.

"I don't like being wet." Olivia stood uncomfortably and brushed away the drops of water from her face.

Emily reached out and softly wiped away a trickle of water running down her cheek before smoothing back the thick dark hair. She tucked a particularly stubborn strand behind Olivia's ear. They both paused, looking deeply into each other's eyes. They both hesitated, and it seemed the rain on the metal roof thundered louder than her heart. Then Olivia cupped Emily's face and softly kissed the fullness of her mouth, still damp from the rain. Emily leaned in to the kiss, her lips moving instinctively under Olivia's. The thought that their mouths were warm and fit together perfectly flitted through Olivia's mind—and then Emily was breaking the kiss, moving away, taking a small step back.

"I'm sorry," Olivia whispered. "I—I just…"

"It's my fault." Emily looked flustered and vaguely apologetic. "I know I must be giving you mixed signals."

"It's my fault. I'm not good at reading signals."

"That may be true, but I know I'm not making it any easier for you." Emily ran her fingers through her wet hair and pushed it back behind her ears. "Like I said before, I need some time."

"I understand, and I'm here whenever you're ready. I know I want this."

Emily licked her lips nervously. Olivia wasn't an open book most of the time, but here she was, laying her emotions out for Emily to see.

"I think I do too," Emily admitted, to both Olivia and herself.

"Then maybe I should be asking you out for that drink?"

Emily smiled. "That would be lovely. How would next Monday evening suit you?"

Olivia smiled brightly. "I'll clear my schedule."

"Good. I'll come to your office—shall we say around six o'clock?" Emily asked.

"Yes, that sounds wonderful."

Luckily, the rain shower was short-lived, and the rest of the afternoon was filled with sharing shy smiles while they spent time with Henry. After just an hour with the giraffes, Henry had declared that he wanted to be a zookeeper when he grew up. Olivia responded by asking the female keeper about training programs, job openings, and salary guides until Emily informed her that Henry would probably change his mind several times before embarking on a career path and reminded her that he had yet to even start school yet.

As Emily had predicted, when it came time to leave, Henry didn't want to go and folded his arms and pouted as he looked up at his mother and begged her to let him stay. The female keeper told Henry that he could stay, but anyone staying after a certain time had to clean out the giraffe toilet. One look at the corner of the enclosure where the waste was stacked up had Henry's eyebrows lifting off his face. He agreed it was time to go.

He hugged the keeper goodbye.

"You've a wonderful boy," she told Emily and Olivia.

Olivia was about to correct her when Emily said, "Thank you for giving him such a wonderful time. He'll remember this day forever."

❖

On the way out of the zoo, Henry began running in a wild zigzag while Emily and Olivia casually strolled behind him, exchanging warm glances. Henry screamed in excitement as they neared the exit and rushed into the gift shop, making Emily and Olivia hurry in after him.

An entire area of the shop was dedicated to the giraffes, and Henry stood staring at everything in reverence.

"Henry," Emily said in a warning tone.

"Mommy, please," Henry begged.

"Henry, you know that we can't afford it," Emily told him plainly.

"I…" Olivia started to speak.

Emily held her hand up to prevent her from saying anything else in front of Henry before addressing the boy again. "You can look, but you can't buy anything, okay?"

"Okay," Henry said sadly and sighed before turning his attention to the cuddly toys.

Emily stepped aside and pulled Olivia with her by the elbow.

"I can buy him a gift," Olivia said.

"I know. But he needs to learn the value of things, and he needs to know that he can't just beg, to get you to buy him things. Because I get the impression you would."

Olivia looked like she was about to argue but then considered her words and nodded. "Yes, I probably would, but what's the harm? I can buy him an eraser and a cup. I don't see the problem."

"The problem is that all these things are just here to entice children. Most of it is crap, and the rest of it no one really needs. The only thing it all has in common is that it's overpriced. I want Henry to learn the value of money and to know that you have to spend it on things you need first, not things you want," Emily explained. "And besides, what about the next time when you're not here to buy him the eraser and the cup? Then how will he feel?"

"But if it's a gift, then surely different rules apply?"

"Not when you're five. All Henry knows is that he either has something or he doesn't have something."

Olivia looked over to where Henry forlornly stared at the giraffe merchandise, taking a moment to hug a pencil case that he seemed to have taken a particular shine to.

"Think of your pig farmer client." Emily saw the struggle on Olivia's face not to run over and fill the shopping basket with everything Henry wanted. "You said he's the big brother of the family and runs the business, right?" Olivia nodded, though grudgingly. Emily smiled and carried on, "Okay, so, say they were doing really badly. The pigs have…I don't know, gotten blight or something."

"Blight?"

Emily chuckled. "I don't know much about pig farming…Okay, the pigs are sick, and the business isn't making money. But let's say Michael's younger brother really wants a helicopter."

"He's got one," Olivia assured.

Emily sighed and took a deep breath. "Okay, let's say he wants a speedboat, a frivolous, unnecessary expense. Pig farmers don't need speedboats, right?"

"Right," Olivia agreed quickly. "He's over a hundred miles from any water source."

At Emily's pointed look Olivia shut up and silently inclined her head in understanding.

"So, Michael has to say no, his brother can't have a speedboat. But what if you came along with a pig ornament one day and said, *Oh, sure, why not? Buy a speedboat, it'll be fun.* Then where would Michael be?"

Olivia looked horrified by the notion. "But that would be foolish because the business would be in trouble with the pigs having…blight." She shook her head at the ridiculousness of it. "He should put off any unnecessary expenditure until the business is more secure and they can afford it."

"Exactly, and Michael would probably not be happy with you for suggesting his brother could have a speedboat, would he?"

"You're Michael," Olivia said with understanding. "Henry is the brother. And I'm…me."

"Yes, and the speedboat is all that hideous giraffe merchandise that Henry is pawing at as if his life depended on it," Emily added with a smile.

"I understand."

Emily noticed as Olivia's hands reflexively came together but before Olivia had a chance to pinch the skin, Emily covered her hands with her own. "What are you thinking?"

"Nothing." Olivia swallowed.

"You do that when you want to stop yourself from saying something. Say what it is. It's okay with me. It will always be okay."

Olivia took a deep breath before looking over to Henry. "I was just thinking that I still want to buy him the whole store."

Emily chuckled. "That's natural. Henry's *pity me* look is very tough to ignore."

Henry let out a huge sigh as he picked up a giraffe ruler and then slowly put it back down again.

"Emily?" Olivia asked softly.

"Yes?"

"Can I wait outside? This is too hard to watch."

Emily grinned. "Of course, we won't be long."

Emily watched as Olivia dejectedly turned and left the shop, and then she turned to see Henry sadly cuddle a giraffe toy. She shook her head as she realised she was going to be caught in a lot of these situations if a relationship with Olivia was in the cards. She bit her lip as she thought about how difficult it had been to communicate with Olivia at first, then smiled at the progress they were making.

The knowledge that Olivia seemed to have no qualms about embarking on a relationship was a double-edged sword for Emily. On one hand, she was finding it hard to keep her feelings for Olivia concealed. There had been a few times when she had caught herself staring at her, wanting to pull her aside, and kiss her senseless. But on the other hand, she knew she had to keep her wits about her. Life was tough at the moment, and she didn't know if she had the time or the energy to properly devote to a new relationship. She chanced a glance outside the gift shop. Olivia was checking her phone, presumably to distract herself from Henry's guilt trip. Emily had to admit to herself that she just didn't know what was for the best, and though she wasn't aware of it, Olivia Lewis was making it very hard for Emily to ignore her.

Henry tugged on her sleeve. "I'm ready to go now, Mommy," he said sadly and started for the door.

As heart-wrenching as it was to see him upset, she knew that it was the right thing to do and that, within the next ten minutes, he would have forgotten all about the gift shop and would be laughing and smiling again.

❖

"Henry, get back here!" Emily shouted across the hotel suite, startling Olivia from the book she was reading.

A naked, sopping wet Henry ran into the sitting room with his mother chasing after him.

"Sorry, Olivia," she said as she pursued Henry around various pieces of furniture while Olivia watched the scene unfold in confusion.

"I won't!" Henry shouted defiantly as he crawled under the large coffee table and curled up in a ball.

"He won't what?" Olivia asked. She put her book down and

watched as Emily sank onto hands and knees and peered under the table at her son.

"Henry, come out right now," Emily told him firmly before looking up at Olivia. "He doesn't want to go home."

"Oh." Olivia was confused. Henry had been happily talking about flying home the next morning. "What changed?"

"I don't know." Emily sighed. "He won't talk to me."

"I'm staying," Henry shouted as he edged away from Emily's grasping hand.

"Henry"—Olivia tried reasoning next—"will you tell me what's wrong?"

"I'm staying!"

"Henry, come out and finish your bath," Emily said softly. "Then we can talk about this."

"No, I'm not going home," he repeated, quieter this time.

"Is it because you'll miss the giraffes?" Emily asked.

"No," Henry said sadly before mumbling something.

"What was that, sweetheart?"

"Olivia," Henry mumbled.

"I'm here, Henry," she said.

"Henry, do you want to stay because Olivia is here?" He snuffled an affirmative. "But, Henry," Emily explained softly. "Olivia's going back to New York too. If you stay, she won't be here."

"She will later," Henry said boldly.

Emily looked at Olivia. "Henry, what if we ask Olivia to come to the park with us this weekend?"

Olivia smiled widely and nodded her agreement. "Yes, Henry, that sounds nice."

Henry awkwardly angled his head out from under the coffee table to look at his mother. "Really?"

"Yes, really." Emily and Olivia nodded in unison.

Henry scrunched up his face and considered it for a moment.

"Okay," he said, before slowly crawling out from under the coffee table.

Emily breathed a sigh of relief. "Right, let's get you in the bath again and then it's bedtime. I'll read you a story tonight because I'm going to bed at the same time as you because of the early start." Emily lifted him up into her arms and mouthed *thank you* to Olivia. "Right,"

Emily said as she carried the boy to the bathroom again. "Bath, pyjamas, and then you have to say goodnight to Olivia."

Olivia watched the two walk away and smiled as Henry looked over his mother's shoulder at her. She offered him a small wave, and he gave him a tiny one in reply.

❖

It was sometime later when Olivia looked up from her book to see Emily enter the living room.

"I thought you'd gone to bed." Olivia clipped her bookmark into place.

"I had. I couldn't sleep." Emily wrapped the luxurious hotel-issued bathrobe tighter around her and sat next to Olivia.

"Oh?"

"I can't stop thinking." Emily paused. "About us."

"Oh." Olivia hesitated, knowing that the conversation had to happen eventually. "Can I help with anything?"

Emily laughed lightly. "You could do something to stop me from wanting to kiss you silly right here, right now."

Olivia felt herself blush. "I'm not sure I'd want to stop you from doing that."

"I know, and that's the problem." Emily sighed.

"This isn't a game for me." Olivia looked down at the book in her hands. "I have strong feelings for you and for Henry. I—I know I'm probably not—"

"Don't! Don't be self-deprecating."

"But I know—"

"Don't," Emily repeated. "Because if you do that then I'll have to tell you how wrong you are and explain how much you mean to me and then I really will kiss you senseless."

Olivia grinned. "I'm a terrible cook. I have no head for heights, and I can't draw giraffes."

Emily chuckled for a moment before turning serious. "I care for you. And Henry is clearly head over heels for you. But my last relationship…it really hurt him. And his pain hurt me more than anything. Every morning he would ask where she was, when he would see her again. It's hard enough having a break-up of your own, but when you're five and your other mommy has left…" Emily stood up and walked towards the window to look down at the street. "And the guilt. My God, the guilt. I cannot put him through that again."

"I'm not her."

Emily looked at her kindly. "I know. I just want to make sure we're doing the right thing. Emotions are high. This situation is bizarre. I want to feel normal again. I want to…"

"I don't have the slightest idea what you're talking about," Olivia admitted. "But I meant what I said at the zoo. I'm here whenever you are ready. If you want me."

Emily looked wistfully at Olivia for a few silent seconds before slowly approaching the sofa and crawling closer to her.

"I want you," Emily whispered before covering Olivia's mouth with hers and sealing the words with a passionate kiss. Before Olivia had time to get her wits together and respond, Emily pulled away. "And when the time is right, I'm coming to get you." With a lingering look she turned to leave. "Goodnight, Olivia."

Olivia exhaled slowly, raising trembling fingers to her lips. "Goodnight, Emily," she sighed into the air.

CHAPTER TWENTY-EIGHT

Olivia sat on the sofa in her New York hotel room and stared at the coffee table in despair. How had the day gone so wrong for her? In the last two hours, she had analysed every interaction with Emily, and played over their conversations again and again to try to figure out what had happened.

She twisted her phone over and over in her hands while she waited for Nicole to return her call, so she could discuss the situation with her best friend. In the meantime, she reminisced over the morning in London when Henry had been jumping around in excitement about flying home and seeing his friends.

While Emily got ready for work, Olivia had kept Henry occupied, and they had spent some time eating breakfast before watching the morning cartoons. Then they had looked out the window to see who could spot the most red double-decker buses.

Olivia, speechless, gazed at Emily when she appeared. Emily was immaculately presented with perfect hair and make-up and wearing her striking deep purple cabin crew uniform. Of course, Olivia had seen her in her uniform before, but that was before anything had happened between them. That was back when there were disagreements and misunderstandings rather than sweet kisses and longing looks.

Family Emily, with her fondness for casual clothes and light make-up, was markedly different from work Emily. Emily offered Olivia a casual wink as she noticed her prolonged hungry stare.

Olivia called the concierge and had their bags taken to the awaiting taxi, and all three piled in. She instructed the driver to take a route that showed a few London landmarks. Henry's curiosity ran at a million miles a second while Olivia pointed to buildings and told him interesting facts about them.

With the London Eye standing high and proud on the other side of the river, Henry pressed his face to the glass until Olivia pointed ahead and showed him the Palace of Westminster with Big Ben striking the hour as they drove past.

Buckingham Palace, Green Park, Wellington Arch, and Hyde Park were passed in quick succession, and mother and son were silent as they stared in wonder at the sights.

They said farewell to each other at Heathrow, and Emily and Henry walked into a staff area. Olivia spent three hours walking around the airport attempting to kill time, suddenly desperate to be reunited with the mother and son duo. Emily had appeared in her life such a short time ago, dressed to perfection in her impressive airline uniform and introducing colour to an otherwise black-and-white existence. For the first time in years, Olivia had been captivated. She could immediately sense that there was more to Emily, and she was eager to learn what that more was.

Olivia had never really seen the appeal of children. Not until she met Henry. The talkative and inquisitive boy had left her little choice but to engage with him, and as soon as she did, she found him as captivating as his mother. If someone had ever told her that she would relish spending time counting double-decker buses with a child, she would have laughed in their face.

Things had changed for her. In a short space of time, she had gone from being a loner to desiring a family. But not just any family, the White family, with all their quirks and routines that she couldn't wait to learn and to be a part of.

The three hours prior to boarding the flight had given Olivia time to realise her feelings and time to reflect on the hectic couple of weeks. Her conclusion was that she simply didn't want there to be any more time apart, not even three short hours.

However, when Olivia entered the first-class cabin, she was confused to note that Emily was nowhere in sight. As Kerry greeted her and offered to take her coat, Olivia saw a man sitting in Henry's seat. She paused for a moment, frowning at the man.

"Is everything okay, Miss Lewis?" Kerry asked.

Olivia snapped out of her stillness and moved to her seat.

Emily appeared in the cabin, escorting another passenger to his seat, before returning to the first-class galley. Soon after, Emily reappeared with a tray of champagne flutes and began to hand them out the passengers, including the impostor sitting in 10K.

When Olivia noticed that Kerry was occupied, she slipped out of her seat and followed Emily into the galley.

"What are you doing in here?" Emily whispered in shock.

"Where is Henry?" Olivia demanded.

"Picking up some duty-free," Emily replied tersely.

Olivia paused for a moment, deciding whether or not the comment was a joke. Emily continued pouring champagne, so Olivia grabbed her elbow and turned her around.

"There's a man in his seat!" Olivia implored her to understand the seriousness of the situation.

"I know," Emily said and shrugged her arm out of Olivia's grasp. "When the passenger was a no-show they offered him an upgrade from premium. Please don't grab me like that again."

"But—" Olivia started.

"Olivia, I appreciate what you tried to do, but it didn't work. Now, please go back to your seat before someone wonders why you're in here." Emily looked around nervously.

"Henry is in economy?" Olivia asked.

"Yes, please go back to your seat."

"Let me speak to your manager. I can explain—"

"Olivia," Emily interrupted. "Please go back to your seat. You're just making this more difficult for me. If anyone sees you here, there will be questions, and I really can't risk my job."

Olivia clenched and unclenched her fists in frustration before finally nodding and turning around to leave the galley.

Olivia sat in her seat and watched as the two flight attendants served the passengers. Her mind whirled for a resolution to the situation, for a way to get the interloper out of Henry's seat and to bring Henry to the front with her where he belonged.

Emily moved around the cabin with ease as she put hand luggage into overhead compartments and served drinks as if nothing was wrong. Olivia looked at her sharply, surprised that Emily wasn't outraged at the injustice of the situation.

Before long, the aircraft was taking off from London to begin its journey back to New York. As the nose of the aircraft tipped into the air, Olivia wondered where Henry was and if he was afraid. Her memory unhelpfully provided her with an image of Henry looking terrified on the take-off from JFK. Olivia could feel her breathing constrict as she panicked.

As soon as Olivia heard the click of the cabin crew's safety belts, she also undid her own lap restraint and followed Kerry and Emily towards the galley. Kerry entered the galley without seeing Olivia, but Emily stopped her in the corridor.

"What are you doing? Go and sit down—the seat belt sign is still on," Emily told her firmly.

"You're up," Olivia challenged.

Emily blinked at Olivia's behaviour. "I'm allowed to be. What do you think you're doing?"

"I'm going back to the economy section to check on Henry. He doesn't like take-off," Olivia hissed.

"I'm well aware. I have someone looking after him."

"I can't believe you left him in economy when I could have sorted all of this out." Olivia shook her head and made a move to pass Emily.

Emily held up her arm to block her way. "He is my son, and he is with a member of the cabin crew who I know and trust to look out for him. I assure you that he is fine," Emily said. "Now, *please*, sit down before I have to inform the captain that you are not complying with regulations."

"Emily," Olivia pleaded quietly. "Let me deal with this. I can sort this out. Henry can sit up front, with us."

Emily took a step forward and stood directly in front of Olivia. "There's nothing to sort out. Henry doesn't need a first-class seat in order to be safe and looked after. I know exactly where he is, and my colleagues are watching out for him. The only person giving me cause for concern right now is you."

"But I can—"

"There's nothing you can do, Olivia." Emily stared at Olivia's face in wonder. "What's gotten into you?"

"How can you not be worried about Henry?" Olivia demanded. "Am I the only person who is willing to sort out this mess?"

"Wow." Emily blinked. "There it is. You want to wave your money around and fix everything, or at least have it the way you think it should be."

"Why does it always have to come down to money? I told you before that I don't think about money the way you do," Olivia explained. "I'm sure I can resolve this. I'll speak with your manager, and then Henry can sit with me. It's ridiculous to keep him cooped up in economy where I can't look out for him."

"And just how will you explain that one? Did everything I told you about cabin crew not fraternising with passengers mean nothing to you?" Emily asked.

"I…" Olivia flustered. "Let me fix this. You're being ridiculous."

Emily stared open-mouthed at Olivia before shaking her head and taking a deep breath. "Miss Lewis," Emily announced loudly. "Please return to your seat."

Olivia opened her mouth to reply, but the curtain from the premium cabin opened and she watched as Iris Winter entered the corridor.

"Is everything okay, Miss Lewis?" Iris asked with a confused frown.

"I…" Olivia stuttered for a moment as she noticed Emily's harsh glare. "I'm just returning to my seat."

The rest of the flight was agony for Olivia. It wasn't lost on her that Emily had switched her usual row with Kerry. She attempted to make eye contact and even pressed the call button a couple of times in the hope that Emily would answer, but it was always Kerry.

When the aircraft finally touched down at JFK, Emily was nowhere to be seen, and Olivia wandered around the terminal building confused, in the hope she would bump into her.

Olivia felt her heart fill with joy when she finally caught sight of Henry rushing across the terminal, but it sank again when she saw him hugging a short-haired brunette who had been waiting in the arrivals hall. Emily appeared from the customs area with their luggage and smiled warmly at the woman who Olivia assumed to be Lucy. Lucy and Emily embraced. Over Lucy's shoulder, their eyes met, and suddenly the warmth was lost from Emily's gaze.

Oliva froze as Emily ordered Henry to stay with Lucy, then stormed across the arrivals hall to meet her.

"Emily…" Olivia trailed off, realising that the hours of practicing what she was going to say had been wasted, and she could barely remember a thing.

"That was out of line." Emily stood in front of Olivia with her arms folded.

"I know. I apologise, but I—"

"No." Emily shook her head. "No, I can't do this. I can't run the risk that you'll do something like that again. Money may not be important for you, but unfortunately, for those of us who live in the real world, it's essential. I cannot risk my job. I think we need to end this now."

"What?"

"You repeatedly challenged me on how to look after my son," Emily hissed. "You came into the galley—you got out of your seat while the seat belt light was still on. My boss caught us talking. You don't seem to understand how important my job is to me and how easily you could get me fired."

"I was just thinking about Henry's welfare."

"You think that's not my number one priority every damn day?" Emily shouted back, before taking a deep breath and looking around to check no one had heard her.

"You...promised that you would try." Olivia's whisper was almost inaudible over the background noise of the loud terminal. "You told me that it would be okay with you, that it would always be okay with you. That we'd find a way to communicate."

"How was I supposed to communicate with you when you were so out of control? I'm sorry, Olivia. I...think this has to end. Thank you for everything you did for Henry and me while we were in London, but we can't do this. I'm sorry."

"But what about Henry. The park tomorrow?"

"I think it's best if you don't see Henry again. Or me, for that matter."

"But Sunday. I'll see you on Sunday night."

"Then maybe I'll move my schedule, or maybe you should think about moving yours. One of us needs to not fly route SQA016 any more," Emily said with finality. "Goodbye, Olivia."

She turned on her heel and left Olivia rooted to the spot. As she watched Emily leave, she saw Henry raise his hand and offer a small wave to her. Olivia waved back and watched the three of them leave.

Olivia blinked and returned her thoughts to more pressing, more current matters. She looked down at the phone in her hand and checked the time before she jumped to her feet.

She stalked around the hotel suite in frustration, her eyes darting around to take inventory. Pulling a small side table away from the wall, she looked at the electrical outlet and snorted a laugh before looking at the light switch with bitterness. She took a step back and slowly spun on the spot as she looked at the suite as if seeing it for the first time. After the second revolution, she picked up her handbag, opened the door, and marched down the carpeted hallway towards the stairwell.

Her mobile phone rang, and she took the device out of her handbag and answered it with relief. "Nicole."

"Hey. Sorry I missed your call earlier," Nicole said. "How are you?"

"Everything is wrong!"

"Where are you? You sound like you're in a tunnel," Nicole asked. "And what do you mean, everything is wrong?"

"I'm in the stairwell at the hotel," Olivia replied as she angrily thudded her way down the stairs, mentally counting them as she went.

"Don't they have an elevator?"

"Yes, but it's the same, exactly the same," Olivia said in distress.

"I'm lost. What do you mean?"

"The elevator, the room, the damn furniture, it's all exactly the same," Olivia announced as she paused on the sixth floor and looked at the painted number on the wall. "The only difference is the stairwell. The stairwell looks different."

"Are you saying that the hotel in New York looks the same as the one in London?"

"Yes!" Olivia cried.

"Well, it's a chain. They're bound to have a certain design specification to keep costs down and create a brand," Nicole reasoned. "Why is it a problem? Surely you've noticed before."

"No," Olivia exclaimed. "I just saw it. Why did I only just see it? It's literally the same save for the light switches, the faucets, the electrical sockets, and the air conditioning panels. I checked."

Nicole whispered something that sounded like *I bet you did.*

"What? I can hardly hear you," Olivia said as she continued walking downstairs.

"Did you call me to tell me that the rooms are the same?"

"Yes," Olivia snapped before sighing. "No...I don't know."

"Why is it bothering you?" Nicole asked softly.

"I didn't notice," Olivia said sadly as she paused on the fifth floor and leaned against the wall. "I've been living in these hotels for years, and today I noticed they were identical."

"You like things to be the same," Nicole pointed out. "That's probably why you chose them."

"I had a bad day," Olivia admitted quietly.

"What happened? I thought you were looking forward to more time with Henry during the flight?"

Olivia sighed deeply and sat on the concrete step, not caring about the dust that would be visible on her black Armani skirt. "I messed it up."

"Ah."

"It all started so well," Olivia said with a small sniff. "But I ruined it. As usual."

"What happened?"

"When the airline realised the seat was a no-show, they sold the seat to someone else."

"Ah. And Henry didn't get to sit with you after all?"

"Exactly."

"But you saw him afterwards?"

"Not exactly."

"What happened?" Nicole asked. "I know you're holding back something."

With a deep sigh, Olivia relayed the story of the journey. Having run the conversations over in her mind for the last few hours, she found them easy to repeat verbatim.

"I..." Olivia struggled. "I was so stupid. I see that now. But at the time I just...I..."

"Wanted to fix things," Nicole said. "I understand."

"I had a lot of time to think." She stood up and slowly walked down another flight of stairs as she explained how she had initially been angry at Emily and given evil sideways glances to the man in Henry's seat. Soon she became all-consumed with wanting to check on Henry and see if he was okay.

The truth was that she was enjoying being a part of a family, and she felt like a part of her was missing. She missed him and enjoyed his company. Even when he was throwing a tantrum and crying and confusing the hell out of her, she still enjoyed his company.

"Is it normal to grow to love a child so quickly?" Olivia asked her best friend. She felt pensive as to what the answer would be.

"Wow, that's a tough one," Nicole admitted. "Kids are lovable, so I suppose it is easy to fall for them."

Olivia nodded to herself before explaining that she had come to the very same conclusion, that she loved and cared for Henry and Emily, despite having spent relatively little time with the two of them.

"Oh, Liv," Nicole said sadly. "I am so sorry."

"I don't think I can fix it," Olivia said. "She was rightfully angry at me. She wouldn't even let Henry say goodbye to me. She left him with *her*."

Nicole let out a laugh. "Who is *her*?"

"Lucy Kent," Olivia said with disdain. "Really, Nicole, you've never seen such a smiling, simpering, cardigan-wearing sap."

"And who is she?" Nicole asked.

"Emily's friend. They live with Lucy and her husband." Olivia sighed.

"Ah, I see," Nicole said. "I wish I was there. I'd come over."

"My hotel rooms are the same," Olivia muttered. "What kind of person doesn't notice that?"

"Someone who's been going through the motions for years, someone who was recently pushed out of their safety bubble and into the real world."

"What do I do?"

"Well, you can't hang out in the stairwell all day," Nicole pointed out.

"I've never been dumped before," Olivia mused. She paused and looked around the stairwell. She came to the obvious conclusion that being there was not productive and turned and walked back up the stairs again.

"Can you really be dumped when you've never been on a proper date?"

"I'm not sure. I feel dumped."

"I'm sorry. And I'm sorry you had a bad day."

"It's okay." Olivia sniffed.

"Can I do anything?"

"No." Olivia opened the door from the stairwell and walked back along the carpeted hallway towards her room. "I just needed someone to talk to."

"Well, I'm always here if you need me," Nicole replied.

"You're a good friend," Olivia admitted as she opened the door to her traitorous hotel room.

Nicole let out a small sigh.

"What?" Olivia asked with a frown.

"I don't know. I may be wrong about this, but I just have this feeling. Emily and Henry were good for you, and I know you can be good for them. You reacted the way you did because you care so deeply."

"What good will that do me now?"

"I just don't think it's over yet," Nicole said softly. "I think this is something worth fighting for."

Olivia considered the matter as she walked around the room and found herself entering the rarely used spare room. Unsurprisingly, even that room was the same, and she looked at the bed, so similar to where she had read Henry bedtime stories, before shaking her head and exiting the room.

"What do you suggest?" she asked.

"Oh, that's not up to me to say," Nicole said. "Sadly this has to come from you."

"Then I'm doomed," Olivia said quietly as she fell back onto the sofa and stared glumly at the coffee table.

"I know it sounds corny, but listen to your heart and then I'm sure things will come right in the end."

"I don't know—I acted appallingly."

"But you recognise that," Nicole said. "Fight for what you want, Liv. You know there's something to this, or we wouldn't be having this conversation. When have we ever spoken about the end of one of your relationships?"

"Never."

"Exactly. They mean something to you, and when something is important, you need to fight for it. Don't just give up. I know it seems impossible right now, but you can fix this."

Olivia heard the call disconnect and looked at the phone with surprise. She stared at the device in her hand for a few moments as she replayed Nicole's advice, then let out a deep sigh.

She sprang up from the sofa, tossed the phone onto the cushions, and started to pace the room. While it was true that she had a terrible track record with relationships, she realised that she couldn't let this go easily. She couldn't go back, couldn't turn her brain back to a time before she had met them.

Emily and Henry had jumped into her life and turned everything upside down in a matter of days. Her outlook was transformed, and she felt as if a veil had been lifted and she could finally see clearly again.

She looked out of the window towards the skyscrapers of New York City and started to form a plan. She was at the top of her game, restructuring businesses worth billions, working with the rich and famous, never backing down from a challenge. In her heart she knew that she could salvage what she had, repair what she had mistakenly destroyed.

There was simply too much to lose to not try.

About the Author

Amanda Radley had no desire to be a writer but accidentally turned into an award-winning, best-selling author. Residing in the UK with her wife and pets, she loves to travel. She gave up her marketing career in order to make stuff up for a living instead. She claims the similarities are startling.

Books Available From Bold Strokes Books

Flight SQA016 by Amanda Radley. Fastidious airline passenger Olivia Lewis is used to things being a certain way. When her routine is changed by a new, attractive member of the staff, sparks fly. (978-1-63679-045-9)

Home Is Where The Heart Is by Jenny Frame. Can Archie make the countryside her home and give Ash the fairytale romance she desires? Or will the countryside and small village life all be too much for her? (978-1-63555-922-4)

Moving Forward by PJ Trebelhorn. The last person Shelby Ryan expects to be attracted to Iris Calhoun, the sister of the man who killed her wife four years and three thousand miles ago. (978-1-63555-953-8)

Poison Pen by Jean Copeland. Debut author Kendra Blake is finally living her best life until a nasty book review and exposed secrets threaten her promising new romance with aspiring journalist Alison Chatterley. (978-1-63555-849-4)

Seasons for Change by KC Richardson. Love, laughter, and trust develop for Shawn and Morgan throughout the changing seasons of Lake Tahoe. (978-1-63555-882-1)

Summer Lovin' by Julie Cannon. Three different women, three exotic locations, one unforgettable summer. What do you think will happen? (978-1-63555-920-0)

Unbridled by D. Jackson Leigh. A visit to a local stable turns into more than riding lessons between a novel writer and an equestrian with a taste for power play. (978-1-63555-847-0)

VIP by Jackie D. In a town where relationships are forged and shattered by perception, sometimes even love can't change who you really are. (978-1-63555-908-8)

Yearning by Gun Brooke. The sleepy town of Dennamore has an irresistible pull on those who've moved away. The mystery Darian Benson and Samantha Pike uncover will change them forever, but the love they find along the way just might be the key to saving themselves. (978-1-63555-757-2)

A Turn of Fate by Ronica Black. Will Nev and Kinsley finally face their painful past and relent to their powerful, forbidden attraction? Or will facing their past be too much to fight through? (978-1-63555-930-9)

Desires After Dark by MJ Williamz. When her human lover falls deathly ill, Alex, a vampire, must decide which is worse, letting her go or condemning her to everlasting life. (978-1-63555-940-8)

Her Consigliere by Carsen Taite. FBI agent Royal Scott swore an oath to uphold the law, and criminal defense attorney Siobhan Collins pledged her loyalty to the only family she's ever known, but will their love be stronger than the bonds they've vowed to others, or will their competing allegiances tear them apart? (978-1-63555-924-8)

In Our Words: Queer Stories from Black, Indigenous, and People of Color Writers. Stories Selected by Anne Shade and Edited by Victoria Villaseñor. Comprising both the renowned and emerging voices of Black, Indigenous, and People of Color authors, this thoughtfully curated collection of short stories explores the intersection of racial and queer identity. (978-1-63555-936-1)

Measure of Devotion by CF Frizzell. Disguised as her late twin brother, Catherine Samson enters the Civil War to defend the Constitution as a Union soldier, never expecting her life to be altered by a Gettysburg farmer's daughter. (978-1-63555-951-4)

Not Guilty by Brit Ryder. Claire Weaver and Emery Pearson's day jobs clash, even as their desire for each other burns, and a discreet sex-only arrangement is the only option. (978-1-63555-896-8)

Opposites Attract: Butch/Femme Romances by Meghan O'Brien, Aurora Rey & Angie Williams. Sometimes opposites really do attract. Fall in love with these butch/femme romance novellas. (978-1-63555-784-8)

Under Her Influence by Amanda Radley. On their path to #truelove, will Beth and Jemma discover that reality is even better than illusion? (978-1-63555-963-7)

Swift Vengeance by Jean Copeland, Jackie D & Erin Zak. A journalist becomes the subject of her own investigation when sudden strange, violent visions summon her to a summer retreat and into the arms of a killer's possible next victim. (978-1-63555-880-7)

Wasteland by Kristin Keppler & Allisa Bahney. Danielle Clark is fighting against the National Armed Forces and finds peace as a scavenger, until the NAF general's daughter, Katelyn Turner, shows up on her doorstep and brings the fight right back to her. (978-1-63555-935-4)

When In Doubt by VK Powell. Police officer Jeri Wylder thinks she committed a crime in the line of duty but can't remember, until details emerge pointing to a cover-up by those close to her. (978-1-63555-955-2)

A Woman to Treasure by Ali Vali. An ancient scroll isn't the only treasure Levi Montbard finds as she starts her hunt for the truth—all she has to do is prove to Yasmine Hassani that there's more to her than an adventurous soul. (978-1-63555-890-6)

Before. After. Always. by Morgan Lee Miller. Still reeling from her tragic past, Eliza Walsh has sworn off taking risks, until Blake Navarro turns her world right-side up, making her question if falling in love again is worth it. (978-1-63555-845-6)

Bet the Farm by Fiona Riley. Lauren Calloway's luxury real estate sale of the century comes to a screeching halt when dairy farm heiress, and one-night stand, Thea Boudreaux calls her bluff. (978-1-63555-731-2)

Cowgirl by Nance Sparks. The last thing Aren expects is to fall for Carol. Sharing her home is one thing, but sharing her heart means sharing the demons in her past and risking everything to keep Carol safe. (978-1-63555-877-7)

Give In to Me by Elle Spencer. Gabriela Talbot never expected to sleep with her favorite author—certainly not after the scathing review she'd given Whitney Ainsworth's latest book. (978-1-63555-910-1)

Hidden Dreams by Shelley Thrasher. A lethal virus and its resulting vision send Texan Barbara Allan and her lovely guide, Dara, on a journey up Cambodia's Mekong River in search of Barbara's mother's mystifying past. (978-1-63555-856-2)

In the Spotlight by Lesley Davis. For actresses Cole Calder and Eris Whyte, their chance at love runs out fast when a fan's adoration turns to obsession. (978-1-63555-926-2)

Origins by Jen Jensen. Jamis Bachman is pulled into a dangerous mystery that becomes personal when she learns the truth of her origins as a ghost hunter. (978-1-63555-837-1)

Unrivaled by Radclyffe. Zoey Cohen will never accept second place in matters of the heart, even when her rival is a career, and Declan Black has nothing left to give of herself or her heart. (978-1-63679-013-8)

A Fae Tale by Genevieve McCluer. Dovana comes to terms with her changing feelings for her lifelong best friend and fae, Roze. (978-1-63555-918-7)

Accidental Desperados by Lee Lynch. Life is clobbering Berry, Jaudon, and their long romance. The arrival of directionless baby dyke MJ doesn't help. Can they find their passion again—and keep it? (978-1-63555-482-3)

Always Believe by Aimée. Greyson Walsden is pursuing ordination as an Anglican priest. Angela Arlingham doesn't believe in God. Do they follow their vocation or their hearts? (978-1-63555-912-5)

Courage by Jesse J. Thoma. No matter how often Natasha Parsons and Tommy Finch clash on the job, an undeniable attraction simmers just beneath the surface. Can they find the courage to change so love has room to grow? (978-1-63555-802-9)

I Am Chris by R Kent. There's one saving grace to losing everything and moving away. Nobody knows her as Chrissy Taylor. Now Chris can live who he truly is. (978-1-63555-904-0)